Praise for Kimberly Kafka's *True North*

"*True North* has the valuable things that every reader looks and hopes for in fiction—characters that you can care about and remember . . . a strong story told in graceful prose. But it also has something more, something special. The author knows and loves the Alaskan wilderness, and she summons it up for us accurately and vividly . . . *True North* is a first-rate novel to be read with pleasure."
—George Garrett

"Savvy and well written . . . Kafka's control of her story, her lean, gorgeous descriptions of the true, uncontrollable awfulness of nature in Alaska, and her sense of tribal politics makes you read slowly, so as not to miss a single fine detail."
—*The Seattle Times*

"Kafka is a great storyteller. She conjures up the feeling of living in such a harsh but beautiful world. Kafka is a writer to watch."
—*The Capital Times* (Madison, Wisconsin)

"In her atmospheric, tightly wrought debut novel . . . [Kafka] excels in integrating wilderness lore, descriptions of the natural landscape, and insight into the harsh lives of people who brave the territory."
—*Publishers Weekly*

TRUE NORTH

Kimberly Kafka

A PLUME BOOK

PLUME
Published by the Penguin Group
Penguin Putnam Inc., 375 Hudson Street, New York, New York 10014, U.S.A.
Penguin Books Ltd, 27 Wrights Lane, London W8 5TZ, England
Penguin Books Australia Ltd, Ringwood, Victoria, Australia
Penguin Books Canada Ltd, 10 Alcorn Avenue, Toronto, Ontario, Canada M4V 3B2
Penguin Books (N.Z.) Ltd, 182–190 Wairau Road, Auckland 10, New Zealand

Penguin Books Ltd, Registered Offices: Harmondsworth, Middlesex, England

Published by Plume, a member of Penguin Putnam Inc.
Previously published in a Dutton edition.

First Plume Printing, March 2001
10   9   8   7   6   5   4   3   2   1

 REGISTERED TRADEMARK—MARCA REGISTRADA

The Library of Congress has catalogued the Dutton edition as follows:
Kafka, Kimberly.
True north / Kimberly Kafka.
p.   cm.
ISBN 0-525-94530-X (hc.)
0-452-28223-3 (pbk.)
I. Title.
PS3561.A3619 T78 2000
813'.54—dc21   99-047296

Printed in the United States of America
Original hardcover design by Julian Hamer

PUBLISHER'S NOTE

This is a work of fiction. Names, characters, places, and incidents are either the product of
the author's imagination or are used fictitiously, and any resemblance to actual persons,
living or dead, business establishments, events, or locales is entirely coincidental.

For Alyson Hagy—true heart, true voice. And yet another tip of the trick hat goes to the Girl in a Black Raincoat Gang.

HERALD: Submit, you fool. Submit. In agony learn wisdom.
—Aeschylus, *Prometheus*

TRUE
NORTH

1

That morning Bailey started the generator for the first time in weeks, had to hand crank it because the cold had long since sapped the battery. She'd let the weak, spring sun warm the motor beforehand, a small trick learned after five years of living in the Alaska interior, one of many tricks that came of learning to think about everything one did, no matter how trivial or insignificant. The first trick she'd learned had been to let nature work for her as much as possible because damn sure it worked against her most of the time.

The engine choked, caught, and grumbled fitfully before conceding to run. She recoiled from the sound, then smoothed the grimace from her face. Annoyance cost energy and led to things done too quickly, and things done too quickly could lead to mistakes that cost. You didn't fly for three years as a bush medic without getting that lesson etched into places that hurt. But she'd quit that two years ago when she found this camp for sale and bought it. The prospect of a haven was the reason she'd come to Alaska, why she'd done the medic job in the first place.

She returned to her cabin to lie on the couch that still reeked of dog, even though it had disappeared in February. Almost blind, it must have wandered inevitably into the belly of something hungry, because everything was hungry by that time of year. The wolves had commenced mating and were particularly sharp tongued. That's how she knew what month it was when the dog left: the wolves had begun to give voice, and she imagined them, snouts pointed skyward, poised on high ground in order to send their voices farther. The were trying to connect as they loped, spread-toed, across the river valley, looking for recognition in the voice and eyes of another.

She rued the dog's absence on bitter nights, when it had been good to curl around; missed it, too, when scraps of food had to be eliminated and it was not around to fill the position. Now she had to burn everything to keep the bears away from camp in spring when they would lumber in and eat even the Naugahyde-covered foam rubber seats off her snow machine. On the odd occasion they came in anyway, the dog had been a good sentinel. It could detect a pine marten skittering across late winter snow crust. But its sense of detection didn't stop at the tangible. Finally, that is what she hated about the dog. She could not look at it without realizing that it knew. It knew her, and it remembered.

———➤

It had belonged to her sister, but at least had the sense to get out of the house, though its fur was singed all to hell and stank for months afterward. It had wanted to survive. She only had to drag it away from the intense wall of heat into the field where she'd fallen, pulling it down beside her. It had struggled a little but she held on to it, her nose full of the burnt protein that had been its pelt.

She could smell the burning still, feel Temple's weight balanced against her as she dragged her down the upstairs hall. She imagined her lungs shriveling like raisins. Now she was at the stairs, dragging Temple *bumpety-bump*. One step, two, and that was as far as she'd gotten before the beam came down, breaking her hands away.

Without the counterbalance of Temple's weight, Bailey fell freely down the stairs. She'd hit the floor, heard the air whoosh from her lungs even over the sound of flame sucking up the old wood of their house. Had she passed out? Dampness on her face, the sharp rack of the dog's voice. She found the door handle, pulled. Dark air moved in a cool, insistent column past her and up the stairs where the fire gobbled it greedily. She snaked down the porch steps on her belly, the dog scrambling down her back in a panic, using her body like an escape ramp. Its claws tangled momentarily in her hair and she swung at it, connecting with a hank of its fur that came away in her hand. She grabbed it again, this time finding a good hold, and used it to angle herself to her feet so she could stumble away, dragging the dog with her as she called for Temple, knowing she could not go back there, it was too late to go back. She had felt consciousness slip from her like a dank shroud, ebbing so quickly she was hardly aware of its passing.

The smell of the dog's old body rose redolent around her. She closed her eyes, wishing that ears could also be closed so that she could block out the high, tight voice of the generator. It disturbed the rhythm of her careful world, made her think she had to be moving, doing something, when she did not. At least she was able to keep the machine outside now. It was worse over the winter when she had to keep it inside the cabin, and when starting it precluded being able to stay in the cabin at all. But she was unable to leave it unattended for fear it would cause a fire. She would run it only when the weather was good enough to allow for hours of outdoor chores while it charged the batteries, anticipating the moment it would run out of gas and die.

For a week now the going was too treacherous to do much of anything outside. This close to break up, the ice on the river was rotten as moth-laced fabric. The snow pack on land, though still a good foot thick, was even more rotten than the ice, pocked with air holes left by the receding moisture. Just getting from cabin to outhouse was a chore. Even the snowshoes held no promise of ease as they sunk into the snow, then came out of their holes caked with the clingy, wet mess. This was the time of year she hated most, and this was the time she spent working on the cabin's interior.

When the river backed up, everything on the bank a hundred yards in would be flooded and washed clean. Even the cabin would sit in a few inches of water which was why she did not bother to clean the floor until after iceout. Then she would wash away the river silt, scrub the log walls free of gluey grease accumulated there from long winter months of cooking meat in the small enclosed space, and clean and lube the two outboard motors.

The first boat ride after iceout was always particularly pleasing to her. She was eager to see what the ice had scored or torn away, how the landscape had changed from its winter cloak to its raw, gash-marked spring skin. She marveled at how harsh the landscape looked then. There was no color in it, no varying hue, no life. The fawn-colored flanks of the Nulato Hills were almost indistinguishable from the flat river valley. Standing in the stern of the boat, braced against the wrenching movement of the current at high water, she was thrilled by the tableau. In its deadness, all seemed possible.

She could almost smell the washed-over cleanness of the land when the static-riddled click forked into her ear, as if someone had snapped their fingers directly into it. Her body went rigid on the couch.

"Village to River Camp, do you read?"

She stood, walked stiffly to the shelf where she'd hidden the handheld VHF unit behind a stack of repair manuals, and scrubbed her eyes hard, as if the gesture could rub away the reality of the voice that spoke to her now, unavoidable.

"Village to River Camp, do you read?"

She could choose not to answer, certainly, but the voice compelled her, and she picked up the black box, squeezing the reply bar with a callused thumb. She cleared her throat into the mike, then released the bar without responding. She had not spoken in so long once the dog was gone, she wasn't sure she could bear the sound of her voice, or that she could speak at all.

"That an answer?" the box asked.

She pressed the bar again. "This is River Camp. Go ahead," her voice remarkably normal, not graveled as she had expected.

"Roger that," Raina said. "Sounds like you made it through winter okay. How's the ice look up there?"

"Rotten. Another week, maybe."

"Sounds about right. Well we got a little problem maybe you can help with, over."

She could picture Raina clearly—long hair glinting darkly, eyes dropped down when talking until finished, then fixed on the face opposite her as she listened to the response, a habit peculiar to the native Ingalik of the region. It had unnerved her initially, having been trained from childhood to look somebody in the eye, for that was when you could tell best if someone was lying, and so her gaze had grown steady, then immutable.

"Still there?"

"Yeah. What's up?"

"Kash's plane's still gettin' checked out in Anchorage. When you planning to fly the Cessna in?"

"Couple of weeks, I guess," Bailey said, but the hand holding the radio set had drifted away from her mouth.

"Come again," Raina said, "I can't read you."

"Couple of weeks I'll come through," Bailey said again, the handset now in range of her voice. "Somebody need a ride into the city?"

"It's people wanting to come out from Anchorage is what I'm talking about."

The possibilities blew into her ear. She did not respond for fear her voice would crack.

Again, Raina broke the long silence. "River Camp, did you copy?"

"Roger that," Bailey said.

"They'll be staying up at the Lodge. Something Kash is tryin'. You know him and his schemes. He woulda done the flying, but like I said, his plane's out. You been missing those little visits?"

Bailey hesitated. That fall, Kash had begun to fly up every couple of weeks. He didn't radio to let her know he was coming that first time nor did he on successive visits. At first, she waited for him to state his business—it was inconceivable to her that one would waste time on an aircraft engine for a social call. But there was only small talk and a gift here and there, functional, of course. He stayed long enough to unsettle her completely, then left.

She had begun to listen for his plane, could recognize the sound of the Cub's engine from a distance. She started to take a little more care with her appearance, made sure she had on a clean shirt, found herself shaking out her hair, smoothing it with fingers unaccustomed to such ministrations. As something like the Yukon's most eligible bachelor since his wife's death a year and some previous, his interest might be physical. She searched for signs but gleaned none. At first she was insulted but squelched that immediately. It was a waste of energy. She was thirty-five years old. This was not her first time at the rodeo. Nevertheless, she had continued to see to her appearance and swallowed the extra work of washing more clothes as a result.

"Don't get all clammy on me," Raina said. "I'm just fooling on you."

"Wouldn't think otherwise," Bailey said cautiously. "Anyway, I'm too busy, thanks to you, to mess in that horseshit."

Raina laughed and made a point of keying the mike so Bailey could hear it. That was good. Without Raina's good graces, it was hard for her to operate. In spite of Raina's occasional drinking bouts and not so occasional bad taste in men, she liked the woman.

"So, about these kids, now. They'll pay," Raina said. "Figured you could use the money."

"Who is it?"

"Couple of kids from out East," Raina said. "Fellow and his girlfriend want a 'wilderness adventure.' They'll get that, all right, flies and all. But Kash'll make sure that's all they get."

Bailey knew what Kash was worried about. He headed one of twelve regional corporations set up by Congress when land disputes with Alaska natives settled in '71, and was in the position of playing arbiter between the white power base and the seething animosity and despair of his people. Hostility raged through rural Alaska in a giant backlash against faults inherent in the settlement, faults that threatened native control of their land, their way of life. Kash's politics did not lean to the radical faction, some members of which resided in Ingalik Village, that was violently anti-white. While he was utterly pro-native, he was a realist. White incursion in their culture was inevitable. History bore him out on that point. His ideas about letting whites into their country but controlling the access as tourism had gained him the stamp of being pro-development. It was not a complimentary term.

"Hey," Raina prompted her. "It's not like you got a lot else to do, and you could use a little social life, you know?"

"Yeah. Like a hole in my pointy little head."

"Lighten up," Raina said. "It's just a ride they need. No big deal."

"When are they coming?"

"June first."

"Okay," Bailey said. "But you'll have to do something for me."

"What's that?"

"Call my mechanic and reschedule my appointment for that morning."

"No problem," Raina said.

"I'll stop in the Village on my way out."

"Roger that," Raina said. "Ingalik out."

Bailey turned off the handset and shivered. She had tried as much as she could bear to contribute to the community in positive ways: she gave freely of her airplane time and her medical training when someone was lost or hurt in the bush; bought her fuel and as much of her food as possible from the Village, even though the cost was twenty percent higher than in Anchorage; and didn't abuse the privilege of living there by mining or trapping or bringing other people in for those purposes. She hunted and fished for herself and the dog and that was all. The natives could allow that, she hoped, because it made sense to them. She did everything she could to be a useful, positive presence, but her motives had little to do with altruism. To her, people were like the proverbial albatross; if she could control the amount of contact she had, life was bearable.

But if Kash's tourism schemes became reality, her haven was threatened. The native corporation had bought out the doctors who built the lodge on their site only five miles upriver from her camp. They had intended to bring in upscale hunting and fishing clients by float plane. The fish and game were good there, no doubt, but above her camp, the river's character changed. The upper watershed configured itself tensely, gushing through tight channels or, where the river widened on the plains, spread itself thinly over gravel bars. It did not allow for a straight, deep stretch of water on which to land a float plane when the water was low much of the summer. The Lodge was still accessible by boat, but eighty long river miles separated it from the Village. Most wealthy sporstmen would not tolerate such inconvenience, but Kash's guess was that a scaled-down clientele would tolerate it, and enjoy the experience to boot. Eco-tourists, he called them. He had read all about it.

She shivered again. The woodstove needed stoking. She managed to pack down a decent trail in the mush from woodpile to cabin and before long found she had amassed almost half a cord without realizing it. She pulled the maul down from its nail pegs on the wall and began splitting what she had hauled over. Each wedge set was considered, precise, and while the spruce and larch was mostly twisted and difficult to split, she needed few strokes.

She was fit and clean-limbed as an athlete, but she did not have the bulk and muscle to spare on ill-considered motion. She used to look at herself and admire what she saw. With shirtsleeves rolled up even in the dead of winter as she went at the demanding task of cutting wood, she would regard the corded muscle in her forearms, biceps clearly defined, hands thickly veined from the work and strangely attenuated on a body that was characterized more by blunt ends than elegant tapers.

But her body was no longer something to admire and appreciate so much as a machine to maintain scrupulously and to curse when it could not perform what was required of it. There was seldom anything she could not do as long as she had her mind and a few basic tools: chainsaw, axe, pulley, and winch. Compared to what her responsibilities had been so much of her life, the mental and physical challenge of surviving alone was a pleasure.

After Temple's death, it had taken a couple of years for the habit of her old burdens to slough away. For too long, she had expected to feel the near constant touch of her sister's warm fingers, to see the idolatrous gaze, hear *I love you* over and over, all of it so seamless, ceaseless. When she shook the memory away, her skin gone clammy, the voices would remain. Her mother, the smell of her sick body, and the voice launched from a face set with pain, with no expectation of reprieve before inevitable death: *Take care of your sister. She hasn't got what God gave you.*

Yes, and thank God I don't have what you gave her, she'd thought a million times as she heard those words flipped at her so automatically that they had lost weight, become the meager mantra of a sick woman who was too tired to blame herself aloud anymore, as she surely must have in her soul. Outwardly, though, it was always her father's fault that her mother had been drunk that night; her father's fault for having screwed around with Black Label Mable in the double-wide trailer down the road—her father had sold the woman life insurance and worked a little harder than usual to sign her up, apparently—his fault that her mother tried to drive home, that she was doing forty-five when she fishtailed onto the dirt road that led to their place and never recovered from the skid.

Two pine trees took the brunt of the collision, along with the six-month-old fetus that sloshed hard in her womb. Miraculously, it had lived, though it spent the rest of its gestation bundled up hard under her mother's breastbone, unmoving, until it tumbled reluctantly into day. Temple was three when her parents admitted there was something wrong with her. "Fetal Alcohol Syndrome" had not been coined; in those days, she was simply "retarded." When Bailey was born that year, her mother had had her checked fanatically for similar symptoms. Had thought, she later told Bailey, that it was in her blood and not, as the doctors insisted, a result of one night's exceptionally poor judgment. Bailey understood it all more clearly when she finished nursing school.

As Bailey split wood precisely, rhythmically, she planned the task of returning the float plane to the water as soon as the river ice cleared, and worked her way around the darkened place in her brain to which the radio contact had been relegated, the place where past and future could not torment her, nor threaten her present refuge. When her camp was in order for the day, and she had maintained the machine in which she lived, she would open the dark place and examine it with ruthless curiosity, as she had seen raccoons do when examining objects of potential danger.

She hated landing on the slough behind the Village in the spring. The water stayed muddied year-round there at the confluence of the Ingalik and the Yukon, and in spring the debris that washed down from above was concealed by roiled water. She had circled low four times already and still unease kept her aloft as she strained to detect the ghostly outline of a tree trunk or branch, water-logged and hanging just beneath the surface, that could puncture one of her floats.

Her flight instructor, Whip McClintock, had been very thorough. On arrival in Anchorage one spring, learning to fly had been Priority One; the solitude she sought depended on it. She researched the available pool of instructors; McClintock's name surfaced repeatedly.

She was rebuffed on her first approach. He told her she could enroll in one of his classes that didn't begin until spring. No classes, she had told him. She wanted private lessons and then offered him a sum that was enough above the going rate to surprise him. He had peered at her for an uncomfortably long, silent time before agreeing.

The recommendations had been on the mark. Though he was technically precise ("fussy" was the word some had used), he was also an intuitive pilot. He could think quickly in an emergency and improvise. Of course, he had pointed out to her, his "fussiness" precluded him getting in many of those situations in the first place. "Think ahead," he'd tried to impress on her. "There are always signposts along the way to a bad decision." One of the most important of those signposts, he had told her, was an emotional one. "Unless you are absolute master of your emotions, do not fly when you are exceptionally riled. If you catch your man in bed with another lady, do not jump into your airplane and expect to have a hundred percent at your fingertips." She had let go with an uncharacteristic laugh at that advice. "Oh," he had responded. "Obviously your man is one of the trustworthy ones."

"No," she'd said, still laughing. "*My* fussiness precludes me from ever getting in that situation in the first place."

By December she had completed her ground school and wheeled training. She would have to wait for spring to get her float rating. She spent the winter apprenticed to a mechanic Whip recommended so that she could get certified to do most of her own maintenance. Nights kept her in a grim efficiency apartment near Lake Hood studying manuals and anything she could get her hands on to read. She collected brochures, newspapers, flyers, magazines—anything that would give her a better sense of the place, the country. In addition, she badgered the hapless employees of the Department of Natural Resources, and Fish and Game. She attended any open meetings hosted by native organizations and read all their publications, because the more she learned, the more she realized that nursing work for the clinics in rural Alaska guaranteed involvement with natives.

When she began her training in float planes, it felt like what she'd been waiting for. She had been fascinated by them since she was a child and watched one land on the river in front of their house. It belonged to a bear-hunting guide who hosted his clients at his camp upriver. He used the plane to scout for game from the air, and to take his clients into remote areas other people could not reach. She would watch the plane lift off in a shower of spray, its slightly recurved pontoons dangling from its underbelly as if a snow skier had been lifted from the mountain by a giant hawk. *Places other people could not reach.* She wanted that.

Finally, she radioed to Raina that she was coming down. She had marked the villagers on the beach working on their boats when she made her passes; though they would not stand and watch her overtly, she knew they were watching. A stiff crosswind toyed with her trajectory and she practically stood on the right rudder pedal to keep the plane straight. She concentrated on her depth perception and kept her eyes on the surface of the water, no longer aware of the people on shore. Now her body was part of the plane, when it seemed that if she shifted her hips, the plane would shift with her.

The rear of the pontoons dug into water, sending up huge walls of spray. She coaxed the nose down to level once she had slowed enough to let the pontoons go horizontal. No one looked up as she let the plane drift close to shallow water, then cut the engine. Curan, Raina's son, waited at water's edge. Bailey splashed into the water in her hip boots to tail the plane up on the sand.

"Mom's up at the store," he said.

"Thanks, Curan," she said with a smile that pulled her mouth tight across her face; the feeling of it, the smile, was as foreign as if somebody had touched her skin.

After tying the plane off to a scruffy clump of alder up the bank, she perched facing backward on Curan's ATV for a ride up to the Store. Wind eddied into her eyes. Between slitted lids she watched the dogs chained to their worn patches of dirt. They lunged against their restraints at the passing distraction, their faces worn dull by equal doses of outrage and boredom. Kash's store was the only one in town serving the population of one hundred and twenty-five people. His sister, Raina, pretty much ran the place. She was the liaison to most of the commercial flights landing on the gravel runway on the hill behind the village, and transported any freight, mail, or passengers the two miles between town and airstrip. She was also secretary to the Native Corporation of which Kash was president. She had access to all of the meetings and all of the paperwork. A VHF marine-band radio hulked in the corner behind the counter where Raina sat now, talking to the commuter flight on a separate aviation-band unit.

A young boy scooted out the door as Bailey walked in, shrinking away from her. She didn't waste a smile on him. Ferrin hulked over the desk in front of Raina. He had been the Village cop at one time, before the Corporation board decided having a cop in town incited more bad behavior than they originally had. Ferrin worked on the North Slope oil field now, two weeks on and two weeks off, making eighty dollars an hour. He was one of the minuscule minority able to function in a cash-based economy. He moved like a wrestler, thighs so overly developed he walked slightly spread-legged, as if he were not yet used to walking without snowshoes.

Bailey nodded at him as she stopped at the desk. He walked out, eyes on the floor. Raina shrugged when Bailey turned to her, then flung out a casual hello as if nine months had not elapsed since they had seen each other.

"Plane's comin'. Head on up," Raina told Curan. He jogged out, drafting in his wake the smell of the cheap leather jacket that hung loosely on him. She turned to Bailey and moved her eyes frankly over her. "That a new shirt?"

Bailey fought the blood down from her face. "I wash my clothes from time to time. I'm not just sitting up there eating chocolates in a pile of dirt." It was all she could do to keep from purposefully messing up the long rope of hair she had braided so carefully before flying down.

"Okay," Raina said, leaning over the counter with a pad of paper. "Thing One: Got that fifty pounds of dog food you wanted."

"Don't need it."

"Got that dog on a diet or something?"

"No," Bailey said. She took off her cap and settled it again on her head. "What's Thing Two?"

"I got a list of supplies these kids said they wanted. I figure it's going to take you more than one trip between them and their gear and this stuff." Her eyes stayed glued to the paper as she spoke, then wandered to Bailey's face.

"What do you think they're really coming out here for?"

"Better not be for the wrong reasons. They're on Ingalik land up there and hell's the price if they go back on their word. It ain't the old days anymore. They signed a contract and we will enforce it."

"Contract?" Bailey asked.

"Kash's idea. Anyone wants to use our land for recreation purposes has to sign a waiver of responsibility, plus an agreement to leave it like they found it, haul their trash and shit out. Strictly forbids hunting, trapping, or mining. Plus we charge a daily fee, just like them big paper companies do in the lower forty-eight and Canada, is what Kash told us. He started advertising for people to come in. You know. Like tourists. Least we can control it that way and make some money."

Bailey turned away, one hand hooked over the crest of her

shoulder to work her fingers into tensed muscles. Gruesome images of incompetent, curious, sociable people surging up the river, wave upon wave, washed across the backs of her eyes. Sweat tickled down the small of her back and she flinched involuntarily as if already their needy fingers were upon her.

Bailey willed a smile to widen her mouth as she spoke. "So about these kids now. Think they'll stick to the weight restriction?"

They all knew that folks from the outside could not imagine a situation in which all that they deemed vital in the world could not be hauled into the bush, that they had no concept of a plane smaller than a 747.

"Hope so," Raina said. "I'd hate to see the kind of shaking down you'll give them. That gal's hair dryer and high heels'll be at the bottom of Lake Hood, sure." She paused a moment. "Seen Kash yet?"

"No," Bailey said, "but I've got to find him to get the keys to the fuel pump. Need to top off the wings before I head out."

"Oh," Raina said, stretching the vowel way out. "Guess he hasn't had a chance to check with you then, eh?"

"What about?"

"He wants a ride into Anchorage to get those people moving on his plane. Got a couple of meetings, too. And he hasn't seen his daughter in a month."

"I won't be able to ride him back with the load I'll have," Bailey said, almost talking over Raina's last words.

"He'll fly his own plane back. Think he's at the Corporation office now. I saw him drive past before you landed.

"Okay."

"Here's the information on those kids. I told them exactly what you told me about where to meet you and when, but you should know where they are and stuff, in case they're late."

"They don't show up at the right time and place I won't need any information because I'll leave on schedule," Bailey said, remembering to tack a smile onto her comment. "It's good of you to organize everything like this. I hope you're getting paid for your trouble."

"Wasn't much," Raina said. "They paid for the phone calls and stuff and I don't have nothin' much else to do till commercial fishing starts." She looked up at Bailey, then away. "They seem nice enough."

"Most folks are nice enough until you get to know them," Bailey said, hoping she sounded cheerful.

⌒⌒⌒

She walked up the hill from the Store, sloshing through the streams created by the onslaught of defrosting earth. She kept her cap pulled low to her brow and watched the road as she went. She knew by heart the tiny, prefabricated structures along the way, didn't need to see the dogs that persisted in straining at her, choking their own barks back into their throats. They all looked the same, anyway, dogs and houses alike. Looked particularly forlorn this time of year with rotten mounds of dirty snow heaped anywhere the bulldozer had been able to pile them, bare earth still frozen to rock consistency only half an inch down, the raw top layer roiled and churned into mud that found its way into everything. Her boots were already two pounds heavier with it.

As people passed her on the road she kept her eyes down or gave a short sound that sounded like "hi" or a subtle nod. Nothing more was needed here, especially if you were white. With her eyes down she heard him before she saw him.

"Looking for my keys, I bet," Kash called from the tiny porch of the Corporation's offices. His smile was broad and welcoming. But he was a worldly man, she had to remind herself. He did business with big shots, handled the Corporation's millions of dollars in investments, and was used to wheeling and dealing with whites. He was one of the few natives she knew who looked at her when he spoke. She was so accustomed to dealing with the Ingalik, or mostly with no one at all, it made her uncomfortable. Made her particularly uncomfortable coming from him. She looked up, shading her eyes against the flat glare.

She was reminded again that he was not a tall man. There was bulk to him, though, a hard, sinuous fullness to his body that reminded her of the huge old oaks back east. She had thought, at times, that even her long fingers could not encircle his arm—not that she ever meant to test her supposition.

"Happy spring," she said.

"Always a good occasion," he said.

"Hear you might risk riding in with me."

He laughed and brushed the hair back from his forehead. She watched it feather slowly forward again. "Yeah, I'm still thinking about it."

Two adolescent boys passed her, distaste palpable in the cant of their heads away from her. The sickeningly sweet vapor of airplane glue muscled into her nostrils as they passed. They creaked up the steps past Kash on their way into the office, at least a head taller than he. He spoke softly to them in dialect and they responded each with a "yeah" before disappearing inside.

"Thought I'd top off the wings and be on my way. You ready to go?"

"Pretty much," he said. "If you'll wait a minute I'll grab my stuff from the office, then ride you down to the store."

The scene played itself out, unbidden. Her behind him on the ATV, arms clasped lightly to his sides, the half-inch space between them turned to boiling air. The clean air smell of him whorled over her face. And then there was Ferrin and Raina and Curan staring at them.

"How's about I walk down now, get the chariot all ready. I'll meet you at the plane."

He shrugged, unzipped his coveralls down to the crotch to scrabble in his pants pockets for the right keys, then underhanded them gently at her, laughing when her groping hand missed the catch. She bent to pick them out of the dirt, tried to make a joke of it when she straightened. But his eyes had an unusual sheen, his mouth, pursed gently at the corners. He had seen something he liked; a sign.

She turned and started back down the hill, the keys gripped so hard in her hand they almost drew blood. Curan came slopping along on the ATV, the little trailer rattling behind. "Ride?"

"Down to the beach?"

"Yeah," he said.

She sat back to back and signaled him to go on. Kash still stood on the porch, not smiling. She raised the edge of a flattened hand to her brow in flippant salute. There. I got your sign.

He watched her go, remembering the time he first met her. He'd known she was coming, knew she was alone and therefore, he'd figured, she was probably homely as hell. She had flown into the Village once or twice for the Clinic, given vaccinations, checked a few wounds, but he'd always been away. She arrived the day after the ice left the river and set the red Cessna down on the muddied slough, a bit awkwardly, he thought. Overly cautious. A 185, to boot. Lord, she was probably humongous as well as homely. But she looked nothing like he had imagined based on . . . what? The sort of woman who would do something like this had to be big, raw, unattractive. The person he met looked tightly bound, compact.

She introduced herself with an outstretched hand. He tracked her name across his tongue, *Bailey*, and tried to decide whether she was of God or the Devil. When he drove the fuel truck down to the beach so she could top off her wings, the airplane was loaded to the ceiling. A dog stared morosely out the window. After she finished fueling, he suggested she taxi out to the Yukon so she'd have plenty of room for takeoff. She had looked at him, head cocked slightly and said, "I planned on it." Her eyes showed him only what they saw reflected there: a plan.

When the land claims settled out for the second time in '88, one glitch was not remedied, but the concession was so minuscule in the big scheme, he dared not oppose it. The glitch had entailed the omission from a native claim of any parcel of land held by a patented deed. For the most part this was negligible; most privately owned parcels were held by standard deeds and could be rescinded by the government for any reason it deemed important to its greater interests, such as oil or mineral strikes. But patented deeds could not be rescinded, which left the Ingalik territory with two small outholdings in its vast millions of acres, specks on its glimmering armor. One hundred acres among millions did not seem like a big deal to anyone else in the community, but Kash was a seer. He knew an infinitesimal flake of rust could spread like cancer to consume huge structures, that one moth could render useless an entire garment. He knew, too, that if the Lodge were to become operable without native control, the inevitable clashes would end in unpleasant reckonings if the local radicals had anything to do with it.

When the previous owners of the lodge went belly-up, he managed to manipulate corporate funds into a chunk that would enable the Corporation to buy the lodge. He got no argument from the board on that. None of the community liked the fact that white people paid other white people to come in and shoot the hell out of native game; the natives were the only ones who lost in that arrangement. He'd thought getting the other parcel would go just as easily.

But the board didn't see the little camp as threatening, not like the Lodge had been with its blood-happy sportsmen who shot moose and bear for the trophy, then left the meat to rot. What could it hurt, they argued, to have that parcel sit empty up there, even if the Corporation didn't own it? Nobody was going to buy it anyway, not for the asking price. It was on floodplain and bears had reduced most of it to nothing more than a porcupine den. Even if someone were fool enough to buy it, they wouldn't last long in that inhospitable locale. No, the board would rather use the money on a dozer for snow removal, converting the electricity generator plant to diesel so it would be cheaper and more efficient, and how about seeing a few bucks on their corporate dividends? He hadn't been able to argue that. As usual, the immediate outgunned the long-term.

He had presided over the remainder of the meeting, making the automatic responses, then left the office and went to the ceremonial ground on the hill. He walked the clearing, fingertips burning, and shook his hands into the air. He had experienced setbacks before and on a much larger scale, but for some reason this little speck of land ate into his heart.

There was something of a reprisal when, the very next year, he got word on the grapevine that someone from out East had bought the land. The fist in his chest tightened and then softened until he could breathe when he found out it was a woman. He felt certain the spirits had smiled. This country was hard enough on a man, let alone a woman who had it in her blood, let alone a white woman. She couldn't last long, a year at the most. And then he would raise the issue again to the board, this time with an example under his belt. *You see?* he would say. *This is how easily it can happen, and none of it under our control.*

After her arrival, he had waited surreptitiously, sensing that she was not someone who could be pushed, waited with the patience of a predator for his prey to weaken and stumble. Surely it would take no more than one summer with the mosquitoes, and a winter of isolation and hardship to send her on her way, but after the first year, he'd had to rethink his course. In the months after his wife died, the new strategy went into effect even before he knew consciously what he was doing: flying up to the Lodge unscheduled, uninvited, small gifts in hand. *Here,* he'd say, handing over a box or a paper-wrapped bundle. *Some of us thought you might need this.*

Kash courted Bailey and said nothing of his intentions; he knew better than to give the opposition a foothold. Once he had surmounted this impediment, he would achieve his goal quickly, quietly, and the land would be whole again.

He gathered some files from the office and shoved them in a battered, soft-sided briefcase. The door opened and closed softly behind him and he couldn't help smiling. She had come back. Another sign. He composed his face as he turned to encounter round-faced John Knik. His mother was Eskimo and had passed her physical features on to John. The roundness and a gentle blush on each cheek gave him a perpetually cheerful look, though from the set of his shoulders at the moment, he was anything but chipper.

"John," Kash said with a nod. "How's Girlie?"

"Getting along okay, I guess."

John's wife had to be medevac'd to Anchorage a few months before when her appendix exploded, pumping poison through her system at an alarming rate. They had almost lost her, and she spent a month in the hospital before she was stable enough to fly back to the Village. John was beside himself, unable to afford to fly back and forth. Kash had given him a ticket, and tried to give him another, but it was too difficult, John had said, to make sure their five children were taken care of. Girlie had not yet regained her strength and the medicine was costly, not to mention the hospital bill, even though some was covered by government subsidy.

It wounded Kash to see the young man struggle. He was one of the few who made an effort to keep himself on the straight and narrow. He had sworn off alcohol years ago when Girlie threatened to leave him and take the children after his drunkenness led to a fight that left her with a broken arm. They had worked hard to assimilate their kids while still keeping their feet firmly rooted in native culture. John himself had no schooling, but he was uncomplaining, earnest, and willing to work had there been any jobs. Kash worried that depression and alcohol would reclaim

John if one more slash were made in the gentle fabric of him, and he dreaded the news he was about to deliver.

"I kinda don't know what to do here," he said haltingly, then shoved a smudged envelope at Kash. "Damn Fish and Game people told me I'd have to go on the limited entry permit lottery to commercial fish this year. I filled out the forms as best I could, but heck, they was twelve pages long, and I couldn't understand half of what they was asking me. I just got this today," he said, gesturing at the letter that hung limp in Kash's bronze hand.

"Christ, John, whyn't you come to me? I would've filled it out for you."

John looked down, turned his body to the side, "You was busy then, Kash. Had them big meetin's in Seattle and all. Who couldn't fill out a application? But that letter there says I didn't do her right and now my permit's denied for the season. We open tomorrow and I took out that loan so I could get my nets ready and get that new motor. I'm screwed." He settled a hand across his forehead like a compress and sighed.

Kash almost put a hand on his shoulder, but John was too old for that now. It would have been an insult. "Listen," he said instead. "I'm flying into Anchorage tonight. I've got meetings tomorrow but I'll get over to Fish and Game no matter what and see what I can do."

"It ain't gonna do any good, man. It never does."

"Just hang in there. Let's see what happens."

John let his hand drop from its place on his forehead and settled his cap back on. "Gotta check on Girlie. She didn't take the news too good."

"Tell her I said hello, will you? And tell her we'll handle this."

"Yeah, okay."

Kash folded the letter grimly and put it in his briefcase. There was a new commissioner now, a real Republican toady whose agenda, Kash knew, was to whip into shape the sorry mess that had become of the state's control over fish and game rights. Furthermore, Kash had come out against him in highly uncomplimentary ways when the imminent appointment was announced; the man showed not one ounce of support for native subsistence hunting and fishing rights. But what the hell. It would be another fight in a long, long string of them that he never minded suiting up for, not where the people were concerned, and certainly not John Knik.

2

It was all the money she had: a thousand dollars, scrupulously saved over two years of teaching elementary school, tutoring on the side, and taking care of an elderly doctor in return for the use of a cabin on his property. So when Zach proposed his plan to spend the summer in Alaska to look for gold, Alpha was—well, she wasn't even sure skeptical would be the right word. She understood his desire to do something to get ahead of the game, the frustration of building the same cookie-cutter furniture day after day just to keep his business going, going to the point where he had no time to do anything better. She knew that kind of battle. She was fighting it herself.

She wished she knew more about any of it. She wished she could question the friend, Arnie, from whom Zach had received his information about the stream in the wilderness where he was certain nuggets could be had for the taking, but she didn't dare. The friend had been trained as a geologist but left school for the adventure of working on the great Alaska oil pipeline built in the late '70s. *He knows what he's talking about,* Zach said. *He was there. He knows.*

At least she'd got up the nerve to ask why Arnie hadn't gone after it himself if he was so sure it was there, and she had felt like a complete jerk when Zach explained that he had lost a leg in an accident on the job. One of the huge sections of joiner pipe had rolled and he hadn't been able to get out of the way fast enough. *It was winter,* Zach explained. *The snow slowed him down and then he slipped and fell.* The friend had gone over the maps with Zach, taught him as much as he could, helped him figure out what equipment he'd need to do the job on a very small scale.

But even on a small scale, he couldn't come up with a budget of less than two thousand dollars to make it happen. What with outstanding business loans, a thousand dollars was all he could free up. Alpha had thought about it long and hard, particularly the part about the beer bottle. At today's gold prices, Zach said, they could fill a beer bottle with gold and come away with ninety grand. She could not help picturing the house they could have, a big yard for the kids to play in. Zach had murmured things leading up to such an outcome. A house of her own, kids running around happy and squealing with orange popsicle stains framing their grinning little mouths—nothing like the way she'd grown up. She couldn't change the past, but she could darn sure make it right in the future.

So in the piney darkness of her cabin loft, curled into the curve of Zach's body, she had been thrilled beyond anything she thought possible once she'd said *Yes, let's do it.* Fingering the bulk of his arms, she loved the way her hand only reached halfway around his bicep, the grainy feel of the work hardened fiber beneath smooth skin, the way he twitched and groaned as he plunged into sleep. This adventure was by far the most exciting thing she had ever imagined, and she was ready to make it real.

They had talked about his furniture-building business two towns away, which was how she met him in the first place. She had needed a small hutch to give her more storage space in the tiny corner kitchen. She spotted his advertisement in the weekly regional paper and liked the simple and disarming way it was worded. Of course, he had convinced her to let him build something a little different from what she thought she needed, but he was the carpenter. He ought to know best.

She liked the smell of his shop, the light layer of wood dust that covered everything, even the hair on his arms. She first glimpsed him as he looked up at her from the clatter of the table saw. A white paper mask covered the lower part of his face, showcasing the cast of his eyes, brown under slashes of black, a forelock of sandy brown hair spilling down his face. She could feel his work in the rough surfaces of his hand as she shook it and felt, too, how he smoothed to silk the surfaces of a white ash desk, cherry table, maple bedframe, or splintered to pieces the errant wood that refused to be worked.

She had thought she would go anywhere with him the first time she had him to dinner. She laughed through the meal as he entertained her with stories of the people he knew, his customers, the kid, Hank, who worked for him. The whole thing was smooth and tangy all at once, like one of her best lemon meringue pies, like the apricot custard tart she'd served him for dessert. Later, lying in a lounge chair on the deck, cool night air raising the hair on their bodies to protective buoyancy, he spoke to her with more urgency in between long, thirsty drafts of beer. They lay outside, she tucked into the vee of his legs, while his hands moved over every inch of her that he could reach.

She listened to him now as he choked himself awake and then settled back into a steady rasp. She wanted to talk about the trip, but she knew how much he needed the rest. After deciding that she would never be able to sleep, she lay on her back with her hands behind her head and dozed off.

———

She had decided to tell her third graders first.

Jen Allen had burst into tears and was taken to the principal's office until she calmed down.

"Big deal," Richard Rodriguez grumped from his back row seat with his arms laced tightly across his chest; Alpha sent him along after Jen.

Her class at Groton Elementary was such a mixed bag. In her education courses at the University of Maine, she had been taught that everything worked according to levels. First graders were like this, and fifth graders like that. It was as predictable as the seasons according to the books. In reality, her class consisted of advanced kids of Bostonian surgeons as well as the hungry-bellied progeny of working-people.

The precocious, towheaded surgeon's son piped up, "One of the largest and most ferocious predators in the world roams the wilds of Alaska."

"Really?" Alpha asked. "And that would be?"

"Grizzly bears," he said. "Actually, grizzly bears are the largest carnivorous predator on the earth."

"What's that mean, smarty-pants?" Priscilla Barnes sneered.

The boy was unruffled. "It means they're as big as a house," he said, "and they eat people whole. Alive, too."

The children gasped.

Alpha laughed. "Well, I don't think they eat people as a rule," she said. "If they did, they'd have starved to death long ago. You see, there aren't any people where we're going. It's the wilderness."

"What's that?"

"What about the grizzly bears?"

"When are you coming back?"

"Who lives there? There must be *some* people there?"

They began firing questions all at once; it was a good distraction from the regular lesson plan.

Alpha went to the front of the room and pulled down the map of North America.

"We're here," she said, flicking her finger against the heavy, latex surface of the state of Massachusetts. She moved to the left and reached five fingertips to the upper corner of the map. "This is where I'm going. Alaska."

⌒

"*Alaska?* Have you lost your Christly bitten mind?" her father had shouted, then turned immediately to her mother. "Has she lost her mind?" It was his favorite conversational ploy, to turn to the one person who wouldn't dare answer him, effectively silencing the one who might.

She had taken her whole weekend to drive home to Lincoln, Maine, to tell her parents, a weekend she could have spent with Zach at the cabin, or making up her lesson plan for the following week. But there she had sat with her parents in the stuffy kitchen that smelled of too many years of boiled meat and cabbage, her father indulging in the usual harangue preparatory to the brick-wall treatment.

"This freakin' Zach is a lunatic," he said to Alpha. "I told you he was a lunatic, didn't I?" he shouted, pointing a reedy finger at her mother. Her mother looked him steadily in the eye, her mouth drawn straight across the bottom of her face. Once, it may have been the effort to resist reply that had drawn it so, but now, Alpha was sure, no words welled behind the thin slash.

"Christ, girl, I knew it would come to this," he directed himself back at Alpha now. "You move out of the house because you think your big shot education has made you something. You don't know diddly about diddly and you never will. Just like your freakin' mother except she got sense enough to stay home."

Once Alpha had moved out and become more independent, she had taken the tack of responding reasonably and rationally to his blustering, though she never got to finish. Even now when she tried to reason with him—that Zach was infinitely capable and that she could learn, Zach thought she could or he wouldn't be taking her—he cut her off by stalking out the door. She stood in silence with her mother, both of them well aware the dust had not settled. They could hear him knocking around in the woodshed next to the house, boots scrunching the late winter muck as he returned.

He slammed in, not even pausing to take off his mud-clumped boots, and hurled something heavy to the floor behind her.

"There!" he shouted. "Let's see you do something about that."

Her mother's hands crossed themselves over her mouth before she turned away. The scene was escalating to the dreaded level. Sweat trickled lightly down the trough of her spine to the waistband of her jeans. The woodstove blazed away in the corner of the living room, and Alpha turned to the window as if to project herself through the ripply glass into air she could breathe. But she was trapped by his anger, just as she had always been, so she forced herself to turn, to turn and face it.

The huge chunk of spruce lay in the middle of her mother's carefully braided rug where he'd dropped it. With the toe of his unlaced Sorrel, he flipped the wood on end, then raised the axe over his head in the familiar swing and let the blade fall. It bit into the flat, chainsawed surface and held. He backed away, gesturing to Alpha. "Go ahead, Miss Alaska. Split that up so you can make a fire."

Alpha could feel her mother's back turned to it all, but her foremost thought was to keep from hurting the rug that Alpha knew she prized. Alpha walked to the middle of the room, rocked the axe handle up and down until finally the bite let loose. She put the axe down and hefted the spruce, cradling it in the crooks of her arms. "Bring the axe," she said to him, then turning to her mother, "We'll finish this outside."

She heard him clumping out the door behind her as she moved carefully across the yard. She could have walked away; she could have gotten in her car and driven away from the whole stupid thing. Her brother did it all the time, but something in her would not allow it. The image of her mother's flat-line mouth was vivid, and she rejected it.

She set the wood down with a grunt. The open door shafted a wedge of light across them, her mother inside, stooping over the rug, whisking the detritus of her father's temper into a dustpan. Though she couldn't see his face, she knew it well enough: the left cheek a wrinkled sneer that hooked up the corner of his mouth.

She took the axe. "Stand away then," she said as she'd heard men say a million times in her life.

A snort. "Stand away, my ass."

She hacked at the wood for a good twenty minutes before he tired of the game "And that's not even hardwood," he said. Satisfied that he had won, he went inside and slammed the door shut. She dropped the axe and stood in the dark listening as he continued his tirade. *"Who the hell does she think she is? She can't make a Christly fire, she don't shoot guns, she wouldn't know a food animal if it up and licked her."*

Alpha didn't feel the cold, only the relief of knowing she had not backed down. The sky to the east glowed sulfur yellow from the lights of the pulp mill that labored twenty-four hours a day. Once as familiar as the rhythm of her heart, it ground at her ears now. The smell, too, like welled-up sewage, was stench to her after the sun-shot smell of the forest where she lived in Massachusetts. It was all a part of her father.

She wandered to what was left of her garden. Her mother did not grow things — didn't want to deal with the mess, she always said. But Alpha had bored her fingers into earth from day one. She had begun with a tiny plot and slowly enlarged it every year. She could breathe within the slatted fence her brother had built with staves salvaged from the pallet plant, safe from the people who had no interest whatsoever in finding out what she could do.

The tiny enclosure once hummed with sunflower and morning glory tepees, vegetables, and wildflowers. The ground still gave to her weight. She had turned it and aerated it religiously every spring and fall so that it was springy and rich, the perfect medium for growth. She knew she could make life like that for her children.

Eyes closed, Alpha could smell the pungent tomato plants as she harvested the perfectly colored Best Girls that were her favorites, feel their silky skin in her rough palm. The feel of grown

things in her hand always soothed her; she never tired of looking at the colors splashed over her skin. Orange, green, yellow,
each color with its own smell and texture, life shaped in her cupping hands.

She kneeled and pulled brittle stalks away from the day lilies
that used to rim the perimeter with their bloom-laden spikes, tears
dripping on her hands, furious to find that her father could still
provoke her so. He would say nothing more with words now, only
with silence, or sniggers, or gestures. The old brick wall routine.
In spite of her tears, she did not dread it anymore. She had begun
the process of breaking out and away two years ago when she
moved to Massachusetts to take her teaching job. That first step
was good but it was not enough. The more her senses were stimu-
lated, the more they craved. In spite of her fear of losing all that
she had saved, she trusted Zach. She had to. She couldn't get
where she wanted to go without him.

She rose, swiping dirt clots from her knees as she walked back
to the house. All was as she expected inside: raucous snorts from
the couch where her father lay asleep in a crumpled mess, her
mother in the armchair close to the woodstove, trying to cook the
cold from forever frozen bones. She could not believe she was a
part of that picture. The smell of woodsmoke was strong in the
room; she must have just stoked the fire before Alpha came in. She
crossed the braided rug to her mother's chair and leaned over to
plant the customary kiss on her cheek before going to bed. Her
lips went rigid on her mother's cool skin.

" 'Night," she said, and turned to the dark hall that led to
her room.

"He don't mean anything by it, Ally," she heard her mother say
softly.

Alpha stopped in the gloomy hall, canted her head sideways, let
the lie bounce harmlessly against her thick hair and fall away. She
closed the door to her room and stripped off her clothes before

crawling into bed, all without turning on the light. She didn't need it. She knew exactly what she was doing.

⌒

Zach had worked late that night so he had to make the calls from the shop phone. He had a big order due on Monday. It was best that Alpha had gone to her parents' for the weekend because he'd have to work straight through. One of the big furniture stores had taken a shine to the CD racks he made, and they were selling well. They'd called him early that week for an order twice the size of the previous one, and they were hoping to have them in stock by Monday and could he manage? *Sure*, he'd said. Allrightyroo. He'd have them there before opening Monday morning. This kind of gig was his bread and butter, and it bored him spitless.

But just now, as he was trying to make some sense with this guy on the phone, his apprentice chose to bevel shelf slabs on the router, which had to be the loudest machine in the shop.

"Jesus H. Christ, Hank, I'm on the phone to Alaska. Shut it down!" but he'd ended up having to wing a chunk of oak at him to get his attention. "Hand sand something, will ya? I'm on the phone here." Hank sulked across the shop and clamped a slab of pale ash to the bench before going at it with a hand plane.

"Lookit," Zach said to the official at Fish and Game in Anchorage. "I'm having a hard time getting this stuff straight, you know? Now, what's the deal again?"

"Just tell me where you want to go," the guy told him. "That's what I need to know first."

Zach could feel the heat spreading down his neck. He didn't know how much information to give up. If he told the truth, would it screw up his chances of going to the stream he had decided would most probably yield gold to his pan? His friend Arnie didn't really know what was required. As many magazines as he had read and videos he had seen, none of them really spelled out the legal situation, saying only that a prospector had to contact local authorities as to the proper course of action and what sort of permit was required.

Finally, he confessed to the guy where he wanted to go and what kind of prospecting he planned to do. There was a long pause on the other end during which he could hear papers rustling, and *clackety-clack* as the computer was consulted.

"Hmmm," came the response from Anchorage.

"What's that mean?" Zach asked.

"The good news is you don't need any of our permits there."

"Good. Great," Zach said. "I take it there's bad news?"

"The bad news is you don't need our permits because you won't be on State or Federal land."

"What other kind of land is there?"

"The private kind. You'll have to contact the Corporation directly for permission to do anything on its land. The Ingalik Native Corporation, to be exact."

Natives? Zach thought. Arnie didn't say anything about natives. He'd said they might have to get permits from the government or something, but never natives.

"How do I go about that?"

There was a pause on the line.

"Hello?"

"Uh, yeah, I'm here," the official said. "Listen, buddy, do you know anything about what's going on up here?"

He could practically feel the steam rising from his back. Hank slithered out for a cigarette and Zach let him go.

He cleared his throat. "I'm not sure what you mean."

There was an audible sigh at the other end of the line. "This state's about to explode," the man said. "I'm talking mini civil war. Natives want priority in all subsistence hunting and fishing, plus they want their own governmental control over their people and their land. Sovereignty, in other words. It's way more complicated than that, and it's been coming to a head for a long time. It's a lot of politics. You know."

"Yeah, sure," Zach said.

He swiped the scrap wood onto the floor and was satisfied at the clatter. From the corner of his eye he caught Hank peering in at the door. "Shut the goddamn door. You're letting all the heat out." Hank disappeared. Zach spoke evenly into the mouthpiece, "I was only gonna dink around with a pan, *maybe* a rocker box."

"Still gotta get permission from the Corporation, and that isn't going to happen, not the way things are going out here."

Zach had been afraid of this, which was why he had been hesitant to say where he was going. He definitely had no desire to provoke the native people, but this was the stream he had set his sights on.

"Any chance a fellow could just mosey out there, inconspicuous like, and not get bothered?"

"Look, man, there's a hell of a lot of territory to this state. People always think there's nobody out there, nobody will find you. But there are people out there, and word travels like wildfire in the bush. You'd only have to be spotted for a second and . . ."

"And what?"

"There'd be trouble."

"How much trouble?"

"Some areas, it's hard. Where you're going, the head of the Corporation is kind of pro-development. I believe he's trying to encourage tourism. Camping, photography, rafting, stuff like that. But the CORE is strong in that area, too, and some unpleasant situations have developed out there."

Zach's neck prickled. "What's the CORE?"

"The radical native faction. They're pro-native, anti-white. Period."

"Well," Zach said, "I'll be very careful in my dealings with the Corporation."

"That would be smart," the man said

When Zach hung up, Hank appeared at the door.

"Let's get those shelves routed," he said.

He would have to contact the Corporation for permission to camp on their land, and pay for that privilege, the Fish and Game guy had said. Camping fees just for starters, and mining fees, not to mention a tax that would be levied on anything they might find. But he had to decide whether or not to tell them he wanted to pan the stream. Hell, it was just a tiny stream and it wasn't as if he was going in with a bunch of dredges and high bankers. There was every chance he would come out empty-handed with two thousand bills down the sink for his trouble.

He had been thinking of big country and panning for gold since he'd read about the 1897 Klondike gold strikes in his schoolbooks. He hadn't realized how much that little information had festered in his brain until he overheard Arnie talking in the bar one night. He'd bought him beer after beer to keep him talking until his speech became unintelligible. Zach came back, night after night, feeding him beer to get him warmed up, gathering as much information as he could until he'd thought, *Hell, I can do this. I gotta do this.*

Zach had never been much of a reader, but when he was interested in something, he would read everything he could find until he was satisfied he knew it all. He spent many of his Sundays, the only days off he allowed himself, at the Boston Public Library on Copley Square, devouring every prospecting magazine they stocked. Of the thousands of glossy pictures he scanned, none looked so alluring as Alaska; it seemed like the kind of place where a person could get lost and pan undisturbed. He wanted to be out there, of that he was certain. The country was big, big enough to breathe in, roam in, make a life in.

He had no desire to make a big operation of it, or join one of the organizations that frequently took people on summer trips to Nome and other places in the state to prospect on a club's leased territory. The idea of going on a tour with a bunch of rock geeks was out of the question. An individual operation was the best way, he was sure, and with Arnie's information, he had a pretty sure bet. But the idea of doing it alone was not so appealing. He thought of other men he could fold into his idea, but the thought of letting someone else in on his big plan made him feel like lifting his leg on a tree. And that's when he thought of Alpha. She would go with him, help out in any way she could and she would not try to one-up him.

He realized he hadn't even told the guy at Fish and Game he was planning to bring a girl with him. As far as she knew, their time in Alaska was a vacation. They would simply pan for gold and come away with a bankroll big enough to set them up together, married, with a home and large shop where he could build the kind of furniture he really wanted to build. Alpha never questioned his decision to leave the shop temporarily, and this was something that stood her in good stead with him. It was his business, she'd said, and she would mind hers. He decided to tell Alpha of his plans to lie to the Corporation about their activities on the stream, but he would not tell her about the CORE.

3

The beach was crowded with men readying their boats for the commercial fishing season that opened in two days. Though he had made her wait an hour, Bailey was careful to greet Kash with a smile when he came down to the plane.

"Ready?" Bailey called to him. "I'd like to get in tonight. Weather's supposed to hold."

"I'll call my daughter then, let her know I'll be in tonight so she can pick me up."

"Good deal," she said.

"You got food with you?"

"Enough for me for three days. Better bring something along."

"Hate to get stuck and fight over food with you," he said. Often when he came up to the Lodge he had managed to stay over for a meal and could not let her forget that she ate as much as he did. Her metabolism was high and working in the bitter cold burned calories fast.

"No doubt you'd lose, so make sure you bring plenty," she said.

He seemed pleased with the repartee and probably construed it as flirting.

The cockpit was noisy and she did not have an extra set of headphones that would have allowed them to back-and-forth it without shouting. Climbing over the Yukon, then the Innoko River,

they saw moose and black bear that had come down to the Delta
for tender spring forage, but no grizzlies. They tended to stay upriver, where there was less human activity.

They crossed the Alaska Range at Merrill Pass since the weather
was good and the ceiling high. The usual updrafts and crosses gave
them a good ride through the peaks, but neither of them was
prone to airsickness. Pity, she thought. She would have liked to see
him squirm a little. Once over the mountains she connected frequently with air traffic control. She could see plenty of traffic
around them already. Lake Hood in Anchorage was the busiest
float plane base in the world, which made sense in a state the size
of Alaska that had few roads. They landed on the lake without a
problem. She was careful to adhere to the established though unmarked traffic lanes. It was pure entertainment for her when
yahoos came in without consulting and crossed the lines. The
invective-laden garble on the radio was delightful.

She taxied to the public landing first to unload Kash. There was
a pay phone there where he could call his daughter.

"Jeanette says she's got plenty of room," he shouted from the
phone. "Need a place?"

Bailey had never met the girl, young woman, really; had no
idea what her leanings were. She had graduated from University of
Alaska at Anchorage with a degree in wildlife biology and was in-
terning with Fish and Game for the summer. Eventually, she
hoped to get a position on the Yukon so she could be close to
home. Probably she was nice as pie. But if she was like most
daddy's girls, she wouldn't appreciate Daddy bringing home a
woman for the night, even a platonic one, much less a white one.

Bailey tugged absently on the bill of her cap, turned to look at
her plane bobbing gently on the lake.

"Guess I'll stay with the plane," she said, though her aching
body would have preferred a comfortable bed.

Kash returned to move his duffel farther up the ramp. "You're aware of the crime rate here?"

"Here in particular?" she said, letting her eyes encompass the lake, "or Anchorage in general?"

"Both," he said, looking at her steadily to ward off the glib comment he obviously sensed bubbling behind her lips.

She shrank from the sincerity in his face, did not even experience a moment's difficulty swallowing the opportunity to let loose a barb, and responded with equally steady eyes, "All the more reason to stay with the plane. Besides, I'll be sleeping with the best protection I know of. I won't worry a minute."

"I know you think you're tough enough to hunt bear with a baseball bat, but I hope your 'protection' is a little more substantial than that."

She did not feel insulted in the least. Smiled sweetly and said "I believe it is."

"Good," he said, grinning back at her. "Listen, I'd be happy to test your appetite against my wallet tonight if you're not otherwise occupied." He'd said it quickly, pushing the words over themselves as if to overrun his panic at saying them. His eyes refused to touch hers, to give her the satisfaction of the visual sign.

She had not even been out in public, unless Lake Hood or Ingalik could be counted as public, much less been out with a man, for six years. For a flash of a moment she considered it. Broward had taken her out to dinner, listened with the patience of Job as she talked about what she had to deal with. She had been so relieved that he didn't mind Temple, she had granted him access willingly, surprised to discover that the body she considered merely a tool was also a woman's body, and horribly surprised to realize that Temple's body had changed, too. She should have known.

As quickly as the possibility danced before her she repelled it. She would not take the risk and almost said it aloud, *I wouldn't risk it,* but caught herself in time to say instead, "Nice of you to ask in spite of. my appearance," spreading her hands to indicate her battered Carharts, boots, and heavily napped sweater, "but I've got an early start tomorrow with the mechanic and a long day after that taking care of your errands," but said it smiling, as graciously as she could, so as not to gibe him overmuch.

"I'm sorry about that," he said, and she thought he'd meant about not having dinner with her and then he said, "but you will be paid for time and expenses, don't worry about that. And they have instructions on how the systems operate up at the lodge. At least that kid said he understood everything, said he knew how to deal with propane. You do nothing more than drop them off . . . Damn, there's one more thing."

Bailey rolled her eyes.

"Could you stop at the Village and pick up the radio for the Lodge? Raina has it at the store. Fuel the plane while you're there, on the house."

He was as close to being apologetic as she'd ever heard him get.

"Deal," she said.

"A good one," he said. "A hundred bucks worth of fuel for a ten minute stop."

She couldn't argue that. "Okay. A *good* deal."

When his daughter arrived, Bailey pasted on a smile and waved at the beautiful young woman she could barely see through the tinted windows of the Bronco; she didn't expect a response as would be the case in the bush, but Jeanette waved back and smiled. Kash hefted the duffel to his back and walked away. Bailey turned to the plane, heard the door slam behind her, but then Kash was calling out, "When you taking off?"

She turned back to him. "Tomorrow night, soon as those kids show up and weather permitting."

He nodded, a heavy arm dangling down the outside of the car, and stared at her from a face empty of anything she could interpret. So intent was his gaze she almost missed the hand bending backward at the wrist, fingers parted slightly, in a gesture of such diffidence she doubted she had seen it. Her eyes watered as if they had been touched.

⟶

After the plane was squared away in a slip at the Aviatec docks, Bailey acknowledged the outstanding headache that had begun to plague her. The first few flights of the season always did it. So much light. So much horizon. After the long darkness and half-light of winter, it took some getting used to. She removed the passenger seats in the rear of the plane, then unrolled her sleeping bag and pad. She had washed up earlier at the bathroom in the hangar, compliments of some poor slob who was working late on repairs. Her mechanic had seniority in the company, and never worked late anymore, though he liked to start early. The man was eminently competent and she respected competence; insisted on it when it came to her airplane, her survival.

She zipped herself into the sleeping bag—red, like her airplane—and felt deliciously safe, a raw cardiac muscle in its pericardial sac. Her hands stayed crossed behind her head, just under the occipital curve where the weight of the cranium would contribute to pressure pointing her headache to a more manageable level. Though it was midnight, the sun shafted relentlessly in. She left the near door ajar to keep cool air circulating through the cabin. She liked to sleep cold, probably a habit she picked up from her childhood. Fresh air, her mother had insisted, was good for your health, though she could hardly be trusted as a spokesperson.

To combat the onslaught in her brain, she tried to breathe evenly and focus on the comfort of being in her airplane. The blunt outline of the .20 gauge snuggled securely to her leg, the grip at hand's easy reach, shell chambered and ready. Again, she went over exactly what she knew about the two people she would have to bring back to Ingalik tomorrow night. They were coming from Massachusetts, some small town near Boston and Raina said they had accents she found hard to understand. Bailey smirked inwardly at that; she knew well what happened to the language in the mouths of certain New Englanders.

The woman, the girlfriend, was a complete unknown. The man's name was Zachary Scott. Raina had said he seemed nice, polite, though hardly up on his bush skills. Didn't know the difference between a brown and a grizz, nor did he realize that black bears also occupied this habitat. Didn't know it stayed light twenty-four hours a day during summer. He'd learn and do it the quick, brutal way. Necessity and shame could mainline knowledge into the heads of rubes more efficiently than any other method. But it was pointless to relish that if she ended up being the one to have to teach it. They would only be five miles upriver and you could just damn betcha the woman would be on Bailey like a bird dog. Chatter chatter chatter, show her the flowers. She would have to figure out a way to lay down the law. Put on the smile, fly them upriver and drop them off and, excuse me, I'm busy forever after that.

Thinking about Zachary Scott and his girlfriend in this cursory way relaxed her. The pounding in her skull ebbed to a level that would allow sleep. Float planes roared in and out regularly, raising wakes that undulated to the Phoenix and rocked her in its blazing red belly.

⟶

They were staying in a campground on the outskirts of Anchorage; hotel prices during the tourist season were outrageous and, what the hell, this was a good way for Alpha to ease into camping. He consulted his watch which, he was amazed to realize, he could actually see clearly at 1:00. At midnight, he'd crawled out of the tent to piss but had to trudge to the Porta-Johns because the light offered no privacy.

Twelve more hours and they would be so close to his dream he could hardly stand it. He looked at Alpha, turning carefully so as not to wake her, and wondered for the jillionth time whether it was a good idea to bring her. She had been born and raised in rural Maine, and she was accustomed to a rigorous lifestyle of sorts, but, being a woman, her body had not been subjected to the hardships of outdoor life. She raised food in a garden, prepared the meat and fish brought home by the men in her life, canned and cleaned, knew how to keep a woodstove perking, and could cook like a dream in his estimation. But she had never used an axe, much less a chainsaw, did not know how to crank an outboard or know Thing One about motors at all.

That was the way a woman should be, but, given their time limit, she would not be able to hang out in the cabin all day while he busted his ass in the wash of the stream. She would have to be right in there with him. No doubt about it, time would have to be spent in educating her about survival, and time was scarce. They could only afford two weeks at the Corporation's lodge on the upper watershed of the Ingalik River.

As if awakened by his thoughts, Alpha opened her eyes, lids sliding up over sheets of green so unearthly it always made him open his mouth a little, suck an extra breath. She looked at him, face hard and blank until the sun rose behind it and she smiled back at him, then frowned, blowing errant bangs away from her forehead. *"I must look like shit, because my mouth sure feels like a dog crapped in it."*

He laughed. It just cracked him up when she tried to talk dirty.

She tried to soften the clamped set of her jaw when she realized that Zach was watching her, then managed to bring herself back enough to smile at him. She had never been one to lose sleep over life's questions and lack of answers. Sleep had always come to her, immediate and profound. Zach teased her about it. The sleep of the pure, he called it. She never thought about it, really, at least not until she had started to think long into the night once they bought the tickets for Anchorage.

Somehow she had imagined Alaska would be like the Westerns

she used to watch with her brother on Saturday afternoons, pictured herself stepping off a plane onto a dusty main street edged by wood-framed buildings with horses tied out front. But so far, Alaska was like everywhere else—Wal-Marts, video shops, endless strips of stores punctuated by ubiquitous fast food chains. Urban areas lacked the charm of cities back East. She wondered if it was because the cities themselves were so young, like the guidebook said. Anchorage itself was only around eighty years old. And when it went up, it went up in a hurry, the bulk of the expansion a result of World War II and then the Cold War. Though the city itself was ugly, it couldn't have been set amid more natural splendor. The snowcapped Alaska Range half-circled it, opening out onto Cook Inlet. "Dramatic" was the word that came to her mind, like the travel brochures said.

The whole state was dramatic. It had the highest mountain in North America, the richest oil deposits, and the most land. It was bigger, even, than Texas. But the place was downright crowded with people from all over the world. The airport was worse than Logan in Boston. Every concourse seethed with people carrying gun cases, fishing equipment, and plastic coolers smothered in duct tape. She could not figure out where they all could possibly go without running into each other at every step.

Zach had been very worried about stowing the guns while they overnighted in the campground. He took great pains to bury the hard-bodied gun cases underneath the duffels in their tent, and then threw a blanket over the whole caboodle. She could feel him worrying about the gear even when they took a short stroll around the campground after a meager dinner of reconstituted goulash. He would not be able to relax until they loaded the float plane at Lake Hood.

———

Zach couldn't believe he was being driven around Anchorage in a taxi that was a station wagon. When the guy first pulled up at the campground office, he thought it was a joke. Alpha laughed right out loud. *Look,* the driver had explained defensively. *You wouldn't believe the shit people come out here with. Everybody's got guns, rods, tons of camping gear, pretty much like this pile I'm looking at right here. Didja think I could stuff it all in the trunk of a friggin' Pinto?*

They had driven past all the aviation buildings on Lake Hood, and still could not find the one Raina had told them to look for. *Be on time,* she had told him, *'cause Bailey don't wait.* Alpha sat stiff-spined on the edge of the seat, neck stretched taut in her effort to find the right building. She seemed nervous, and he knew there was something he should be doing, talking to her, perhaps, or some such shit. But he just couldn't focus on it now when their flight out to the Village was possibly in jeopardy.

He asserted himself a little more firmly with the smart-assed cab driver. "Look, man, if you don't know the place as well as you thought just pull over at a phone booth and I'll call the hangar for directions." And why hadn't he thought to do that in the first place, just to make double sure? It never occurred to him that a taxi driver would not be able to find the place. He was about to mess with the guy's ego a little more when Alpha yelped and jabbed a finger at the window.

"There," she said. "It's that little building right behind this brown one."

The driver swore, and turned around until he found a place to maneuver the overloaded station wagon to the rear of the building. It crept down to the lake, sandwiched between the building and a high, chain link fence. As they inched slowly around the corner, a bright red float plane tethered to a short floating dock came into view.

"That's the plane," Alpha said. "I bet that's her."

"Where?" Zach asked. The only human he could see was what looked like the back of a small man standing on one of the plane's pontoons, hat pulled low on his head, wearing a ratty old sweater against the chill wind coming off the lake. He was operating some sort of bicycle pump that was sucking water out of the pontoon. He didn't seem to have noticed them pulling up. But Alpha was already out of the taxi and bounding toward the plane.

Over the whoosh and rush of the pump, Bailey didn't hear her coming and nearly pitched into the water before catching herself by slapping one hand flat against the Phoenix's tail section. At least she hadn't let go of the pump, which would certainly have sunk to the grungy bottom in five feet of water. She managed to limit her reaction to the smack of hand on metal and the satisfying hiss of a swear word.

Behind her, the girl babbled away. Blah blah blah late, blah, inconvenience, taxi, blah blah, confusing, blah expensive, blah name's Alpha. That got Bailey's attention. Alpha? Had she heard right? When the girl with the funny name finally fell silent, Bailey said quietly, *Be with you in a minute,* and continued to pump the last of the water out of the float. As she shoved the handle against the pressure of air and water she closed her eyes, breathed through her nose and gushed the exhalation in time with the water. She must turn and meet this situation, turn and meet strangers, smile and be cordial.

Bailey resolved to try with a smile smeared across her lower face like clown paint. But she could never have prepared herself for what she saw. The hand she had thrust out to this babbler, this Alpha, remained frozen in mid-air as the girl took it, grasp light and sure, and let that high-wattage smile scald the darkened interiors of Bailey's eyes.

It was Temple's smile, the face that made people feel like a million, long as they could forget she wasn't playing with a full deck. Temple delighted everyone, Bailey knew, but she could never understand why they took it seriously once they knew that that sumptuous, unctuous love was completely undiscerning, that it was freely available to anyone and everyone. Which only reminded

Bailey of the man who took advantage of it; but that was later, when Temple was eighteen, so radiant. But long before that, Bailey had had her hands full keeping them away as they prowled in, low-bellied, like sneaking dogs. In spite of her efforts, there was the one sonovabitch, the one who'd slipped past all her smoke screens. She had to take care of that, too, and Bailey believed that Temple had experienced grief for the first time in her life and had keened when they took it away. Once the keening ceased, she could not tell how much Temple remembered, if anything, of the pregnancy, the birth. But Bailey remembered it all, and sometimes felt as if the weight of the memories were doubled; that she had to assume the burden of the memories Temple could not retain. She imagined, sometimes, that her heart bristled with poisoned needles that could never be removed.

She held the girl's hand, did not speak, tried to and stammered, feeling still the smear of her mouth. *Grab it,* she told herself. *Get a chokehold.* She had learned to handle fear that way as a child and it was the only technique she knew.

Had she sucked in her breath, or did she imagine it? *Hold tight. Squeeze with all your might,* said her child's rhyme.

She dropped the clasped hand, her own trembling as it drifted back to her side, and turned away, saying to the girl aloud, "You're late."

No kidding, Alpha thought. Didn't she just finish explaining that very thing and the reason for it? Had she not, in fact, also apologized for same? This woman had been in the woods too long, was Alpha's immediate reasoning, but she had seen something, too. Had watched something light behind the woman's eyes and felt the hand turn wooden in hers. It was as if she recognized her, but almost instantly lost the light and turned with nothing more than that obvious remark. She felt a chill, and wiped a damp palm down the leg of her pants.

And then Zach was there beside her, thank God, setting down a load of equipment. He eyed the plane and swiveled around for a look at the mountain of stuff still back on the asphalt.

"Hope it'll all fit," he said. Then, "I'm Zachary Scott. I guess you're Bailey the pilot."

And now the woman turned to him with a normal smile on her face and stuck out her hand like she was a regular person.

"Hi," she said, smoother now, then frowning as she noticed the mountain of gear behind him. "Won't be able to handle all that. Got a backup plan?"

"Well, not exactly." Zach seemed like a little kid all of sudden, awkward and unsure.

"Rule Number One," Bailey said. "Always have a backup plan when you're out in the bush. But you'll figure that out. And you'll also figure out that all the rules are Number One." She said it smiling, not gruff like before, and Alpha felt her shoulders release from where tensed muscles had sucked them into their sockets.

Bailey seemed anxious to get going and offered the backup plan herself. "Sort through your gear. Figure out what you'll need first and foremost, survival-wise, what you'll need to set up camp, food, et cetera, and have the rest of it air-freighted out to the Village. It'll cost you some, but I'll wager you were smart enough to set some money aside for an emergency." She said the last part like a question, and Alpha was gratified to be able to answer that yes, in fact, she had insisted on it, but they didn't have much.

They called the air freight company to come over for the excess baggage, catching them, luckily, just as they were about to close, unluckily for the fellow who had to drive out to the lake for the freight. Zach and Alpha stirred up their belongings, selecting what they thought they'd need, keeping as much as possible, while Bailey leaned quietly against a wing strut, watching them. When they'd done, she picked up a load and carried it to the plane. They followed her with as much as they could carry. Alpha tried to make small talk, but soon gave up against the wall of businesslike silence that entombed their pilot.

Zach sat stiffly beside Bailey in the passenger's seat, and Alpha sat behind him, gear piled to the roof around her, even under her seat and legs. The racket in the plane was unbelievable as they took off. Alpha kept her hands clamped over her ears while they taxied out to the proper side of the lake, but found herself gripping the back of Zach's seat, eyes wide and unblinking as they roared up the lake toward a tiny island that began as a speck but loomed close as all hell now and still they had not lifted from the water.

Bailey had pumped the yoke in and out a couple of times to no obvious effect, and Alpha could only assume it meant they weren't going to make it. Her eyes were transfixed now on Bailey's other hand, which gripped an inside strut on the dashboard and seemed to hold her up enough out of her seat so that she could see out. How could she fly the plane if she couldn't even see out? Alpha focused on Bailey's hand, the unnaturally long fingers curled around the metal, almost folding back on themselves, blue veins stark and wriggling across shifting bone and tendon. She was aware of the huge wall of spray outside her window, and in the distance beyond the hand the low, scrubby island looming very close now.

Bailey pumped the yoke again and then the spray was gone and they were passing over the island, Alpha didn't know how. They were so close she could see the expressions on the faces of the two men who were there, Bailey had told them, to tend the pigs. The Department of Fish and Game had planted them there to eat the eggs laid by seagulls which were becoming a nuisance, not to mention a hazard, to the air traffic around the lake. And then she even saw the pigs, one with a dark spot on its back, as they ran for their lives through the brush. But the plane was up now, she realized, and going higher. She craned her neck to the side and watched the earth rush away.

She had felt, until now, that they could stop any time they wanted to. That they could change their minds and go home. Now the noise and the shuddering airplane felt final to her. She could not go back now. Had she wanted the plane to fail on take-off so they could abort the trip and lay the blame on something else? No. She was determined to make the best of this. And just now, approaching the mountains they had gawked at from Anchorage, she could see forever, the late evening subarctic sun so intense it seemed to illuminate every speck of the universe. Occasionally, she could see tiny cabins at the edges of bright ribbons of water; no roads led to or from them. Her heart whomped her ribs a little harder at the prospect of living like that. The fresh adrenaline felt good. They seemed to be flying into a long valley, perhaps the pass Bailey had said would take them through the mountains and into the big country. She strained her body up as far as it would stretch to see ahead of them, to see where she was going.

───

Zach spotted the slim, glinting line of the Yukon River half an hour before they reached it. He was a little confused when they crossed a fairly large watershed before they reached what he thought was the great river. He checked the aeronautical chart he had folded and refolded to allow for their progress. He tapped Bailey's shoulder, then pointed down and screamed "Yukon?"

She shook her head and shouted "Innoko." He went back to his map and found the Innoko River on it, then peeled his eyes again for the distant ribbon. Even after four hours of flying through country that would make color covers of the glossiest outdoor magazines, he thought his heart would stop when they crossed the Yukon, Alaska's main artery.

And then he saw Ingalik Village nestled into a hillside, protected by a high bluff formed over centuries by the Yukon's muscular current. He pointed to the buildings and mouthed, "Ingalik?" to Bailey, who nodded, shouting "We'll have to land there for fuel."

This woman was sure as hell enigmatic, he thought. He'd felt almost clumsy next to her machine-like precision. There was no wasted motion in her movement. She had climbed all over the plane, lifting and loading things even he had strained over, and Alpha had looked almost ridiculous as she scrambled with awkward armloads of things to the plane, then teetered between the dock and pontoon, one time actually dropping an armload of stuff, half of which splashed into the water.

Alpha had tried to make conversation with them both in an effort to keep up with Bailey who hadn't responded at all. He could tell Alpha was confused by his behavior, but he would have to make it up to her later. Normally he was proud of her warm, gregarious nature. For now, he felt as if he were back on the playground in elementary school, forced to taunt or ignore the geeks in order to be accepted by the crowd. Instead, he was in country that could only be inhabited by men of backbone and character, and he harbored what he considered inferior feelings toward the woman he loved and on whom he would have to depend for more than love in the next couple of weeks.

4

Bailey felt as if her axis had tilted forty-five degrees. She did battle with her natural self, but could not seem to do any better than adopt an air of silent concentration. She felt the cold ooze from icy seams but the girl kept chattering, her desperate attempts at rapprochement increasingly feeble until finally she had shut up altogether and doggedly stumbled back and forth with her inefficient armloads of gear. Maybe she was more nervous than friendly, Bailey couldn't be sure yet. Perhaps the girl's rapprochement was false; believing this would have helped Bailey cast off the spell that enveloped her the minute she saw Alpha. It would have allowed her to be more congenial, to pin on the smile.

That hair, that white gold stuff waving thickly from her scalp, was only hair, Bailey reminded herself, and there must be hundreds of thousands of people on this earth with hair like that. She reacted to it so strongly only because she was accustomed to the darkened visages of the Ingalik. Six years was a long time, she reasoned, a long time to be away from the world. There was bound to be a time when her careful seclusion would be punctured, and she needed to make allowance for that. Expect it. Then she would be prepared

By the time they reached the Village, she had coaxed herself back to a vertical axis. She had to land before going on. A light headwind had dogged her the whole way out and she did not have enough fuel now to allow a margin of safety. She circled over the slough a couple of times to check for obstructions, noting with a twinge of unease that the beach was loaded with people. The commercial fishing season was coming up and that certainly kept fishermen out repairing nets, restoring winter damage done to boats and fish wheels. But the people she saw below were not engaged in any such activity. Had Raina mentioned some kind of celebration? She tried with no luck to raise her on the radio.

Even at 10:00 P.M. the sun pelted the landscape as freshly as if it were ten in the morning, so Bailey had no trouble landing the plane with good visuals; this, however, did nothing to ease her growing irritation at the idea of having to deal with a crowd in the company of a couple of white kids. She'd have to find Raina to get the radio and the keys to the fuel truck, and this would entail either dragging the kids around with her, or leaving them there amid a possibly celebrating and therefore liquored-up crowd. She decided to play it safe and told them to stay in the plane.

And then she saw Zach splash into the water on the other side of the plane. Was he that stupid or just overly cocky? Either way, he'd have to fend for himself. She was too distracted to herd him back into the plane.

Alpha was exhausted and nervous now in spite of the talking to she had given herself during the flight. Though Bailey had told them this would be a brief stop to refuel, Alpha wanted to unfold herself from the cramped position she'd had to hold for four hours. She crept awkwardly around the seat in front of her, then stepped down onto the pontoon. Her limbs were sluggish, but she was unprepared for total rebellion, and found herself sinking uncontrollably to her knees, one leg slipping from under her into the water. Zach, already wet to his crotch, splashed into the water to help her regain balance, but she snapped him away with her voice, and managed to stand until blood found its way into the crevices of her muscles.

She walked stiffly from the pontoon onto the beach and looked around. Coming from rural Maine had accustomed her to poverty, but this was beyond what she had grown up with. Dingy shacks lined the road leading away from the beach, and all manner of cast-aside vehicles and equipment lay twisted into the dirt and melting snow piles. Water coursed in runnels across the muddy beach, forming a pale, widening cloud in the already roiled water of the slough. Small mountains of blackened snow were visible here and there, mute reminders of the recently deceased winter.

"Not much like Massachusetts, is it?" Bailey said, with her eyes pinned on the tide of people that had sagged away from the plane.

"Where I grew up . . ." but Alpha was cut off by the roar of a jonboat skittering around the bend of the slough. She and Zach watched as the driver gunned the motor and then cut it off, causing the boat to scrape almost completely onto dry land. He didn't look at them, even glance their way; it was clear to Alpha, who smiled eagerly at him in her usual friendly way, that his avoidance was a conscious effort. She heard Bailey calling after the man in a voice that was barely stronger than its normal tone, "*Peter,*" so that the man, without ceasing to move on, turned his head to the side enough to acknowledge that he had heard her. "What's happening?" she asked.

He stopped, still not looking at them directly. "John Knik. Found him downriver in his boat this morning. They're layin' 'im out now." He turned away and continued up the muddied beach, not bothering to pick his way among the threading rivulets of water.

Alpha could feel her resolve slipping away, replaced now by queasiness, and a dull thump behind the bridge of her nose. She looked at her watch. It was 10:30. Bailey stood on the sand holding the plane by its tail rope as she scanned the crowd, tense, alert, watchful. Zach stood next to Bailey, hand smoothing his hair repeatedly. Alpha turned to see what was going on.

The edge of the crowd that had retreated now seemed to be

swelling closer to them. A small woman approached, moving very carefully, decidedly. When she got within five feet of them, she stopped and said Bailey's name by way of a greeting.

"Bad news about John Knik," Bailey said to the woman.

"Damn right," the woman said without raising her voice. "Damn right it's bad news when we lose our people to this Godawful shit."

Bailey held up her hands as if to ward off the weight of the words but the words came on.

"John Knik. Another drunk Indian screwed up. That's what you think. Truth is, John Knik was a young man who shoulda been full of hope. He had a wife and five kids and he's dead because he killed himself." She swayed hard as if the words had pushed her. "This kinda shit never used to happen. We survived because life was precious. Now these children, hell, all of us . . ." Her voice had not risen but the rage knotted in her throat gave the words distinct, clipped beginnings and endings. "Losing control of our land will kill us. But we will not let that happen. We remember."

Alpha was transfixed by the woman's eyes. They looked molten, as if they might seep darkly down her face. Bailey's voice had dropped impossibly low, "Just needed some fuel to get upriver," she was saying. "I'm flying for Kash. They're staying upriver," she gestured at Alpha and Zach, "like Kash agreed. They're paying you to stay there."

"Whadja bring 'em here for, eh? Think anybody here's got the time to waste on these people," the woman said, louder now, eyes squinting tightly so that her face appeared a grimace. And then Alpha registered the smell, like Zach smelled when he returned from one of his "steam-blowing" trips. This woman was drunk, and almost simultaneously Alpha realized that the men standing around in tight knots on the beach had begun to spread themselves out in a line.

Alpha stepped closer to the woman, stuck out her hand.

"Hello. I'm Alpha and this is my . . ." she stumbled a moment on what she should call Zach, then settled on "this is Zach. We're very happy to be here and grateful for . . ." she trailed off.

Stunned by this non sequitur, the woman was silent. She peered at Alpha's smiling face, and outstretched hand, examined them closely, and swayed a bit from the effort of shifting her focus from face to hand before exploding into rant.

Alpha's smilie was frozen across her face which only seemed to enrage the woman further.

". . . standin' there smilin' like a bunch of idiots. Get out. Leave."

Alpha heard the sound very distinctly in the split-second silence, the solid thunk of something hitting metal behind her. The identity of the sound didn't register until she saw one of the men on the beach raise his arm in a leisurely fashion as if to throw something, then heard the thunk again behind her.

From the corner of her eye she saw Bailey pivot and disappear then heard a brief wheeze before the engine caught. Zach had her by the hand now, and they had to splash, high-stepping, into the water to make it onto the tail of the retreating pontoons. Something bit the back of her outstretched arm, and it took her a minute to realize one of the rocks had struck her. Zach tugged at her, shouting over the engine noise, *get in*. She struggled to get her foot onto the step but her wet, muddy shoes kept slipping back. She saw rocks splashing into the water around her, ricocheting off the body of the plane, saw one fall onto the pontoon and remain there.

Finally she was in and scrambling over the top of the seat. She ended up on her knees on the seat, her cheek mashed into the maroon cordura material of a backpack. Her face was turned to the window where she saw another rock smack the pane and, beyond that, boats launching off the beach. *My God,* she thought, *have we been caught in a time warp and gone back to the days of the Wild Wild West? But no, we are in an airplane, not a stagecoach, and there are angry*

natives chasing us in motorboats, not bareback on mustangs. She saw
Zach on the wrong side of the window, perfectly silhouetted
against the wall of spray created by the plane speeding along the
surface of the water, fighting the door open against the onrush-
ing wind.

Alpha struggled to right herself, thinking that maybe if she just
got sitting forward in her seat, all this backwardness would re-
arrange itself. Halfway around she became aware of Bailey's voice
booming, *"Get in."* And just as she got herself straight, Zach was
in, water flying from the ends of his hair like a sprinkler, and then
the world muted somewhat as he slammed the door shut and
jammed the handle down.

"I told you to stay in the Goddamn plane!" Bailey shouted
at Zach.

Alpha cringed, tried to shrink farther in to her seat.

They were up now. Alpha had felt them lift off the water and
Bailey had the yoke practically jammed into her belly, forcing the
Phoenix to rise against its load, against its will, against all the
gravity that tried to hold them down.

Bailey's hand moved over the instrument panel, checking
switches, a long forefinger poking at one gauge after another until
the hand seemed satisfied, then her body twisting this way and
that, trying to see if there was any damage to the exterior of the
plane. She straightened, seemed to Alpha as if she had frozen like
that before erupting in a fury of movement, stomping the one
foot that was not engaged on a rudder repeatedly on the floor-
board. *"Goddammit,"* she yelled. *"Goddammit Goddammit Goddammit."* Alpha gazed idly at the blur of her pilot, thinking she
had never heard a woman cuss quite like that.

———

She had lost it, pure and simple, for the first time in—how long
had she been here now? Six years? It rattled the hell out of her and

she sat now as still as possible, trying to compress the rage that swelled her ribs so hard it hurt.

She had never seen the people in such a foul humor. She knew the history of their anger; it was the same from the time Russia sold Alaska to the United States in 1867 as it was now. Russian entrepreneurs crossed the Bering Sea, landed on the Aleutians, and promptly enslaved the natives there because of their skill at acquiring fur pelts, much as England's Hudson's Bay Company had done to aboriginals all across Canada. Not all of the encounters were physically cruel, but slavery was slavery, and the damage done to the human mind and spirit was more devastating than the agonies accreted by the flesh. The history of usurpation in Alaska was long, often bloody, and always sad; it was the kind of sadness spawned when you allowed yourself to examine in pure light the chain of cruelty intertwined irrevocably in your fiber, regardless of what you would do to break it in the course of your own, infinitesimal lifetime.

Contact with whites had brought nothing but misery and confusion. So what if you were one in thousands who tried to correct that, or simply not to interfere. The truth was, you interfered simply by being there. Bailey had realized this clearly the moment she made eye contact with Raina back on the beach. As she submitted to the barrage of heat from Ferrin's wife, she had caught Raina's eye at the back of the crowd where she stood resolutely, arms stitched across her chest as if to say, *If I come out for you, I come out against them*. It didn't matter which side of the good guy–bad guy equation you occupied. When the shit hit the fan, blood was blood.

The Village had turned against her but only because she'd had Zach and Alpha with her. Alone, she was no threat, but once the white faces began to multiply . . . The memory of Zach leaping into the water, and then the girl teetering down the pontoon as if she was out to pick flowers, all against Bailey's orders, made her wish she'd left them there for Kash to clean up. She rubbed a hand

across her aching ribs. Kash. He was going to get a big, hot, earful in the very near future.

In the meantime, what to do with these two people who
crimped the lining of her world unbearably? The weight of them
seemed to tilt the plane to starboard, though one glance at the
gyro told her it was balanced; even so, she had to stifle the urge to
peck at the port rudder pedal.

The immediate concerns were water and fuel. When she had
reconnoitered the upper river after iceout, there had been plenty
of water to enable her to land in front of the Lodge. With the scant
snow cover they'd had that winter, she knew the river would drop
more quickly than usual and farther, but she did not count on it
dropping this quickly. From the air, she eyed the river banks she
knew so well and realized that she had failed to adhere to Rule
Number One.

Now she was faced with the prospect of a difficult, perhaps impossible landing. And she could only spare enough fuel to make
one pass. And then what? Pain coiled tightly around the crown of
her head. In a few minutes, she would know one way or the other.
She trimmed her flaps and ailerons and prepared to go down.

They circled once before the plane leveled out and began to climb
again, heading away from the lodge. Zach felt his stomach hit
bottom and glanced at Bailey, making his eyebrows into question marks. He waited to see if she would bank again, turn back
to the Lodge, but she only continued to climb in the direction
from which they had come. He looked at her questioningly again,
then shouted "What's up?"

She still did not turn to meet his gaze but moved her mouthpiece aside and said clearly without seeming to have to raise her
voice, "Low water."

Zach craned from side to side to get a glimpse of the river, panic rising in his throat as he shouted at her "Whaddya mean, low water?"

She swung her eyes to him and spoke again in that voice that seemed to rise above the roar of the engine without straining itself. "Not enough water. Can't land."

"Are you sure?" he yelled at her, desperation pitching his voice high and twangy.

She turned to him again, looked him straight in the eye and said, "Yes."

Alpha leaned into his ear from behind to ask what was going on.

He turned as far toward her as he could and told her that they would not be able to land because of low water. He tried to compose his face in a mask of efficiency and control because he felt sure she would need to see that.

Then she had to ask, "What now?" and he thought that his chest might explode from the effort to remain calm.

"Dunno," he answered, "but I'm sure as hell gonna find out."

"What now?" he asked Bailey.

"Can't exactly fly around until it rains. We're low on fuel," she said.

"Is there someplace we can land?" he asked, trying to return his voice to a masculine octave.

"Yes," she said.

He heard in her voice the annoyed patience one exhibits to a child who simply cannot understand something that should be easily understood. He was tired of this woman's inscrutable act. Here he was in the middle of hell and gone with Alpha to take care of, spent every last of their dimes on this trip, come all this fucking way, been driven at a gallop out of the Village by angry natives and couldn't land because there was no water? He was dumbfounded. This cranky, stone-faced woman was screwing around with him and how the hell would he know if what she said was true? He felt trapped between helplessness and the desire to get what he wanted, what he came for.

He was shaking and dull-headed, afraid that Bailey would take them back to Anchorage, and equally afraid that Alpha would demand it. Scrapping the whole endeavor was the most logical course, for Alpha's sake. He couldn't believe he'd had this crazy idea in the first place, bringing a woman into the wilderness when he had not clue one as to what the situation would be. But he could not bring himself to quit until he was certain there was no hope whatsoever, until every shred of possibility had burned to ash. So he waited to see where Bailey would take them, and tried to steady his trembling heart.

Bailey had to decide in a hurry. She wanted to take the kids, kit and caboodle, back to Anchorage and to hell with Kash's schemes and contracts. She had a cache of AV gas at her camp, but it wasn't nearly enough to get back to the City. Her only choice was, of course, the least desirable, the one that left her responsible for these people for who knew how much longer.

If she kept them overnight, she would have to get them up to the Lodge herself, which meant she would have to supply them with a boat, too, her backup. Did they know anything at all about handling a boat on a river like this? No and hell no, so she would have to teach them. Zach hunched in his seat like a defiant child, hair dripping onto the thighs of his blue jeans. She could not see Alpha, but sensed her balled up tightly in the backseat. Oh joy, this was going to be such fun. Not only would Kash get an earful, he would have to sweeten the monetary pie on top of it.

Ultimately, necessity decided her course, that and the fact that she was not what Whip McClintock would consider "one hundred percent." She had banked east, heading downriver to her camp. By the time she swung around the ridge that jutted into the river just above her place, she was back in control. She let the Cessna rock gently in the crosswind—the motion sweet and soothing—before she set it down, mosquito light, on the surface of the glacial river.

———

"Well," Bailey said as they stood in front of her cabin, "I wasn't expecting company." She looked right now like one of Alpha's fourth graders who'd been asked to stand in front of the class and recite something, hands jammed in pockets, one booted toe scuffing the ground.

Alpha couldn't figure out why she was apologizing if, in fact, that had been an apology. The place was just charming, like cabins she must have seen on some prairie show, the logs weathered gray-brown but clean-looking, as if they had been scrubbed by hand. Two small windows peered at her like curious eyes. A shed roof jutted out to one side that was topped by a thick bristle of grass and some tall, spiky plant she didn't recognize. The clearing was free of debris, looked as if it had been washed. And all of it coated in unctuous, golden light. *Midnight sun,* she thought. *This is it.*

"Wow," was all she'd been able to say.

"It'll look better in a few days," Bailey said. "Grass. Trees. Flowers. Everything all greened up."

"It is totally charming," Alpha said.

Bailey ducked a quick look at her. "Thanks."

"Let's get some shit straight. Do we gotta pay you to stay here tonight on top of paying for the Lodge? Because I mean I already paid that man, Dash, or whatever his name is, for two weeks at the lodge, starting tonight."

With that the twisting nausea in Alpha's stomach returned, the feeling that had dissipated once she'd stepped off the plane onto solid, quiet ground and laid eyes on something peaceful and pleasing such as this cabin. Why on earth did he want to bring that up now? Why insult this woman who had their lives in her hands?

She was embarrassed and startled by the feeling. She had always been proud of Zach. Relied on him, particularly now, to be the smart and capable man she had believed him to be. But he was none of what she believed right now. In fact, he hadn't been much of any of it since they'd got here. Or had it started before that? She searched his face for an answer, wanted to say something, but managed only to exhale fully the breath she had held in dismay. He stared back at her, eyes shifting and sullen.

"Look, sonny," Bailey said. "Thing One: An attitude check is in order. Thing Two: If you don't like the situation, go someplace else. Thing Three: I am getting paid to fly you to the Lodge, not baby-sit your ass at my place but, hey, here we are," hands flung up. "Thing Three you're getting for free, so I suggest you button it up while you're working on Thing One."

Now Alpha stared at Bailey as if she had just been dressed down herself. She was amazed at the way Bailey had lashed back against a man's anger. Alpha had spent her life as peacemaker, smoother of prickly prides, and she felt obliged to move into that role now, but frankly she really didn't feel like making the effort; she could have used a little pacifying herself. She felt like flinging up her hands, too, as if to say, *I don't even know this guy. He hopped on the plane at the last minute.*

Surprisingly, Zach didn't attempt a response, only stood there with his face looking like a just-popped balloon. Bailey had gone down to tie the plane more securely to the still leafless cotton-wood that overhung the river. Alpha joined her on the riverbank. Bailey hopped down to the pontoon. "I'll get this door off so we can unload the gear. We'll do it bucket-brigade style, with one of you on the bank." Alpha couldn't help noticing her eyes as they skipped past her to Zach, then back to Alpha.

"Zach," Alpha said. He ambled over. "Mind if we unload now?" and she couldn't help it, swore she'd never be like that with her man, words full of bitter sarcasm. But the tone was there, all right.

Alpha eased herself onto the pontoon to form the first part of the brigade. She felt a little high, kind of intrepid, just pitching in.

It took fifteen minutes to unload what had taken them an hour to pack in.

"Dig out your sleeping bags," Bailey said. "You did bring sleeping bags?" Alpha nodded. "Good. I'll just taxi the plane up to that backwater and secure it."

When Alpha scrambled up, Zach reached out to help her but she brushed his hand away. Alpha rummaged through their gear to get what they needed for the night then sat on the pungent earth to wait for Bailey. Three rafts of ducks flew by, wind whistling through pinfeathers. Zach sat beside her, slumped to two thirds his size and continued to smolder in silence.

Finally, "That bitch." Just those two words, flat, without any true acrimony.

Alpha felt her jaw tighten. She had hoped Bailey's speech had smeared some sense into him.

"You realize that she was going to leave us back there in the Village?" he continued. "If we hadn't jumped aboard we would have been road pizza by now."

It was all still a jumble that she had not been able to sequence, but never in any of those whirling parts had she included the possibility that Bailey would leave them. She remembered hearing the plane start up, and Zach grabbing her arm and then splashing through the water to leap onto the pontoon. She remembered Bailey's voice, rough as the straining engine, *Get in,* and Alpha's stomach feeling rougher than any of it, conflated in fear.

"You think?"

"Yeah, I think," Zach said.

"Maybe she was yelling at us to come on and we didn't hear her. I don't think I would have heard anything. Because that's crazy to think she would leave us. You're just mad because she put you in your place and, Zach, I've got to say this, you deserved it. You were acting like a complete jerk, not the man I know and love."

Zach let out a loud shallow breath. "We've only got so much time, you know?"

"Yes, I know, and how do you think I feel?" Tears swelled her eyelids and she turned away. She didn't want that; it made her feel like she was with her father.

Zach sighed again, draftier this time. "I know, hon," he said, his roughened hand snagging her shirt as he moved it softly down her back. "I'm sorry." She turned to him, squinting against the light; he put his mouth on her forehead, and curled her against him. "It's okay. We'll get there tomorrow," he said, failing to realize her fear and doubt were directed at him, not the situation. Now she really felt like crying until she heard the polite cough at the edge of the clearing. She peeled herself away from Zach like one of her fourth graders who'd been caught holding hands in the cloak room, stood up and swiped the dirt from the back of her pants.

Bathed in that remarkable light, Bailey looked almost pleasant. In fact, she could be considered quite attractive when one took the trouble to look past the hat and the clothes.

"We'll grab a bite to eat," she said. "Then I'll show you where you can rack up. I'll split wood, get supper going."

"Great," Alpha said, hurrying after her. "I'll help you."

Bailey stopped at the low-hung door and looked at Zach. "Can you handle an axe?"

Alpha detected the flush in his cheeks even from fifteen feet away, and quickly chimed in, "He can knock up a cord of wood, lickety-split."

"Well then, lickety-split some of that wood on the far side of the clearing," Bailey said. "Don't need a whole cord. An armload will do. Axe is on the wall around the corner there." She went inside, letting the door bang shut behind her.

Zach looked at Alpha, his face in a corkscrew. "I'll just lickety-split this wood and then get lickety-split on inside. I wouldn't want to leave you alone too long with the troll."

"I'll be fine," Alpha said. "I'm not the one who can't get along with her."

"Well since you two are so close, see if you can find out what the hell's going on. We need to get up to the Lodge pronto."

"I'll try," Alpha said. She looked at the cabin, trying to bring back some of her former enchantment with the scene, and caught instead Bailey's face in one of the tiny windows, stark white in the subarctic sun filtered through glass. Alpha could not tell if the twist of her mouth was a smile or a grimace.

The move from bright sun to the cabin's interior blinded her. The back of her neck prickled uncomfortably against the soft flannel of her shirt collar; she jumped when Bailey loomed suddenly out of the shadows with dishes and eating utensils and started to set the table.

Alpha held out her hands. "I'll do that."

Bailey stared at her. "I'm not used to that."

"To what?"

Bailey looked confused. "Help, I guess."

"It's just common courtesy. The way I was raised."

"Of course," Bailey said.

As she set the little table by the small, dingy window, she peeked discreetly into the gloom of the kitchen where Bailey moved in and out of deep shadow as she prepared the meal. Alpha jumped again when the meat hit the hot fry pan.

"Hope you don't mind moose meat," Bailey said.

"Not at all. My father and brother both hunt so I grew up on the stuff." Alpha relaxed a little at the prospect of familiar conversation.

"Seems like we were always running people from Massachusetts off our land in hunting season," Bailey said.

"That's funny," Alpha said. "My father always complained about people from Massachusetts, too. 'Massholes,' he called them. And he never misses a chance to remind me that Zach's a . . ." She trailed off when the white oval of Bailey's face bloomed abruptly from the dim back of the cabin.

"Where did you say you were from?"

"Maine, originally," Alpha said.

"Raina said you were from Massachusetts," Bailey said, like a cop trying to catch her out in a lie.

"Zach is. I moved there a couple of years ago for a teaching job." Alpha was flustered by the interrogation.

Bailey's eyes focused intently on something just over Alpha's shoulder. But for their own stirrings in the cabin and the distant *kack, kack* of the axe, there was no subliminal noise, no sound of insect or bird, wind, motors, or the white noise of civilization. Bailey continued to gaze out the window, stroking her throat with one long-fingered hand. Alpha felt as if she was watching a television with no sound and she couldn't help clearing her throat. The rough rasp deflated the silence abruptly.

"Well," Bailey said, "where in Maine are you from?"

"Lincoln," Alpha said. "Chester, really, right outside of Lincoln, but nobody ever knows where that is so I just say Lincoln. Come to think of it, most people don't know where Lincoln is, either."

"Lincoln," Bailey said dreamily. "Home of loggers, pulpers, and skidder drivers. Not to mention foul air."

Alpha's eyes felt hot and watery. "How do you know that?"

Bailey looked down at the rough plank floor. "I'm from Milo," she said softly. "Medford, actually, but nobody ever knows where that is, either, so I just say Milo."

"Holy shit," Alpha squeaked, then excused herself for cussing. "That's only, like, fifty miles from Lincoln."

"I know," Bailey said, and sank back into the gloom.

Zach flung open the door carrying an armload of wood. "Where you want this?"

"By the stove's fine," came Bailey's voice.

"Something smells great and I'm starved," he said after stacking the wood neatly.

Bailey made no response from her shadowy crypt. Alpha piped

up nervously, "She's cooking up a regular feast. Should be ready any time now."

Bailey appeared at the table with the skillet full of meat. Alpha asked hesitantly if she could help. Bailey only shook her head and gestured at Zach to sit.

They feasted on moose steaks, canned beets, and rice. It was classic northern fare that both Zach and Alpha were accustomed to. At first they ate in silence, which wasn't unusual for eating with Zach, anyway, whose focus zone encompassed the distance between his face and the plate. Once he'd flung his fork down as if he were throwing a spear and begun searching his teeth for bits of food, he was good for a little conversation.

Though everybody seemed to be avoiding what happened down in the Village, Alpha could not help bringing it up. Zach gave her a hard look.

Bailey tried to explain the incident. The people didn't get liquored up en masse very often, but when they did, the effect could astonish outsiders who happened to get caught in the crossfire. The problem with natives and alcohol had been the same ever since liquor was first introduced into their culture when the Russians crossed the Bering Sea. The personality change was remarkable, she said. Whites had such a ludicrously romantic vision of Native Americans living in tepees, wearing skins, and hunting bare naked on horseback, that they were always surprised by reality.

"So, you're saying they threw rocks at us because they were drunk?" Alpha aked in disbelief. "But what did that woman mean about losing control of their land, and that man killing himself?"

"You people know anything about Alaska history?" Bailey asked.

"Zach's done quite a bit of reading," Alpha said.

"Did you read about the Land Claims legislation?"

"Nineteen seventy-one and nineteen ninety-one the natives settled with the government, right?" Zach asked.

"Seventy-one and eighty-eight," Bailey corrected.

"Whatever," Zach said. "Natives got forty-four million acres of land plus a billion dollars for other lands lost."

"Roughly, yes."

"But that's good, isn't it? Why would they be mad about that?" Alpha asked.

"The government sure as hell wanted it to look good." Bailey paused.

"But?"

Bailey pursed her lips and exhaled slowly. "I'll try to simplify. These land claims were structured by whites for an entire culture that we've been trying to make white for hundreds of years. According to the terms of the settlement, the government required natives to set up corporations to manage the money and the land holdings. Natives themselves don't really own anything. The corporations do. Kash, or Dash as your boyfriend likes to call him, is the president of this region's corporation, by the way." Zach looked at her sourly, but didn't respond. Bailey continued.

"This arrangement was supposed to force natives to start operating in a cash economy when the only economy they've ever known is based on subsistence and barter." Bailey could see the question coming up and waved Alpha down. "Subsistence is a word we've created to describe the act of living from the land. They never had to 'buy' food. They killed it or foraged for it as best they could. Now, they have to buy licenses, or go into lotteries to compete for licenses with international commercial fishing concerns that have millions of dollars to commit to the process. Remember, only the corporations received money from the settlement, not individuals. People were supposed to get dividends, but the money started to evaporate when natives had to hire professionals to help them figure out how to deal with all the bureaucracy. In some cases, the process actually bankrupted the corporations."

"That's why the Village looked so . . ." Alpha trailed off, not sure what word would be most polite to use.

"Poor?" Bailey supplied the word. "And Ingalik is one of the more prosperous regions, thanks to Kash having managed its funds better than most."

"What's so great about him?" Zach wanted to know.

Alpha closed her eyes and groaned inwardly, waiting for another harangue from Bailey, but she only smiled in a way that suggested she was being amused by a puppy.

"He was educated outside, as in the lower forty-eight. Prep school in Seattle, college at Dartmouth, an institution you probably haven't heard of," that with a lugubrious smirk, "and like most gene pools, some folks get better DNA than others," that with a sharpening of features that made her look almost sinister.

"So he's an Oreo, is what you're saying," Zach said.

"You're in the wrong gene pool, my friend."

"You know what I mean."

"He's pro-native, but he's a realist, is how I see it."

Alpha started to question her, then stopped, embarrassed that she didn't get it.

"He is dedicated to the survival of his people, their culture, but he knows there's no way around white people. We're here and we're coming whether anyone likes it or not. His idea is to control our incursion into Indian country. Try to profit from it. Which brings us to why you're here. You're the first contributors of tourist dollars to the Ingalik Native Corporation."

"If we're bringing in money, then why is everyone mad at us?" Alpha wanted to know.

"The CORE disagrees with Kash's tactics. They are anti-white, period, even whites with money."

"CORE?" Alpha could feel her knee jittering under the table. She looked at Zach imploringly.

"Hon, she's just talking about politics. It doesn't concern us."

Bailey peered at Zach, seemed about to laugh.

"Doesn't concern us?" Alpha said. "It almost darn sure concerned us to death a couple of hours ago."

"Now, hon," Zach said, stretching his arms behind his head

while his probing tongue made his cheeks look as if they were about to explode.

Alpha glared at him. Only an hour earlier he had been the one to grumble dourly that they were almost street pizza.

"So, I hear you're a Masshole," Bailey said in a complete change of subject.

Alpha turned to gawk at Bailey. Had Bailey thrown a quick wink her way?

Zach sat up. "I'm from Massachusetts, yes," he said in an awkward attempt at dignity. "Where you from?"

Alpha would have kicked him under the table if she could have reached, but Bailey surprised her by singing right out, "I'm from Maine, just like your girlfriend. I guess she hasn't had a chance to tell you yet."

"Terrific," he said. "I am surrounded by Maine-iacs. *Female* Maine-iacs."

"Bailey grew up in Milo, Zach," Alpha said. "Medford, actually."

"Oh yeah, I remember seeing an exit sign for Milo when we drove up to meet your parents," he said to Alpha without taking his eyes off Bailey.

"The very exit I took out of there," Bailey said. Her eyes appeared to smile but her mouth did not follow suit.

"If it's anything like stinkin' Lincoln, I woulda got the hell out of there, too. Question is, why'd you come here? Follow your man out, then get ditched?" Zach asked.

Alpha cringed. This was worse than those ridiculous wrestling shows Zach loved to watch.

But Bailey laughed.

Zach's voice rose a few decibels, "I mean, it's not exactly normal for a woman to move out in the middle of nowhere because it's her idea."

"It's not *usual*, no."

"Well," Alpha said, squirming uncomfortably, "that supper was really wonderful."

Zach grunted and slapped the flat surface of his belly. "Yeah. I needed that. Guess we all did," then segued awkwardly into, "Any idea how we're going to get up that river tomorrow?"

"No problem," Bailey said. "You can use my extra boat and motor for a couple of weeks. For a small fee, of course. And the cost of the fuel and oil. You *are* old enough to rent a vehicle, aren't you?" It took Alpha a second to realize she was trying to be funny. Zach, however, took her seriously.

"I'm twenty-five, if that's what you consider 'old enough'," he said. "And how much would that 'small fee' come to?" he asked.

Bailey shrugged. "Fifty bucks a week would do it, I'd say."

Zach frowned.

"That's fine," Alpha cut in curtly. "Fifty dollars a week would be just fine."

Bailey looked at Alpha, her eyes squinting a fraction of a second before returning them to Zach who was at last too tired to pursue it.

"Yes. Fine," he mumbled.

Alpha stood, taking a moment to swipe some crumbs from the table into her cupped palm. Bailey watched her intently, head cocked to one side. Alpha caught her stare, interpreted it as negative. She apologized, explained that she had been responsible for cleaning detail since she was a little girl. She wanted desperately to lie down.

"You guys'll be sleeping out here. Just unroll your mats and your sleeping bags and I'll disappear into my room. Oh, and the outhouse is behind the cabin. You can't miss it. I'll take my turn now if you don't mind."

Finally everyone was settled for bed. Alpha and Zach stripped off and wriggled into the big sleeping sack. The down filling lofted comfortingly over them. The river quarreled over its stony bed; dusky light filtered in through the windows.

She tried to relax, but could only sigh and flip from side to side until Zach, exasperated, asked her what the heck the problem was.

"Well, for starters you were really living up to the perception 'Maine-iacs' have of people from Massachusetts."

"Hey, she started that shit, not me!" he hissed.

"We're out in the middle of nowhere and this woman is the only one who can help us. When she does help us, you act like she's trying to kill us. For Pete's sake, all our money is tied up in this. We're so close, Zach. Don't blow it."

She felt him go rigid from her scolding. Reflexively, her hand reached out to stroke his hair; her mouth almost opened to apologize for her outburst, but she just couldn't bring herself to do it. Darn him, it was the truth and she said it out loud, "You know that's the truth. Don't pout."

He kicked his legs roughly against the confines of the sleeping bag. She shrank away.

"She just pushes my freaking buttons! You *know* how I am about that." He paused, more angry thrusting of limbs. "Oh hell, long as she rents us a boat and we can get out of here tomorrow, she could be the monster under the bed for all I care." He turned to her, slipped an arm under her head and spread his hand over her belly. "I'm so *tired*," he said. "I don't think I've ever been so tired."

He was asleep within seconds of his pronouncement, his hand still splay-fingered across her belly. She lay quietly under it, afraid to move lest she awaken him. She thought of how weird Bailey had gotten over the fact that Alpha was not from Massachusetts as she had supposed. How she had clammed up after discovering Alpha was from Maine, like being from Maine was some kind of honor only Bailey was allowed to have. But then Bailey *had* become more willing to help them, Alpha was sure of that. She tried to go over the scene again, but she just couldn't concentrate. She was as tired as she'd ever been in her life. Zach's hand grew heavier on her belly, the weight of it spreading until it seemed to cover her entire torso, until she felt as if she might evaporate under its pressure.

Before they left Bailey's that morning, they had moose steaks again for breakfast, but Alpha hadn't minded. She needed the protein. Between that and a healthy mess of home fries, she had regained a little spunk.

"What about the bears?" Alpha asked. "Will we see any?"

"Long as you develop good safety habits, you won't see any bears."

"But I'd like to see some," Alpha said. "Get some pictures."

"Did you bring any firearms?" Bailey asked.

Zach lifted his chin defiantly. "My deer gun. Thirty-thirty. That oughta do it."

"The average deer in the Northeast weighs one hundred and fifteen pounds. Grizzlies go upwards of five hundred pounds. You pop one of those guys with a thirty-thirty it's likely to feel like a mosquito bite."

"So we brought the wrong gun?" Alpha asked.

Zach ignored Alpha. "What do *you* use?"

"I try not to use anything. If you want to know something about bears, you should know how to avoid them. If you absolutely must engage in an activity that heightens your chances of an encounter, then make sure you've filed off your gun sights. That way, it won't hurt as much when the bear shoves your gun up your ass."

Alpha stared at Bailey. Was she supposed to laugh or be frightened?

"My point is that unless your encounter with the bear is planned—i.e., you're hunting it—you're going to be mighty surprised, the bear's going to be mighty surprised, and you will not have the time or the poise to raise a rifle in what will probably be close quarters to make a kill shot. In fact, most of the time, it takes many planned kill shots to drop one of these monsters when they're mad or defensive. This time of year, they're still cranky from winter, or you've got cubs to deal with, or both."

Zach started to expound, but Bailey just cut him off. "It's good to have a gun with you in case you're lost and need to get food. If nothing else, it just makes people feel more confident, like they have some control."

Now Alpha wanted to know exactly how to avoid bears, and what to do in case of an encounter.

"Gee, hon, I'm going to get the boat loaded. You can fill me in on the way up."

"Do you need help?"

"No, no," he said. "You girls just continue your school session here, and I'll take care of business."

Alpha had smiled at Bailey sheepishly and apologized for her lack of knowledge. Bailey knee-jerked a crack about her boyfriend's lack of foresight in preparing her. "Well," Alpha said. I should have taken the initiative and asked for information."

"You're right," she said.

"Maybe this is lucky. Maybe I'm better off asking you. You live here and know the place. Long as you don't mind my asking."

Bailey ducked her head, squeezed the back of her neck with one of those long-fingered hands.

"Whatever you can tell me, I'd be grateful," Alpha said, "like how to avoid bears?"

"Oh, well, you need to know their habits, their physiognomy . . ." she trailed off, then looked up briskly. "Don't leave food around. Burn all your garbage. They have poor eyesight but supernatural snouts. Don't give them anything to home in on, smell-wise. If you're out hiking, make your presence known. Usually they'll bolt if given the time and distance. Talk or sing or whistle every so often. Watch out for tall brush that might hide a snoozer. It wouldn't hurt to learn how to use a map and compass."

"I sort of know how to use a compass. My brother tried to show me one time."

"Did you bring one?"

"I think Zach did."

Bailey sat a minute, then got up and went to her bedroom. When she came back she held out to Alpha a square black plastic box dangling from a red string. "Take this. Always keep it on you when you go out, but make sure you orient yourself in camp. Figure out which way's which so if you get turned around away from camp, you'll know the general direction to take to get back to the Lodge or at least the river. It's west, by the way. If you're on this side of the river, you'll need to head west to get back to it."

Alpha held it on her flattened palm. It felt substantial, solid. She opened it like it was an antique music box. It had a mirror in the top lid and she thought that would be handy. "This is really nice," she said. "I'll take good care of it."

"It's a spare. Don't worry about it. Do you have a backpack?"

"Yes, I got one at the Army-Navy store in Boston." At last there was something she could say that she had done to prepare herself.

"Never leave sight of your camp without it. Keep supplies in it: map, string, candle, matches, nonperishable food, rain gear . . . Anything that would be useful in an emergency."

"Like bug dope?" Alpha said, smiling. She had heard that the mosquitoes in Alaska were outrageous.

"Yes. But if you run out, I'll tell you a little secret about bug dope. Find mud and smear it on. Works wonders."

Alpha laughed. "Natural facial."

"Exactly."

The door banged open. "Al, you ready?"

Her smile faded. She rose, smoothed her clothes, and put the compass string around her neck.

"Tuck it into your shirt so it doesn't bang around and drive you crazy," Bailey said.

"Good idea," Alpha said. "Wish we had more time," and wished she hadn't said it. It sounded wimpy.

"You'll be fine," Bailey said. "I'll talk to Zach about the boat. I don't know if he's done any river work, or if he knows how to use a jet unit."

"Apparently, we need all the help we can get," Alpha said.

5

Kash had just returned to Jeanette's from a late, after-meeting get-together when the call came from Raina. He had started telling her the message to give John Knik right away—how his application would be re-reviewed after Kash had gone over it and fixed the appropriate mistakes, and in all probability, would be approved by tomorrow—when she cut him off and said it was too late.

"Too late?" he said mindlessly, for he couldn't fathom what on earth that could mean.

"He's dead, Kash," she'd said simply, and he could tell by her voice that she was sober or he wouldn't have believed his ears.

In fact, he still hadn't believed his ears and said, "What do you mean?" thinking maybe she'd meant to use an expression of some kind like *dead tired* or that he had mis-heard her telling him John's new boat motor was *dead* or, still another possibility that made more sense, his wife was *dead*. But he couldn't put together "dead" as in no more, and "John Knik" until she said the words again.

"John Knik is dead. Peter found him in his boat early this morning. They looked for him all night. Left after dinner to run his boat and never came back and Girlie called some people to find him. Drifted way down to Mission Slough before the boat caught up in an eddy. Empty bottle of rum in the boat. Fell and knocked himself out, we guess. It was pretty cold last night. Bit of frost."

He'd slumped to his knees halfway through her report, unable to respond even after she stopped talking until finally she'd started again.

"I tried to get you as soon as I heard, but you were already out to them meetings."

Did he imagine the accusatory tone?

"Yes," he said, "and the meeting where I was trying to save John's life. I was at that one, too," he defended himself reflexively.

"I know," she said. "We just got done layin' him out and what-not. Ceremony's in the morning. Can you make it?"

His mind whirled. There were no more commercial flights to the Village until the following afternoon. He would cancel his meetings tomorrow, of course, and try to get the FAA mechanic to put the Cub first in line tomorrow morning, but . . . "What time?"

"Noon or so."

"Shit," he hissed it under his breath, and then said it so she could hear him, "I can't fly until the plane's checked out. I'll do everything I can to get it done first thing in the morning and hope for a good tailwind. There's nothing else I can do."

"I'll stall it off long as I can," she said. "I know it'd mean a lot to Girlie."

Though he'd left Anchorage as soon as the Cub checked out with the FAA mechanic, a feat that had required him raising some holy hell, he still missed the ceremony by a good two hours. His absence would not be looked on kindly. He spent too much time "outside" as it was, and there were those in the Village who liked to point this out. Were those others to succeed him, they would spend more time outside, and for all the wrong reasons.

Kash had spent a great deal of time away early on, but it was necessary to achieve the status and business acumen he would need to assume leadership of the Corporation he was certain would be part of the Alaska Native Claims Settlements when they were finally won. He had spent time in the most forsaken milieu imaginable—Dartmouth College—but it gave him status among the people with whom he would have to forge alliances, from whom he would be forced to seek professional advice. Four years or ten years at Dartmouth could not prepare him to be a lawyer, tax expert, investment banker, real estate broker, politician, sociologist, and historian. Yet he had to be all of those and a little more in order to manage the Corporation.

Two months after his return from college, he married. Eighteen year-old Susan Dogrib was not so much beautiful as she was handsome and, most important, smart, stoical, traditional. Susan was not radical in her adherence to their culture. She practiced their ways by example, and worked hard to help the community retain its identity and maintain a vision.

Kash could not have been more pleased with their union but for one setback: they had not conceived. Without progeny, he would lose respect, and worse, his soul would not be projected into the future. It was a bad sign.

They decided to adopt an orphaned child. The mother had died of exposure one winter as she kneeled, puking, behind a massive snowbank in the parking lot of a bar in Bethel. The temperature had hovered at fifty below zero so that death had been mercifully quick, freezing the vomit in her throat.

He and Susan were determined to keep Jeanette from the clutches of dissolution. She was put to tasks early on that would give her a sense of her culture, her place in the community, and of her undeniable place in the world. When most of the youngsters fought to go out, she fought to stay in the Village when it came time for her to go to school. She ran the trap line with Kash in winter, had a natural hand at preparing furs, sewing skin clothing, and creating decorative artwear, and when she went away to school, she took her work with her and began to make a name for herself in some of the Anchorage galleries.

After getting her degree, it had been her idea to stay in the City to work for Fish and Game. Eventually she hoped to get a field position close to home. Though he did not dwell on it, Kash was proud of her. When she'd brought him back to Lake Hood that morning, he had hugged her briefly, kissed her forehead and walked away. But he always turned back to watch her, stride purposeful and proud, black braid swinging like a metronome across the back of her jean jacket.

The Village looked deserted when he came in. Though Raina had Curan park the quad-runner on the beach so he wouldn't have to walk, he walked anyway up to the ceremonial ground. All of his young life it had looked the same; as elders died and were put there, a few new piles of earth and stones sprouted, but it always seemed to look the same. Recently, they'd had to bulldoze another half-acre to accommodate the onrush of death. That part of the clearing was raw and bleak, and he saw immediately the pile of freshly chunked earth where John lay.

He sat cross-legged on the cold ground and rested the weight of his upper body on the hands he had pressed respectfully over the grave. It would have looked to a bystander as if he was praying, but they would have been wrong. Because, in fact, he was cursing it all—the wind and the tides that brought the Russians here to begin with, the richness of his land with fur and ore and timber and oil that kept them coming, British, American, German, but cursed most of all, the only thing all these people had chosen to bring to Alaska in return for the treasures they took away, brought it by the barrelsfull.

He had dabbled with alcohol as a boy. But as he watched his people die of it, sometimes violently, other times with slow, pernicious certainty, he vowed that he would not let it kill him. There was too much life riding on the success of his own. In this very clearing he had kneeled in the snow one boreal night and dug his fingers into the flesh of his abdomen until the skin gave a little, every crimson drop reminding him of the thin thread of blood on snow that connected them all.

He touched the pile of raw earth under which John Knik lay, thinking, *My blood to yours, brother.*

Kash walked down to the store to check in with Raina, who was talking with the pilot of the afternoon freight run who had called in for runway clearance. He was standing by the desk, fingers drumming clear spots on a dusty edge, when he saw the Lodge radio on the floor, cord still wound neatly around the frame as he'd left it.

"Sonova*bitch*," he said.

Raina signed off and swiveled her chair to face him. "What's your problem?"

"What's that doing here?" he asked, pointing at the radio by her feet.

Raina looked at him. "That ain't but half of it, brother."

He couldn't bear to ask the question out loud *what happened?*, only gestured with his hand for her to tell it.

"Everybody's freaked about John, you know?"

"I know."

"He was a good guy."

"He was."

"You know how it is when everybody's upset. Out come the secret stashes and pretty soon there's enough booze in this town to float a musk ox."

Kash stared balefully at her.

"So everybody's partying down at the beach when Bailey comes in with them people. Course, Vida was there."

Kash groaned. Everyone knew to stay clear of Vida when she was toasted because she'd chew you a new one before you knew she'd broken skin.

"But that wasn't the worst of it," Raina continued.

"Oh boy," Kash said.

"Yeah, man, it was serious."

"Go on."

"So Vida's popping off at Bailey who's trying to defend herself which she couldn't know was pointless since she don't know Vida, and them kids is milling around like a couple a hammered steers and then somebody, I'm still not sure who did it first, starts hummin' rocks at 'em."

"At the kids?"

"All of 'em. The plane, too. Bailey finally gets the picture and shoots that thing off the beach, them kids was crawling on the pontoons trying to get in, people are jumpin' in boats to chase after the plane . . . It was outta control. The whole crowd, just outta control."

"And you?"

"Me? Oh no. You don't go that route with me, buster. Like I coulda made a difference to that mob, anyway."

He turned away, stared blindly at a shelf of canned goods, and cursed the drink for the second time that day, the first time for taking John Knik in spite of himself, and the second time for making a shambles of the community in front of those white kids. It would not be good for business, but that aspect of it had gone slightly awry even before this. He knew from those who had advised him on this business start-up that these people expected their goods and services to be delivered exactly as advertised. He would have to fly up now to deliver the radio, smooth things over, but not before he stopped at Bailey's to see how she was.

———

He filed his flight plan with Raina before he took off.

"Hey," Raina had snagged him on his way out the door. "Tell 'em their extra freight won't be in until tomorrow."

Kash shook his head. He'd have to add that to the list of grievances.

"You gonna talk to Bailey about last night?"

He didn't look at her from his perch half out the door. "Yeah."

Raina brushed some imaginary dust from the top of the humming short wave unit beside her. "Tell her that I . . . Just tell her it don't mean nothin'. Nobody meant to hurt her."

"Whyn't you tell her yourself," he said pointing his eyes at the radio she was now actively cleaning.

She snorted. "FCC catches us chit-chatting on a live band and we might get fined."

"You sure are up on your regulations when you need to be." She pitched one of those little sister looks at him. "All right," he said. "I'll tell her."

He followed the watercourse on the way up. The riverine valley here was beautiful, bountiful, with plenty of moose and bear. Some years, the migratory route of the barrenland caribou traversed the watershed and there was plenty of that for their freezers, too. This tributary boasted the heaviest run of chum salmon of any river in Alaska, and it was all within their purview. Almost all.

Flying lower to the river now, he spotted a cow moose with calf lunging through the muck of a beaver drainage, startled by the sound of the Corporation's Piper Cub. Sunlight shattered the water flying up from the heaving bodies of the huge, clumsy creatures. The cow probably ran nine hundred pounds if not more, enough to feed a small family for part of the winter.

He homed in on the ridge that bisected the river just upstream of Bailey's camp, then banked the Cub hard west so that he was heading downriver, into the wind. He coasted, throttled way down to facilitate his descent.

<hr />

Bailey had the throttle wide open in an attempt to run cleaner through the fuel line. Irritation oozed into her blood like poison. The cooling system was still inoperable and the motor overheated.

There were so few hours on it—scrupulous hours, with scrupulous hours of maintenance to back it—that this should not have happened. She cursed herself for buying the Yamaha and wished she had stuck with Johnson. They were comparable to the Yamahas now, cost less, and were easy to work on; you didn't have to have a fancy set of metric tools to do the job.

She had planned to go fishing that day—she was damned sick of moose and caribou—but she hadn't been able to crank the motor. This wouldn't have been a problem if she had her backup as usual, and she would have her backup, as usual, if it weren't for these damned kids. Poisonous irritation wended its way inexorably to her hands, causing them to twitch like puppets.

The mild weather that day had prompted the season's first hatch of mosquitoes. Her hands looked like pincushions as she worked. Periodically she inverted them and smudged their backsides against her pants. Normally, the sight of the pulped, bloody mess made her smile.

She flung the socket wrench onto the moist and still partly frozen earth, where it rattled across the dirt before settling into a bright puddle. *Stupid,* she hissed under her breath. She would have to waste even more time and energy to pick up the wrench, and wash and dry it so she could put it away without fear of it rusting in its case. But she walked away instead, past the row of tools hanging on the log wall of the cabin—six-pound maul, two wedges, smaller axe for kindling, chainsaw, a couple of number three leg-hold traps that needed repair, the galvanized washtub that is the hallmark of every cabin in Alaska—moved sightlessly past them and into the cabin where she lay on the couch.

The smell of the dog was so clear, she was certain that if she opened her eyes, it would be lying there on the swept-clean boards, head resting on the joint of one foreleg crossed over the other. Its eyes would meet hers just as they always did, one blue one brown, as if it had been formed by an attempt to combine two creatures that had not quite been able to coalesce completely, so that two beings looked out at her, the one mutely accusing: how could you leave her? How could you?

Leave her? Which one? The faces whirled, began to blur and meld, straw hair weaving a bright, rushing ring around her, dog smell overwhelmed by the clean, guiltless scent of a child.

Bailey folded both her hands over her face and pressed down hard, the rasping coughs so pained they could hardly be construed as sobs. She rose abruptly, blotting the dampness from her face with a flanneled sleeve. She found the box under her bed and brought it to the table where she dumped its contents onto the worn wood. She sorted the photographs into neat, sequential piles before picking them up one by one to peer at each visage.

Over the years, it had seemed as though the face had almost lost its features, the burning smile had faded, the eyes sunk back into shadowy sockets so far as to disappear entirely, or that the surface of the face had been whitewashed by overexposure to that white-gold hair gleaming at her from the photo paper. It blinded her to the point that she usually had to close her eyes. When she looked at them now, though, she realized the pictures had not faded at all. The figure, the face, was as clear as the living girl had been only a day ago.

When the girl said she was from Maine, Bailey's heart had lumped a few beats together. But when she'd found out the boy's age, the black edges of her suspicion broadened. If he was twenty-five, the girl had to be close to that. Since the agency had been a private, local institution, Temple's baby would have been placed within the state. She had let it go so completely at the time, she could not now remember the year exactly. She kept trying to do the math, a simple equation, but her mind would not let her get past it. Her belly told her with sickening regularity that it was possible, but her mind would not allow the possibility to be confirmed by fact.

She based her life on facts, the neat and orderly progression and consequence of them. She did not count on the possible, did not succumb to spiritual inclinations, the significance of the hair rising on the back of her neck. She looked around the cabin: the smooth half arcs of the logs repeated themselves endlessly around her, the bulging sides of the barrel woodstove, the humped, leafbrown tops of the bread she had baked mindlessly after Zach and Alpha left. These shapes flung themselves at her square, linear mind until she thought the wildness of sound that boiled in her lungs would escape, and with it, a soul she wasn't sure she had.

She stood too suddenly, sagged against the table until the spinning passed. The shame of her weakness turned her hot, and she jumbled the pictures together before lifting them as one lump into the box, which she covered and stowed carefully in its hiding place. Face washed, eyes clear again, she returned to the workbench, retrieved the socket wrench from the puddle on the way, and continued the task at hand.

Two more hours of temperate work on the Yamaha and frequent consultation of the repair manual and she pretty much had it fixed. She had smeared cold mud over her exposed hands and face to keep the mosquitoes at bay. It worked just as well as the noxious chemical repellents that cost too much and ate skin and plastic alike; the herbal stuff worked, but was equally costly. She stretched her face, feeling the dried mud crack and fall in chunks from skin that was smooth underneath when she grazed a fingertip over it. She smirked at the thought of the bundles people paid for deep cleansing masks when all she had to do was scrape clean earth from her own yard.

And then her smirk faded as the pulsing hum grew beyond the din of mosquitoes, the sound she had begun to recognize that fall. She dropped the wrench, heedless of its care now, and ran for the cabin. The pump seemed unbearably sluggish when she set the enameled bowl under the spout and laid her weight into the handle. She scraped her cap off. As gently as she could, she wet the caked mud and rinsed it repeatedly. A few stubborn clots had to be pried away with a fingernail, but finally she was able to see in the tiny bit of mirror that her face was as clean as it was going to get. She dabbed a towel over her face and neck, noting with dismay the drooping stain of water and mud that had collected on her shirt. She rummaged through a drawer, selecting finally a clean, green and black flannel that she buttoned as she hurried back to the kitchen. A quick dash to the mirror confirmed the nightmare on her head. A bird's nest projected crazily from her scalp. She didn't have time to brush and braid it, so she settled for just the brush, ripping through the snarls so mercilessly her eyes watered.

"Enough," she muttered, her face on fire both from the violent exfoliation and disgust.

She heard the Cub's engine yowl as he banked—too steeply, she couldn't help thinking—behind the ridge, and she stepped from the cabin in what she hoped was a calm and stately way into the afternoon light, prepared to receive her visitor.

He was so distracted by it that he smacked the water when he landed, completely misjudging the distance. He felt his face flush hot as he muscled the skittish Cub down to a stop, then swung around and opened up the throttle so he could step-taxi back up to the camp. He could not believe that he had never seen her hair loose. He watched her standing on the bank, arms crossed tightly in front of her. He had never really thought of her in terms of size, but now realized how small she was propped up against all that wilderness at her back. He watched her hair in the disturbance created by the Cub's prop as he pulled close to the bank, mesmerized by its fineness and the intricacy of the patterns it weaved in the blow. He had to force himself to watch the bank so as not to jam the nose of a pontoon into the dirt and completely embarrass himself.

Once he cut the engine, she had leaped onto the pontoon with a rope she kept tied to the old cottonwood. He wriggled his bulk from the cockpit of the Cub.

"Little trouble last night, eh?" Christ, where had that come from? He hadn't planned on banging into the tender spot right off the bat.

"Guess you could say that," she said.

He listened to every inflection, trying to make a preliminary damage assessment.

He balanced his way across the thin wire cable strung between the two floats and stood behind her as she kneeled to figure-eight the rope onto the pontoon cleat.

"How'd those kids handle it?"

"He was in a twist. She was scared. Wanted to know why it happened."

Bailey turned to him, not a foot away. He couldn't help noticing the bright flush of her face. Sweat weaved down his back. He took a slow, balanced step backward.

"Must have been a pretty interesting explanation. They understand there was a . . ."—suddenly he was squeamish about the word—"death?"

"Yes," she said. "Vida made sure we knew about the death." Her arms were still crossed over her chest. This was going to require a little prolonged diplomacy.

He stared at her hair. "I couldn't help noticing you had, well, *hair*. Thought maybe you were born with a cap on your head."

Her hands started to rise, but she resisted the urge and tucked them into her pockets instead.

"Didn't mean to make an issue of it," he said, and then quickly changed the subject before she could get defensive. "A fellow could use a cup of coffee. It's been one hell of a long day."

"Longer than you realize," she said, and jackknifed herself neatly onto the bank before heading for the cabin. As soon as the door closed behind her, he untucked his flannel shirt and unbuttoned it to get some air circulating around his torso. It wouldn't do to have his stink feathering the air of the tiny cabin. He kneeled on the pontoon and scooped icy river water onto his face, then fingered his hair smooth to his skull, noting with a frown that the splashing had wet his T-shirt. He climbed up the bank, using exposed roots as steps, and followed her inside.

He stood by the door, waiting for his eyes to adjust, could hear her clattering around on the other side of the room. He waited in uncomfortable silence as long as he could bear before inviting himself to sit. His eyes were more adjusted now, and he could see the smooth outline of her form as the shirt material stretched taut across her back. She turned and brought cups to the table, a small bowl of sugar and a freshly opened can of evaporated milk. Ah, she remembered that he liked his coffee light. As she moved away to get the coffeepot, he was struck again by her slightness. His hands would cover her bare ass completely. He shook his head to clear it of the image, and turned in his seat to regard the room around him.

As usual, he was amazed at how neatly she had reclaimed the rundown hovel of a camp. Fresh logs had been mended into the courses that sagged, then were scrubbed assiduously so that they were all of a color. The roof had been replaced completely; he remembered well the stream of material that had come in by barge that summer she first arrived. He hadn't believed she would know what to do with it. When he'd got up the nerve to ask her on one of his visits, she'd shrugged, acted flattered rather than offended as he had feared she might be and allowed as how she'd ordered some how-to manuals. They'd been pretty easy to follow. It was doing it by yourself that took the time, she'd said, then added quickly that she didn't mind working alone.

A plate clattered on the table behind him, and he snapped around, causing his neck to complain bitterly. He groaned.

She picked up the cookies that had scattered on the table. "Sorry to startle you."

"You didn't." The lie was automatic and, he realized, pointless.

"I was 'lost in thought' as they say." He tried to smile over the lessening waves of pain in his neck; it felt more like a frown.

"How poetic," she said, thrusting a bit of cloth at him. "Can't seem to dig one up without holes. This'll have to do."

While it had been cleaned and carefully folded, the cloth towel was threadbare. But that was standard procedure in the bush. You used things well and to the bitter end, and even then you didn't throw anything away. There were many tin cans in his storage shed full of used nails that he'd carefully pounded straight for potential re-use.

"Don't think I've been treated to a napkin in this establishment before," he said, taking the cloth from her.

"Don't get used to it," she said.

She sat across from him and shaped her hands to the warm coffee cup, silent.

"So the water's not as low as we thought if you could land that Cessna up there."

"I wouldn't say that," she said.

"You wouldn't?"

"No."

Obviously she would force him to continue making comments until she found the one she could best rejoinder with maximum damage. Since he had no choice but to let it happen, he might as well make it happen.

"You going to give me the story?"

"Which part?"

"The part that's got you so tense you're about to bust that mug in your hands." She put her hands in her lap where he couldn't see them. "Tell me," he said. "You might as well get it over with." A ploy well-used with women when they had something acid on their minds. Expose your throat and invite the slash, get past the cat-and-mouse shit.

Her hand reached behind her head, dug into the muscles there.

"The water *is* too low," she said. "Had to bring them back here for the night. Going back to the Village was out of the question."

His eyes widened. "They're here?"

"No. I sent them up by boat this morning."

"You loaned them a boat?"

"I *rented* them a boat."

"Ah," he said. "Good thinking."

"Glad you approve."

"I mean . . ." Oh hell, what did he mean? He was handling this like a ham-headed idiot.

"Never mind," she said.

"Look. What happened in the Village was a total fluke, no-body's fault. You know that, don't you?" She turned her head aside, so he drove on. "I don't want to put myself in the position of apologizing for their behavior as if they were children. They're not. It's a bad time of year, tensions are high, and now this thing with John . . ."

"I'm sorry about John," she said, her face still turned away.

"No one's sorrier than I am," Kash said, unable to keep the bitterness from his voice. She looked at him. "But I can't help it now. There's much more to worry about yet. And there's you. I'll try to make it up to you, monetarily and otherwise, if you'll tell me how." His hands were open, palm up, on the table between them. Supplication. She eyed them warily, then looked away again.

"I hate that," she said, softly.

"Hate what?"

"That you backed me down so I can't even bite your head off."

"I didn't mean to deprive you."

"The hell you didn't," she said.

He laughed.

"I'll submit a bill for services rendered when I get around to it," she continued.

"That's all I ask," he said.

"Not quite all," she said.

"What do you mean?"

"You're bound to ask whether or not you can land the Cub up there. And I'll tell you I wouldn't say for sure, but to err on the side of caution, I wouldn't try it if I were you. You'll think about that for a minute, look worried, sigh a little, and wait for me to offer to take that fucking radio up for you by boat, and finally, *that* will be all you ask."

Kash rubbed his hands across the gristle of beard just beginning on his face, the harsh rasp sounding amplified in the tense air between them. "At least I'll make the effort to reconnoiter for myself." He peered at the cookie crumbs in his lap, brushed them idly away before standing. "Raina asked me to tell you she's sorry about what happened. Nobody meant you harm."

"Right. They were so drunk they hallucinated me into someone else they wanted to throw rocks at."

He ducked his head, tightened his lips on words that threatened to tumble out, then said, "I thought you understood more about what we're dealing with here."

"I understand all right. I just prefer to do it at a distance."

"Okay," he said with a shallow intake of breath. "But sometimes fate turns up your nametag and you got no choice but to act. As long as you expect that, it won't go so hard when the time comes."

She whistled. "Whatever you say, college boy."

Outside, he rotated his head cautiously to take in the reach of the sky. "Don't think we're going to get any in the next twenty-four. Sure hope I can get this radio to them." He was getting irritated with himself. Why didn't he just come right out and ask her to take it up for him? He'd make it a paying proposition. It wasn't as if she had all that much to do. She hadn't responded so he surveyed the log structure before him. The logs had begun to bleach and gray without regular applications of log oil. Silently he calculated how many gallons it would take to do the whole camp, then automatically figured the cost.

"Mind if I step around the corner? Hate to get stuck in the air with a full bladder."

She shook her head and turned toward the plane.

He moved briskly until he was out of sight, then slowed to look around. He inspected the logs carefully, then got on his knees to have a look underneath at the log floor joists. Frost had heaved up a few stumps that were left when the place was cleared for the building and now forced themselves into the flooring above. But that was remediable. The windows were still square in their frames in spite of all the heaving the structure had undergone; none of them had been squeezed and cracked. He ambled behind the building, before turning to face the ridge that rose protectively fifty yards back. He unzipped and relieved himself, scanning the healthy stand of spruce that spanned the base of the ridge. The mosquitoes homed in on the freshly exposed flesh and he brushed at them absently with his free hand. With a bit of work and a little investment, the place could be a gold mine.

He came around front whistling jauntily. Bailey was hunkered down on the bank and turned to watch him as he came on. As he got closer he could see her eyes move pointedly down his body. He saw a flash of something cross her face, then remembered kneeling to look under the building, wetting the knees of his pants.

"Lotta roots back there for an old man to trip on, but I guess nothing's broken," he said in an effort to explain himself.

She untied the rope, leaving only one wrap around the cleat, and held the plane to the bank while Kash ran a few external checks, then climbed in. Finally, satisfied with his preflight, he pumped the throttle a couple of times to enrich the fuel mixture. *"Clear,"* he shouted, then heard the mechanical reply *clear*; he felt the familiar satisfying tightening in his belly as the engine chuffed, caught, and roared. And that's when he thought of the thing that had gnawed the back of his mind since he landed.

"Hey," he shouted over the roar of the engine. "Where's that dog?"

She looked at him uncomprehendingly, cupped a hand to her ear.

"The dog," he shouted.

She looked away, stretched her eyes upriver, then turned back and drew the edge of her hand across her throat in a slicing motion. He didn't know whether she meant she'd had to kill it because of some injury or whether it had been killed. It didn't matter. Death was inevitable and that was a fact.

He motioned to her to cast off the plane, but she only let go with one hand and made that slicing motion again across her neck. He shut down the engine, listened to it cough and wheeze into quiet, before leaning to flip open the passenger door.

"What's up?"

She looked at him, then upriver, her hair clinging to one cheek in the stillness. "Leave it with me," she said, looking back at him.

"Leave what?"

"I'll take the radio up in the boat. I'll have to do it anyway when you can't land up there. Save some time."

"I'll make it worth your while."

"Yes, you will," was all she'd said.

He wriggled out of the cockpit once again, teetered across the cable, and got the radio out of the passenger seat. He set it on the bank at her feet and, watching as if it did not belong to him, saw his hand grasp her boot before he looked up at her. "Thanks." He gave the boot a little squeeze before letting go. "Think I'll just give the place a little fly-by, you know, see how low the water really is, make sure they haven't burned the place down."

"Dry summer like this, going to make it worse for fires," she said.

"True," he said. "But it's mostly human-generated mistakes that cause the big ones. Stupid campers and whatnot. You're not likely to make a mistake like that," he presented that to her with twinkling eyes, expected a good crack in return, but got only a faceful of eyes that had gone dark and unreadable.

"Well, I'm off again," he said cheerfully. Once more, he stuffed himself into the cockpit, fired the engine, and signaled her to cast off. Her hands on the rope looked big, but only, he figured, because she was so small. He knew they had to be strong, and he tried to settle the gooseflesh that rose on his skin as he thought of how strongly those hands could move over him.

6

Zach had stopped at the Lodge long enough to unload their gear, and allow Alpha to use the bathroom. They didn't have much time, he argued, when she suggested they have a bite to eat and get reorganized before they tried to find the stream. She was a little shaky after their boat ride up; it became obvious pretty quickly that he hadn't listened to a thing Bailey had told them about how to navigate such a river. Either he hadn't listened to her or he was ignoring her advice stubbornly. At this point, she feared it was the latter. Of course, they had ended up grinding onto the first gravel bar that cut the channel, sucking stones into the impeller of the jet unit, which had required them to stop while he took apart the lower unit of the motor and cleaned it. Well, she thought, at least he retained that part of his instruction.

She had tried to remind him of things—shouldn't we stay to the outside of the bend, like she said? don't those ripples indicate water too shallow for the boat?—all of which had bounced right off his grimly concentrated face. She wanted to scream, but she sat rigidly in the tiny space he had left after packing the boat. She didn't really know anything about this and maybe he *did* have a better way.

So she wouldn't have minded regrouping a little before going out to reconnoiter, and when she'd said so, he had just told her she could wait there and he would go out alone. That was out of the question. She wasn't about to stay there by herself, even if there was a solid building for her to stay in. She would go with, thank you.

Then they were off again, upriver, to look for the spot where Arnie's stream emptied into the river. After three hours, though, they had been unable to find the outlet. He consulted the topo maps he had ordered of the area, and they showed the stream mouth entering the river not far up from the lodge. *Fucking maps*, he'd said at one point and flung them down where they floated aimlessly in the oily water that had collected in the bottom of the boat. Finally he agreed to go back to the Lodge so they could assess the situation and think of another plan.

He decided they would hike back behind the Lodge until they got to the stream.

"Don't you think we should settle in a bit? I mean we haven't even unpacked our stuff."

"Look, we're already hours behind schedule. We've got to find this stream, check it out, and see where we need to start. We've only got twelve days and every second that ticks by is another bill floating out of our hands."

"Wouldn't we be better off if we were just a little prepared?"

"Like I said, every second, another bill. What do you think?"

Finally, she had agreed, but not before making him wait for her to get her daypack together. She dug out everything she could get to, borrowed his extra cap and knotted a bandana around her neck which she first sprayed with bug dope. He watched her quizzically. "That something the Grump Queen taught you?" he asked referring to her bandana.

"Actually, my brother taught me that. He gave me this for my going away present."

"Oh," Zach said.

He had found nothing to say about something a man taught her.

"We aren't lost," Zach puffed as he shinnied down the spindly spruce he had climbed to get a look around. *"We're definitely in the vicinity and we're definitely not lost."*

He had to maintain her confidence in him. He needed to reassure himself that she depended on him. From his vantage in the tree he had been able to see a line of tall brush snaking across the tundra that could only mean water.

"It's that way," he pointed. And what the hell was she pulling out of her shirt? "Hey. That mine?"

"Bailey loaned it to me."

"Oh."

She was wearing one of his billed caps, the bandana, and one of her father's old wool Pendleton shirts over a turtleneck. Had he seen a woman dressed like this back east he would not have noticed her, would not have considered her attractive, but the way she wore the stuff . . . He couldn't put his finger on it. Maybe it was her figure. Even her ass looked great in those jeans.

Sweating and winded, they reached the stream in half an hour. Zach splashed into the water, and fell to his knees, only to find himself gasping and grasping his aching balls. He jumped up to the tune of Alpha's laughter. He almost got mad, then thought, No, it's good that she's laughing. He tried to go along with it, shuffling in and out of the water to amuse her. Maybe this way, she wouldn't balk at his idea to head up the stream for a couple of miles yet.

But she balked anyway. It was already four o'clock, she reasoned, and they still had no idea how to work the systems at the Lodge, hadn't unpacked their gear. Nervously she pulled her compass out of her shirt—thanks a lot for that sexy fashion feature, Troll—then looked at the sun.

"I'm really tired, Zach. We could both use a good night's sleep."

"I've got to get up that stream, even just a little ways. Hon, time's a wastin'. I'm doing this for us. Why don't you go back to the Lodge and wait for me there."

She blanched.

"You can take the gun and everything."

"What good would it do me? I don't even know how to use it."

"That's true, but it'll make you feel safer. And lookit, you got your compass, right? You know exactly the direction you need to go. You can really just backtrack our footsteps. It's easy."

She looked away. He pushed harder. "If I could find that ridge where it crosses the stream, I might find something that pleases us very much," he said, splitting his face with a mighty grin. "And besides, what would Bailey say if she knew you were wussing out?"

She looked at him, her gaze casting from one of his eyes to the other.

"Look, sweetheart," he said, "we won't do it if you're not comfortable with it." He placed a soft-lipped kiss on her forehead, his hand firmly at the back of her neck. And she capitulated, as he knew she would.

He had promised to watch her go, keep watching her as long as she was in sight, and convinced himself in mere minutes that it was totally fine. It wasn't far, really. He folded his topo map into a neat square that contained only the area they would traverse, pointing out some of the features they had passed along the way. He waved as she capped the rise that would take her out of sight. Then he plunged on up the streambed. Hell, it wouldn't take him long at this rate. He should be looking for what Arnie had described, but now felt unsure as he realized that all he had seen was in photographs. He slowed down, eyes peeled for glitter.

What if the creek was completely unproductive? He had spent so much of his conscious energy convincing himself that prospecting for gold was just an excuse to get into the country, he was astounded to realize that he counted on finding gold and making money. Why else would he leave his business at half mast, spend all of his savings and Alpha's in pursuit of something he didn't fully expect to find? The realization shook him, and he was glad Alpha wasn't there.

A hundred yards up, the stream narrowed abruptly and flowed briskly between two cut banks, forcing him to scramble up the cut sides to make his way through dense willow and alder. After thirty minutes of arduous travel, he stopped. The day was perfectly windless and every mosquito in a hundred mile radius had flown in for the feast. If he could just get out of this freaking thrash to the open tundra, the going would be easier. By the time he fought his way out of the brush, he was ready to burst into a run. He knew now why animals went mad and ran themselves to death. He tried to calm down and managed to pause long enough to get out the Old Woodsman, which he slathered on thick as he could stand. It made him feel better, though most of the damage was done to the mosquitoes when he smeared them across his skin in the process.

A game trail skirted the edge of the brush. He followed it, moving fast as he could without actually running. Sweat coursed down his back. His skin burned under the thick grease of bug dope. He tried to focus on something other than his discomfort. For once, he could do better than imagine what it had been like for the people pouring into this country in the 1890s. In those days, Alaska was the last frontier, but to take off for Alaska for the sake of adventure alone was not socially acceptable then, nor was it in the 1990s. Then, as now, to abandon one's family, quit a promising career, or throw over a paying job of any kind to search for gold could be done without fear of social stigma. Gold was the justification for succumbing to adventure, and many deluded themselves into thinking the justification was the reality.

He stopped to catch his breath. The whining cloud intensified around him. More than the stinging bites, the sound moiling thinly through the air drove his blood pressure up. Standing there, he did not look around him as he had always imagined he would do once he got out in the country. Instead, he dragged two fingers through the crevices behind his ears and down his jaw where the mosquitoes seemed to collect most thickly; he pulled his hands away, amazed at the sight of his own bright blood on his fingertips.

⌒

She had to admit the head net was a pain in the ass. She had been too self-conscious to put it on while she was with Zach, but as soon as she'd got out of sight, it was out of the pack and over her head. The mesh was so fine that she had to squint to detect anything but general outlines. It must be what people with glaucoma saw, she thought, like looking at the world through a milky film. Anytime she wanted a sip from her water bottle, which was frequently as she trudged along with her clothing buttoned down tight against the mosquitoes, she had to loosen the neckcord, slip the bottle up under the netting, drink quickly, then tighten the neck cord again only to spend another few minutes crushing the droners that snuck inside the net. Though the consuming activity annoyed her, she was grateful for it, too, because it distracted her from the anxiety that made its inky presence known as soon as Zach had disappeared from view.

Much as she would like to kick him, she was angry with herself for agreeing to split up in the first place. Why hadn't she been able to say *No, I don't think I'm ready to ramble around in thousands of acres of wilderness by myself.*

But she had sensed the urgency in his voice, his pushing, and responded to it by taking the backseat, just like she always did, unable to assert herself over the desires of others. Right now it was good to be angry at Zach, because her fear of getting lost threatened to overwhelm her and she had to fight to keep her head.

She wanted to enjoy this, too. She wanted to stop and look at the plants, the tiny mosses and lichens just starting to reinvigorate after the winter, foliage budding sweetly on the low shrubs. She wanted to admire the hills in the distance, and marvel at the sweep of the sky that was like nothing she had ever seen, but she could only observe things insofar as they told her whether she was going in the right direction, and whether the things she observed could hide a five-hundred-pound bear. She tried whistling, but her saliva had turned to glue, so she talked out loud instead and didn't give a damn how foolish it might look. After all, there was nobody around to notice.

She plucked the compass from her shirtfront for the hundredth time and checked her course. Yes, she was going the right way, but it seemed she had been walking far longer than fifteen minutes. Her mouth blotted completely dry. She wanted a sip of water, her bladder ached, and her face was on fire. Surely it seemed to take so long because of the panic. *I'll stop right here, take some deep breaths,* and she inhaled and exhaled as if she were leading an aerobics class. *That's good, keep breathing.* Maybe if she emptied her bladder it would help her concentrate. She looked around, then laughed at herself. *What am I worried about? I can strip butt-naked and it won't make a bit of difference.*

She unshouldered her pack. A little shaky, fumbling, she finally got her pants down and squatted, making sure to keep her clothes out of range. It was hard to balance doing that and flailing the bugs away from the fresh expanse of flesh. In the midst of this circus act, she registered the drone, much louder than a mosquito, and looked up to see the small plane buzzing overhead. She thought at first it must be Bailey bringing their gear up, but this plane was white and blue, not red. Alpha could do nothing but sigh at the irony. Alone in this bottomless place and she gets caught with her pants down. She must look a sight, tiny speck crouched on the tundra. Not only that, but she'd have to pull up her pants and make do with the dampness, for she had nothing with which to clean. She felt so small and shrank rapidly in her mind's eye to the point where she could not even perceive herself.

The little bastard. Bailey stood there with her hands spread wide, palms up, unable to answer his question and already pissed off that she hadn't even got a thank you for the radio before he wanted to know where the rest of his gear was. Apparently, this Zach had begun to view her as the local lackey instead of a person doing him a big, fat favor. Not only that, he'd gone off and left the girl by herself in the bush for the first day in her life with no protection whatsoever other than the words Bailey herself had provided her just hours earlier. When she'd arrived at the Lodge a full hour before he'd got back, she had found Alpha sitting morosely by the river, legs kicked over the edge like an abandoned waif.

It had fallen on Bailey to buck her up. She made her take that net bag off her head and wash her face in the river. Then she took her out back to show her how to start the generator, which almost turned into an embarrassment when she realized it was a diesel. Fortunately, the thing had directions on it; she could make as if she was reading them for Alpha's sake. Then, get her inside and show her the circuit breaker that, voilà, gave her power. She tried to boil some water on the stove, but the gas had been turned off at the tank. Right. Another lesson for the girl who was trying hard to soak it all in as Bailey dragged her through her paces. Bailey let Alpha get the water boiling and tried to find something to put in it. Of course, they'd had to unpack some of the boxes to get that accomplished.

And then Little Lord Fauntleroy himself had wandered into camp looking, Bailey noted with satisfaction, a little worse for wear, what with his face all bloodied and lumpy and his hair scruffed every which way.

By then Alpha had hurried out of the Lodge, ready to smooth things over, something she was destined to do as long as she stuck with the Masshole. She tried to scramble into the exchange, but Bailey wasn't about to let this puke off the hook at the expense of his girlfriend. He'd annoyed her without even being there, and now he had actually made an effort to goad her. There was nothing left to do but give him the business.

"You just don't get it, do you?"

"Get what?" he said, his voice rising into low whine. "I was told I would get certain things that I *paid* for and I'm a jerk for expecting to get them?"

"You're in the bush, buddy, and life doesn't run by a clock out here. It runs the way it will or won't, depending on the day, the weather, psychic or cosmic disturbances . . . whatever. Get that through your head and you will get something out of your time here. If not, you will remain as miserable and ass-backwards as you are right this minute. Your choice."

Purely for effect, Bailey turned to Alpha now, "By the way, the reason I came up was to bring the radio. Thought you guys might like to have it, just in case."

"You mean, we didn't *have* a radio?" She turned to Zach.

Zach flung his hand in the direction of the hunk of metal at his feet. "We do now."

Now, back to the puke. Bailey could not wipe the smile from her face. "You know how to use it?" She could see in the tight stretch of his lips how much he wanted to say he did even though it was obvious he didn't. "Because I'd be happy to set it up and give you a little lesson."

"I would like that very much," Alpha said.

"Okay," she said, glancing at Zach, then down at the radio so he'd be sure to understand that she was not his designated Sherpa.

Bailey had passed the place plenty of times on her trips upriver, but she had never stopped to look it over, look in the windows. The peak of the roofline was a like a ship's prow, making room for two huge picture windows in the front that allowed plenty of light to wash the golden log walls inside. The logs themselves were massive. They must have been hauled in from elsewhere, because the spruce just didn't get that big this far north. Thanks to several coats of varnish, the logs still had their just-peeled brightness. Bailey figured they had used a portable mill to rip out the lumber for the floors and interior walls. They had that rough-sawn look, semi-circular gouges still visible from the saw blade.

Two closed doors marked off one wall, and a single cut the center of the opposite wall. Bedrooms and a kitchen.

Zach came in behind her with the radio. Bailey barely resisted the urge to say "atta boy!" and pointed, instead, to a small table where she had already spied the cable curled on the floor. The antenna itself extended from a tall pole attached to the peak of the roof.

He plunked the unit down on the dusty surface and then planted his hands on his hips.

She screwed the antenna in, plugged the unit to the wall socket, flipped the switch, and prayed. Sure enough, the red power light winked on.

"There are fifty stations on this thing. You only need to remember two. Twelve is the station monitored by the Village; there's a radio in Kash's store where Raina talks to incoming flights and whatnot. That's the station I use at my camp, too. Keep it set on that. If there's a hell of an emergency and you can't raise anybody on twelve, go to sixteen. That's the band monitored by the Coast Guard."

"Why would we need to use that?" Alpha wanted to know.

"If someone were hurt to the point their life was in danger and you couldn't raise anybody in the Village, you can send a mayday on this frequency. If you're lucky, it all works according to plan and they send out a medevac chopper to whisk you off to a real hospital."

Alpha stared at the radio, then at Bailey, the green gloss of her eyes gone a bit pale and flat.

"We'll be fine," Zach said.

Terrific, Bailey thought. They're screwed. And why did she

even give a rat's ass? If they got grizzed to bits or axed off a digit or two, it wasn't her responsibility.

"Terrific," she said out loud now. "I'm outta here." She got as far as the door before he kicked one more over the goal post.

"You never answered my question about the rest of our stuff."

She pointed at the radio. "Call somebody who gives a shit."

She yanked the pull cord on the motor so hard she tweaked her shoulder and the pain was like air to fire. She spun the boat away from the bank giving it all the throttle it would take. The transom dug in so deep she almost had to lie down to stay up. The bow planed down quickly, jumping the wake she'd made in the spin and she had straightened out that way, ready to get back to her camp and away from this gigantic screwup, when she caught the movement from the corner of her eye, the bright hair weaving along the bank. It was the girl, watching her as if Bailey were taking away blood she had promised to give.

She remembered that face, scuttling from window to window, room to room as she headed for the barn, the fields, the car, *away*. The ritual: I point at you. You point at yourself. I nod, *Yes, you.* You nod. I move my mouth, muscles aching in silent exaggeration. *You stay.* Yes, you say with your head so violently your hair flies like spun silk. I believe you because I have to. Because I have to be able to go until you pull me back again.

If she didn't look, she could go still. But the weight of those eyes dragged at her hand, which slowly released its twist on the throttle, and she pointed the boat at the girl who stood now, watching her. The boat moved heavily across the current, edging as close to the bank as she dared. She pointed the bow slightly upriver, giving it just enough power so that it hung motionless, current gargling loudly around the upstream side. The girl tried to smile at her but it looked wilted.

"I'm sorry about Zach," she called out. "He's just . . . He gets cranky when he's tired."

Bailey looked down, watched the bailer float lazily on the water that had collected there, gagging back the words she had in response to that defense, said instead, "If you need anything, use that radio." She knew the girl wanted to hear more, but it was the best she could do.

The girl nodded vigorously. "Okay. Thank you."

Bailey slid her cap brim low to her eyes against the coming wind, and let the boat drop with the current before she throttled up and spun the bow downstream.

Alpha watched her go with trepidation. She turned to the Lodge but couldn't make herself go in there. Not yet. She found a place where she could get down the bank onto a slim gravel spit just wide enough to accommodate her kneeling. She took off her cap and placed it carefully beside her, dipped two cupped hands into the chill liquid and brought it to her face, then dispensed with the hands altogether and put her whole face in the water. Even in this shallow spot she could feel current pulling the wisps of hair that fell forward. She stayed under as long as she had breath, then came up, spluttering and spitting. She shook her head to free the hair of its dripping weight and sat back on her haunches.

With the sun at her back, she could see her outline on the water. She peered at the blank reflection in an attempt to put features to the shape, eyes, skin. But no matter how she shifted to catch the light, only the mysterious outline revealed itself to her.

She walked back to the Lodge, letting the water dry itself on her face. She was hungry and tired and something else she still could not name. The kettle hissed on the stove, at least Zach had done something, so she rummaged through the cabinets for a mug in which to make her tea.

Now to make something to eat, but for the world she couldn't think of what they had brought. She stared out the window, hands resting lightly on the counter, then gripping its rough edge when she heard Zach come in and plunk something heavily on the floor behind her.

"I'm hoping there's some food in these boxes. I'm hungrier than one of those charity kids on TV."

"Me, too," she said, without turning, unable to bring her eyes in from beyond the window glass.

"Well, what say we dig into these boxes and get some grub?"

"Okay." Still not moving.

He paused behind her, just a moment, before ripping into the cardboard. "Ah!" he said. "We'll eat off these tonight to celebrate," and two green, plastic gold pans appeared beside her hands on the counter. More rustling, and then a box of macaroni and cheese sailed into the plastic pan nearest her hand, and a canned ham after that. "Look good to you?"

"Yes," she said.

Suddenly, his hands fell on her shoulders, so heavy she felt drilled to the floor.

"What's wrong?"

Could he have asked a crazier question? It didn't seem possible he didn't know what was wrong. That he had acted like a complete head-up-his-ass fool to Bailey, who was trying to help them when they very much needed help, to teach them some things they would need to know, but that he couldn't take from her because . . . Why? Because she's a woman? Worse was her fear that he really didn't know much of anything other than how to swagger his way through he world.

She felt the liquid welling in her eyes and she scrunched them shut to staunch the flow. She would not cry. She would not cry now.

"Listen, baby, you did great getting back here. Don't let that woman upset you."

She knew it. *That woman. Doesn't know her limits.* She was afraid her voice would quaver like the tears that trembled on her chin.

Bitterness coated her tongue, but her voice was steady as long as she said nothing she wanted to say.

"We'll eat and get some rest," she said. "I'm just really, really tired."

Crooning now with his arms wrapped around her from behind, "Yes, baby, I know. Me, too. We'll get to bed as soon as we eat. Start fresh tomorrow."

"Yes. Tomorrow," though she knew that "fresh" was impossible for them.

She waited for her heart to break, for the hot lead in the belly that came with the realization that everything she believed to be true was not. She waited for the feeling, her eyes squinched loosely shut as if the slap in the face were imminent. But it did not come, not the slap, not the feeling, not the pain.

She recalled a lecture one of the professors had given in a Behavioral Ed. course at the university. There are so many categories people can be placed in, behaviorally speaking. But one of the most important identifications you will ever make are between two types: those who do and need to be watched, and those who watch and expect to be needed for that purpose. Doers seek watchers and vice versa. At the time she had thought it ridiculous to reduce people into those oversimplified categories, but it rang her bell now. She knew now why he brought her along. He had never expected her to be able to *do* anything. She was merely along to watch him succeed. The question was, what did she expect of herself? Which one was she?

She let her eyes relax and flood open before she turned to him.

⌒

He saw how the stress had tugged down the corners of her eyes. "Forget the tea. I'll get supper. You know what with all this hullaballoo I didn't get to tell you what I saw. There's a spot a couple miles up that stream, just like Arnie said. I didn't stay long enough to really check it out, but I'm telling you, the stuff's gotta be there. Tomorrow, we'll go get it." He chattered on like that as he boiled water for the macaroni and cheese and opened the canned ham. Zach went about his preparations with gusto in an effort to cajole away the guardedness that Alpha wore now like a metal jacket.

She was still polite and considerate as she had always been, but the cuddly warmth of her had been replaced by an edge that was a little formidable. He found himself practically dancing around her as he went about preparing the meal. While she usually touched him when the situation allowed it, he found now that he could not resist initiating contact.

After they ate, he took her by the arm and led her into the bedroom where he had piled the rest of their boxes. He sat her on the bed, facing the heap, then rummaged through one, two, three boxes until he found the beer bottle with its rubber stopper in place. He kneeled beside her and set the bottle in her lap.

"Look," he said, *spink*ing a finger lightly against the glass, "this is what we came here for. If we find enough gold to fill this bottle, we'll be set. I know we can do that. I found the spot to prove it. We should be celebrating instead of sniffing each other's butts like pissed-off dogs. I'm sorry if you're upset about today. I can't keep you with me every minute." He watched her profile carefully, looking for a change of expression, anything to clue him in.

"Al," he said, pulling her to him. "This has not been easy, and it isn't going to be easy, but hon, I'm about to blow the odds outta the water. I know it. Stay with me on this, okay?" He moved his eyes over her face as if they were hands, probing, pulling. "Ya with me?" Gently he squashed a mosquito that had landed on her temple, then licked a forefinger and wiped the blood from her skin. "Is this the right time to get out the flask, do you think?" he asked, then kissed her, sucking one lip languidly into his mouth.

"Sure," she said. He thought he felt something ease, soften a bit.

He dug out the flask of Maker's Mark bourbon he had splurged on and sat beside her on the bed; though it was still bright out, he lit a candle that he'd found and stuck it on the table. He stood to unbutton his chamois shirt, exposing his flat, hard belly. It was a view she professed to love. He watched furtively as she undressed, furtively because she was usually so covert about it; but tonight she peeled down as if no one else was there, shaking her breasts loose of the bra with a little flourish.

The bourbon was smooth, excellent, he thought. He swished it around like mouthwash before swallowing with an audible gulp. She had sipped some of hers, then asked him to pour the rest back, to save it for the big strike. Now she lay on her side, head propped on one hand.

"Baby," he whispered hoarsely, "everything's gonna be fine. You just watch." He moved his mouth over her neck, moved himself against her, hard as he'd ever been.

"Okay," she said. "I'm watching."

He scooped her to him with one arm. *Christ*, that's what he needed to hear, though there was something in the tone of her voice that he red-flagged, like she was talking to her students. But he had to put that out of his mind and enjoy this now, right now, front and center.

7

Lascivious old man. He laughed. Old, hell. He was only forty-eight. Lascivious? After the series of dreams from which he just woke, there would be some truth to that tag. It seemed he had dreamed about it all night. Waking from the frustration of one scenario only to fall asleep again so that he could finish it. But each dream only worked him to a pitch, right to the very edge, and then woke him. Or he woke himself. Or something. He didn't know what. He thought of relieving the pressure but decided against it. Let that edginess work for him instead.

He'd had the day planned before he went to sleep last night. The rest of the kids' gear would arrive on the morning freight run from Anchorage; he would make the flight up to the Lodge—making sure he flew low so Bailey would see or hear him go up—buzz the place to see if he could land, decide it was too risky even though yesterday it had seemed as if there were a possibility, then be forced to land at Bailey's with the gear. *Gee, sorry to bother you again but . . .* A nice businesslike excuse that wouldn't shy her off now when the meat was starting to thaw. It had felt mighty close yesterday, close to the point of dispensing with the excuse. Close to the bone.

He heard the rumble of the incoming plane as it passed over the Village before coming around for its landing pattern. Perfect.

He made himself a big breakfast, a rare indulgence, but he

thought he'd need the stamina today. Besides, he could see to it that at least one of his appetites was slaked. Scrambled eggs and a couple of thick slices of caribou heart fried in butter with onions. He savored the dense, blood-rich muscle with his eyes closed, feeling the particles of the animal filter into his own heart, pumping life cleanly through his body.

Raina called while he laced his boots. Kids' boxes had arrived, parts for the town generator, dry goods for the store, twine to finish repairing his nets for tomorrow. . . . Yep, yep, yep. Everything was going according to plan.

He walked down to the store, taking his time. In spite of the chilly reception yesterday, it was good to be home, good to be getting ready for the fishing season tomorrow, and good to smell that smell . . .what was today? Had to be Tuesday. Because that smell could mean only one thing: Lenora Richardson was baking.

He had told her about the small business loans she could get, and helped her fill out the applications so she could start up a little baking business there in the Village. It was a great idea, something she could do (and do very well) to make money, something good for the Village and for supporting her daughter. The girl was actually her granddaughter, but Lenora had taken over the parenting a few years ago when her son had gone through the ice on his snow machine, drunk. The girl's mother had run off long before that. Lenora made enough now to help the girl through boarding school in Sitka, the tuition partially subsidized by the government, and the baking made her happy.

He made a sharp turn into her dooryard and leaped the porch steps like a kid. The window was open, so he just leaned into it and called her name, then walked on in.

"Tell me you've got some of those sweet twists going," he said. "I just ate a huge breakfast but I'd make room for one of those sweet twists," he said. Lenora blushed and looked away.

"Darn you, Kash, you had a nose for them things since you was a little boy."

"You mean they're just for kids?" he teased her.

"I guess not," she said.

He loved this. He loved the privilege of being able to walk into the house of somebody he had known all of his life, somebody who had helped him and whom he had helped, and whom he trusted. He ached when he remembered the years outside, years spent on the outside of locked doors, or behind one himself, places where people didn't know each other or want to. *Keep to yourself,* the locks said, *unless you're invited.*

He spied the tray of twists on the counter he had built for her and reached for one. She smacked his hand before he had hold of it. "No!" she said. "Get one from this end. That fool oven has some hot spots in it. These here rose better." She scuffed one up with a spatula and presented it to him like it was the best of her heart.

Carefully he scooped it into his mouth, closing his eyes as the bread coated his palate.

"Ohhhhhh," he moaned. "They just get better and better," which came out *ay uss et bettuh an bettuh.*

"Yes, just like me!" She laughed, pleased. He reached for another one. "Darn you, boy. Save some for the business."

"Oh, I'm all business," he said, reaching into a pocket where he always kept some crumpled bills.

"Don't you dare," she said, her mouth straightened primly. "Here. Just one more." She scuffed another twist from the big sheet and balanced it toward his outstretched hand. "That's it," she said sternly, smacking his belly with the flat of the spatula. "You're gettin' hefty, you know."

"Owww. Low blow," he said.

"Seriously, boy. I worry about you."

"No need, Lenora. I'm fine," he said, rubbing his belly.

"It ain't the fat I'm talking about." Her face creased as she turned away.

Something in her voice told him to pay attention. He had depended on her before to be his ears in the community. Lenora was outwardly a jolly, kindly woman, but she had a sharpness to her, tremendous pride, and a nose for calumny, particularly when it came to those she loved. Those ears had something for him now.

"What is it?" he asked.

"I don't know but that I'm just imagining this here," she said, which was how she always started, "but I seen a few things the past coupla days that make me nervous."

He leaned on the counter, mindful to keep his eyes down.

"Yesterday, I seen that Match come to town. Thought he was going to see Raina, but he marched right on past her house and up the road. I was on my way up to the airstrip. Special-ordered some flour in, is how I know this. When I went up he was at Ferrin's, all slouched in the door talking to him." She stopped, kneaded a huge batch of dough in silence. He waited. "Now, I know that don't mean nothin' in and of itself, but follow that with the laundrymat this morning." Again she kneaded in silence while he waited. "Well, Vida comes in to do Ferrin's laundry before he heads back up to the Slope next week, and her kids is all over the place makin' a racket. I was there first, see, and had the machines tied up. But first come first serve, right?" She didn't expect confirmation. "So she's out in a huff, some of the kids with her, some still tearin' around the laundrymat making me crazy. I thought she'd gone, but then I'm folding and I hear her right outside the window. She's talking to somebody, not a kid, because she's not yelling. I'm not thinking nothin' of it but I can't help hearing her." She stopped and he could feel her looking at him now, so he looked up. Her lips were pursed, eyes unnaturally wide as she peered over her glasses that had become glazed with flour dust. "She said, and I heard this clear as day: *He's a troublemaker, is all. He don't give a darn about any cause. You could go to jail.* And then I hear a man's voice, but it's too low for me to make out the words, and then she says: *Don't do it.*"

"You see who the man was?" He couldn't help asking it.

"I'm getting to that," she said, and he could have bitten his tongue for the disrespectful interruption.

"I was just about finished, so I got a bag of laundry and started home with it. She come in the door as I was going out, but when I got to the road, I seen Ferrin walking down to the beach. Now I didn't *see* them together talking, but you add two and two . . ." She slapped her palms together, little flour clouds erupting around them. Again, the look over the dusty glasses.

"Yeah," he said. He dug his fingertips into his scalp, rubbing hard. "Lenora, you're a hell of a woman and I love you dearly. Don't forget that."

"I don't plan to," she said.

"I gotta go. Got some flying to do today."

"Yeah, I got more work than I can handle myself," she said.

He had his hand on the doorknob when she called him back.

"I might have said it before, but it bears repeating in light of . . . certain things."

"What's that?"

She pointed a white, pasty finger at him. "Match. He's a skinful of bad blood, you ask me."

"I know it," he said.

"That sonovagun's up to no good and I got an idea what it is."

"I do, too, but I can't prove it."

"Can't prove it? The man's had three airplanes and he's got no job. I'm no math whiz but even I can figure that don't add up. There's only one way to get that kinda money out here without working and that's by peddling whiskey. Weasel's out there spouting all that bullcrud about native rights and oppression and fighting the good fight and he's after killing us all in the same breath."

"I know," Kash said. "But I can't catch him at it. I'd cut into some boxes myself, but I can't afford to get caught doing something like that."

"Ferrin's in on it. Got to be. You should watch him."

"Don't think I haven't been," Kash said.

"And?"

"And nothing. I thought he might route it through work on the Slope, but I can't pin that down. I just don't have time."

"You think Raina has any idea what's going on?"

"She's got to suspect, but I'd bet she doesn't know for sure. He's too slick to risk that kind of leak."

"Tell her to stay away from him."

"She won't listen to me. Still blames me for Drew leaving her."

"Now that was a good man. Curan could sure use him around."

"We all could. He was one top-notch mechanic. Making good money in Anchorage now, though. Does well by the kid."

"I wouldn't expect less of him."

"Best get on with the day then. Those twists'll give me strength."

"Stay in the light, son."

"Twenty-four hours a day," he said.

Children ran up and down the road. Their shouts and squeals gave the Village an anywhere kind of feeling. As Kash walked down the hill to the store, the dogs that normally strained at their chains stood silent in their patches of dirt. Only their eyes followed him as he passed.

The Store was quiet except for the two little girls lurking around the freezer, waiting for a Fudgsicle handout. Ketchup had dried darkly around their mouths, and one girl crossed and re-crossed her legs as if she had to go to the bathroom. He nodded, said their names to them, *"Sadie, Drea,"* before walking over to the counter and leaning toward Curan. He put his hand out and cupped the boy's shoulder. "Got to fly up to the Lodge today. I'll let you know before I leave." He always filed his flight plan with the boy, hoping that the added responsibility would keep him occupied and away from the more damaging pastimes.

Raina was shuffling purchase orders on her desk. With her

glasses on and her hair braided and coiled around her head, she looked like somebody out of one of those television shows she loved to watch.

"So, what sexy television show are you from?"

She shushed him. "Aw, piss pots," she said. "You made me lose my place."

"Sorry."

"Well, you got my attention now. What is it?"

"You called me."

"Yeah, right. Boxes are out on the deck. Have at it."

"What if I don't want to 'have at it' right this minute?"

"Have at it any time you want, far as I'm concerned."

Just then the radio crackled behind her, and a man's voice came thinly to them. "This is Zachary Scott at the Lodge calling for anyone in the Village. Over."

Raina frowned. "Jesus, that kid's been buggin' me all morning."

"You want me to talk to him?"

"No, I'll do it," she said, putting a little spit into the *t* for good measure.

"This is the Village, go ahead."

"That you, Raina? Over."

"Roger that. Go ahead."

"Raina, this is Zachary Scott at the Lodge. Over."

"I got that. Go ahead." She rolled her eyes at Kash.

"Just wondering if our stuff came in. Over."

"Affirmative. Just came in."

"When do you think we can get it up here? Over."

She unkeyed the mike, rolling her eyes again at Kash.

"Tell him I'll be up in a couple of hours."

"Kash says he'll have it up there in a couple of hours."

Silence.

"Lodge, did you copy?"

"Uh, yeah. Okay. We'll wait here. Over."

Without keying the mike, she said, "Like you got anyplace else

to go, buddy," then pressed the lever. "Roger that. Village out."
And chucked the handset back on the table.

"Looks like we got our work cut out for us," she said.

"I'll get to it," Kash said, and ambled out to the deck. The
boxes were piled there as advertised. He'd have to bring the quad-
runner around. He stuck his head in the door. "Curan?"

Curan looked up from his comic book.

"Bring that quad-runner around back, will you? Trailer hooked
up?" The boy nodded. "Okay, bring it around then."

He surveyed the pile of cartons. Good Lord, how much stuff
did these people think they needed for two weeks in the bush? He
shook his head. Curan pulled alongside the deck so that the trailer
was abreast of the load. "Thanks, buddy."

He had got his arms around the first box and was ready to lift
when a volt of pain shot down his lower back. He groaned aloud
and let go of the box, which seemed to fall apart as if it had been
sealed with scotch tape. He could feel Raina filling the doorway
behind him before she said, "You all right?"

"Oh, man," he said. "Somebody just knifed me in the back."
He stood loose-kneed, and pressed his hand over the twisting
muscle.

"Lean over." And she dug her knuckles into the bad spot, held
them there while his face contorted. "Let me know when that
eases."

"Like tomorrow, maybe," he said between clenched teeth.

"You get this from Dad. Same place and everything."

"So it was."

"Better?"

He straightened. "Yeah. Thanks."

"Hey. What are little sisters for besides a pain in the ass?" she
said, and grinned. He patted her on the head and she swiped his
hand away.

"I'll get some tape for that box. Hang on a minute," she said.

He looked at the spilled contents on the deck. Lots of food. That was not good.

He'd hoped they would stock up from the store. He moved the stuff around with the toe of his boot. Extra wool caps. Hip boots. Well, they could fish if they wanted, long as they bought a license in Anchorage. A small stack of magazines fanned out from his probing boot. Looks like they brought plenty of reading material. Something caught his eye on the cover of the top magazine. He bent to it, resting his weight on his knees. *Gold Prospector: A Magazine for the Amateur.* He flicked it aside. *Rock Hound.* Flick. *Miner's Light.* Flick, flick. Two more issues of *Gold Prospector.*

His jaw hardened. Raina's voice floated to him from inside. "Where the hell's that tape? Curan? Darnit all!"

He squatted to examine the box nearest him. The stretch felt good. The tape was good on it, just like the other one had appeared to be. He fingered the flap edges, expected not to be able to run his finger the full length of the crease, but when he did, the edges came away like they weren't even taped.

He examined another box, and another. They had been properly sealed at one time, but it looked as if the tape had been slit, carefully, then only partially or hastily patched with clear tape. Raina puffed out behind him.

"Tape and scissors. Why can't people keep their own stash of it 'stead a stealin' mine?"

Her voice grew louder as she leaned close to him. "Whatcha got here?" He felt the words as air on his ear, but he didn't answer, knew she would see for herself in a second. "Ooohhhh," she said. "Now ain't this somethin'." Idly, he turned the pages of one of the magazines

"It would appear we have some amateur prospectors on our hands."

"There!" she said in that gotcha voice. "That's exactly what the fellas are bitching about. No matter what you do, they're going to take advantage."

"Not all of them. This is just dumb luck. Besides, we got no idea what they're doing, first off, and second off, they aren't going to find much if they find anything at all. Everybody knows it's dead up there. Wasn't good wash in the first place."

"But it's the principle, Kash. They were told specifically they couldn't do shit like that. Signed a contract to that effect. Just goes to show you a treaty now's as good as it ever was."

"Who brought these boxes down from the airstrip?"

"Ferrin did it as a favor. Had some stuff on the flight himself."

"Ah," he said, fingering the carton flap again. *You could go to jail. Don't do it.* Is that what Vida was talking about? Match had Ferrin check on their gear to make sure they were keeping their word?

"Raina," he said her name, pulling her down beside him. With her hunkered there, the look on her face so earnest he felt like they were kids again, squatting in the dirt as he tried to explain the rules of a game. "Whatever bullshit they're filling you with, it's not true. It won't work. I don't know how to explain this any clearer than I have for years. They will come. The world's too small now. You cannot avoid these people. We must be able to control their access in some way or we'll be run over. Do you understand that?"

"There is another way," she said excitedly. "Sovereignty. If we can govern ourselves, be in complete control, then we decide who comes and who doesn't."

"Do you remember how long it took us to get the Land Claims pushed through? And you know damn well we'd still be pushing if it hadn't been for the oil companies wanting to get our claims out of the way so they could haul out all the oil. That was pure luck. Sovereignty was in the Land Claims bill, too, but they struck us down. Not even for the price of all that oil were they about to recognize us as a nation. Sovereignty is way off in the stars. We need to deal with this right now. Get something established."

He watched her wilt under the weight of his words, hope crumbling from her skin.

"I'll take care of this," he said.

"There'll come a time when you can't do it anymore," she said, words floating up from her downcast face.

"Do what?"

"Take care of it. Like always. Maybe that's why I try to take you down a peg. Because I'm afraid for you when that time comes. Afraid for us."

It caught him in the soft of the belly. His knees felt so watery he thought they might start knocking. He sat heavily on the deck, let his chin drop to his chest and felt the muscles pull in his lower back.

"Is that what you're doing with Bailey?" she asked softly. "Taking care of it? 'Cause that's not what people are thinkin'."

"Is that what you think?" he asked, without looking up.

"You're after somethin', Kash. I don't know how she fits into this. I mean she's all right. She don't do no harm. But she's white and she's close. Feels like she's gettin' closer. That part of your plan?"

He couldn't lie to her, so he didn't answer. He didn't think she was ready for the answer and were he to tell her the truth of what he was thinking, it might not stay there between them. She was his blood, but he wasn't sure he could trust her with the knowledge. Not when there were alcohol and hormones involved.

He pressed his fingertips to her forehead. "You are my blood."

She gripped his wrist tightly and nodded. "I'll help you tape these boxes."

He had gutted it out through loading the boxes and getting them down to the beach, but his back hurt more and more. He yanked the gas nozzle off the fuel truck and tried to climb onto the port wing. It took just about everything he had. He leaned heavily on one arm and clutched the hose open with the other. The fuel leaked into the tank at a snail's pace. He cursed. There wasn't much of any kind of fuel left in the Village. It was always this way in spring. They waited and waited for the first barge of the year to get up the Yukon, the one with their summer's supply of fuel on it, and though iceout had come early, the water level dropped quickly, too. So now the big barge was stuck on one of the Yukon's ever shifting sandbars. Who knew when they would bring up two smaller barges that could take a shallow draft, and divvy up the load between them.

Right now, with no back pressure, the wings filled slowly, unmindful of how much it took out of him to lean there and wait. He thought of the years his father had fought this weakness. He never dreamed the man had had to do what he did on a daily basis in spite of this kind of pain. Christ, he just about cried now when the fumes made him cough.

He didn't bother to reclutch the heavy black rubber hose to the truck, just flung it onto the beach and managed to lower himself to the pontoon. He leaned heavily on his knees for a few minutes and cursed between shallow breaths.

"This don't look good." He heard Raina's voice from the beach.

He looked up, half squint, half smile.

"Tell you what," she continued. "I'll radio Bailey, have her fly down for this shit. No sense you killing yourself over some stupid magazines."

"She can't land at the Lodge with that big tank of hers," he said as loudly as he could push his voice.

"So? She can get it to her camp, then take it the rest of the way in the boat. Or have them brats come down to her camp and get it their-damn-selfs."

He regarded the muddied water that lapped lazily against the pontoon. "*Jesus*," he hissed under his breath. He felt ridiculous. But he just couldn't fly like this. It wasn't practical.

"Would you?" he said, one eye squeezed shut. "Radio her? Tell her she'll get paid as usual." As much as he had figured to make off these kids he was pissing away just to deal with them. *"Jesus,"* he hissed again.

"Come on," she said. "I'll drive you up to your house. Get off your feet for a while."

When she'd helped him up the steps he felt like a hundred-year-old man. He would have brushed her hands away, but he just didn't have the strength. She left him at the door, at least that respectful.

"Want me to radio down to Bethel, have 'em ship up some drugs from the clinic?"

"It isn't that bad," he said. "I'll be fine in a bit."

She shook her head. "Whatever." And left him in his misery.

By the time he got himself stretched out in his father's old recliner, he felt he could have passed for the old man. The day had gone to hell in flames. He should have jacked off when he had the chance.

———

She had started out that morning to bag a few of the first chum salmon that had got this far up the river. Her mouth wouldn't stop watering at the idea of a fresh meal. But she'd had a heck of a time finding a pod.

No sooner had she got off the gravel bar and found a pod of salmon than she'd started thinking about Kash. One minute she was sure she knew what he was up to, and the next? Maybe she was wrong. And in the middle of that—*bam,* she missed a perfectly good hit by setting the hook so hard she yanked it right out of the salmon's mouth, practically ripping its lips off. The lure backlashed and hooked her in the shoulder. She got so mad she simply cut the line, got another lure from her tackle box, tied it on and continued to cast until she got two fish; the anger wouldn't let her settle for just one.

Only then could she let herself off the hook. She'd used the pliers to pinch down the barb and still had to twist it this way and

that before she could work it out. Between the dead fish and
her clumsy surgery, the boat looked like a slaughterhouse. She let
the pliers with its jaw full of bloody hook clatter to the bottom of
the boat, ennui settling over her like a thick, suffocating blanket.
The boat moved slowly at first in the eddy, then lurched into the
main channel when the eager fingers of current had it securely in
their grasp.

Her head moved languidly with her eyes. She felt each thrust of
current, saw clearly each worn-smooth stone on the streambed,
and smelled a hundred discrete scents. She wanted to lie down and
close her eyes, but she would have to get up shortly and shove the
boat across the current to its familiar landing. Maybe then she
would crawl onto the sweet, spring grass and lie down.

The boat drew abreast of the camp, her home, and she knew she
had to get up quickly in order to shoot the boat across the current
before it drifted too far down. Her shoulder needed a good washing with Betadine, and she should start a course of antibiotics—

Snortling, snuffling, the muffled thump of cardboard boxes.
Every nerve ending pricked up. Bailey rose slowly to her knees,
then to her feet, and placed the oar gently against the river bottom. With it she could pry the boat across the current in one hard
shove.

She grabbed a hank of roots before the boat *whacked* into the
bank, then she tied the bowline to the gnarled knee of an old
cottonwood and pumped herself lightly onto the grass. She froze
in a squat to make sure she was undetected. No response from the
pit, but she crouched low anyway as she scuttled to the cabin door
and lifted the latch with both hands, slowly, before cracking the
door open just wide enough for her to slip through. She pulled
the .270 down from its pegs and reached for the full clip she kept
on the little shelf above the door. The synthetic stock was cold in
her hands, not warm like the wooden stocks she had used before,
but she liked that; it was a weapon, not a baby doll. The dull,
matte finish of the stainless steel barrel reflected nothing back at

her. She smiled to think of her lecturing Zach on firearms. Like the .270 was anything more than a mosquito bite to a bear. Difference was she knew what she was doing, knew this was not a shoot-to-kill situation. At least, she wasn't planning on it. But with surprise on her side, and if it came to that . . .

She bolted a round into the chamber and checked the safety with her thumb to make sure it was on before bumping the door open with her hip and stepping out silently. The scuffling was louder now and clinking bottles, then glass breaking, added to the din. She moved flat-footed down the path, keeping the brush between herself and the pit. She slowed even more as she drew close and slithered into the foliage, the warmth of the sun that had collected there enfolding her.

There were two of them. They must be two-year-olds by now, she figured, having first seen them when she was downriver her first summer at the camp. She had floated quietly with the motor off around a bend in the river to see them lined up, head to tail on a downed tree, sleeping, while the huge sow bear cuffed up dead salmon that had gathered in the eddy below the deadfall. The cubs had stretched the length of the tree bole, legs hanging like hairy branches. She had watched them through her binoculars until the sow detected the odd shape of the boat and stood up waist-deep in water and shook her monstrous forelegs at Bailey, then snapped her jaws repeatedly. Bailey had been able to hear the teeth clacking even at a hundred yards.

She couldn't believe the two young males were still together, but she was sure it was them. The wind favored her, so she watched them play with the garbage like kids in a sandbox. They batted cardboard boxes at each other, or slapped each other outright, knocking one another down in mock rage. They threw bottles, ripped heavy five-gallon plastic buckets to shreds, and scampered in and out of the pit completely unaware of her. She did not detect whatever signal they exchanged to signify playtime was over, so was unable to move before they lumbered out of the pit and headed up the path that lay within five feet of where she stood.

.Her amusement evaporated along with all the moisture in her mouth. Again her lecture came to mind. Bad eyes, snouts like heat-seeking missiles. She was covered with blood, piscine and human. Why the hell had she come out here, anyway? She had only one thing in her favor and that was the wind direction.

The bears moved quickly, not running, as if they had a mission of only slight urgency to which they must attend. They passed her, their greasy smell strong in her face. She kept her eyes slitted nearly shut and prayed that an odd gust of wind would not give her away. In such close quarters, even a cannon would not have been much use.

They headed for the river. When they were well past her and she could not see their faces, she opened her eyes and shifted the rifle to a more ready position. She sidled slowly around the island of brush without taking her eyes from the rumps of her two visitors, and tucked herself behind its protective edge, leaning her head to the side just enough to keep the bears in full view.

They stopped at the cabin where some of her tools hung. The biggest of the two reared up, braced himself with one front leg, then casually flicked the chainsaw from the wall. It sailed over the smaller one's back and hit the hard ground, finally clattering to a stop thirty feet away. The smaller one was entranced by the movement and the noise and decided to pursue the toy, but the big one merely dropped back down on all fours and disappeared. It had to be heading for the boat where the smell of fresh blood would be too much to resist if it had not fed recently.

She tracked it with her ears, only dimly aware of the smaller bear who was playing football with her three-hundred-dollar chainsaw. Her arms were tiring from holding the gun aloft for so long. She moved the butt slowly to her hip and rested it there for a moment, listening for sounds of carnage on metal. If the big one started to trash her boat, she would have to fire off a round or two.

She had no desire to kill them, but if a warning shot did not suffice . . . Shooting bears out of season in Alaska could get you in just about as much trouble as shooting a human, and the last thing she needed was the ill graces of Fish and Game. Granted, there was nobody around to see or hear her, but things got around in the bush. It was difficult to hide one huge carcass, much less two. She did not favor bear meat at all, so the meat would be wasted; the spring pelts after a long, hard winter were frail and patchy, not good for anything. Just about the only thing that would be useful were the claws and teeth that the natives used in their artwork, but she might as well take out an ad in the *Anchorage Daily News* announcing her deed as start distributing bear parts in the Village.

Suddenly the loner reappeared from behind the cabin, charging at his sibling, jaws agape to scare it away from the toy. He took a good whack at it and sent it flying into the river, where it skipped twice on the surface before sinking to the bottom. Bailey almost groaned out loud. The two bears ran simultaneously to the river's edge, leaping into the water with mighty splashes to swim after the lost toy, which they forgot about once they lost their footing in the deeper water of the channel. The larger bear swam strongly across, but the smaller one appeared to have trouble and kept trying to scramble onto the rear of his brother. Mightily displeased at the added burden, the lead bear reached shallow water, stood up on his hind end and turned to face his hanger-on, who got his footing in time to stand up. They boxed each other with great gusto, water pearling from their rough coats, until they grew bored, and galloped through the shallows before disappearing in the thick brush on the far shore.

Her arms trembled as she made her way on unsteady legs to the cabin. She returned the gun to its pegs and lay on the couch, intending only to rest until the shaking subsided.

Temple had a way of appearing at the moment when frustration had numbed Bailey stupid, when she'd lain in the hay stubble at field's edge, the halo of gold hair reflected on her glazed eyes.

Like she ever believed in angels. Nailed to the earth by the short spikes she had mown an hour before, she regarded nearby the broken hulk of tractor that reminded her she had more to do besides this.

Temple hovered, until the tinkling sound filtered through Bailey's stupor.

B she'd whisper excitedly, and again *B*.

Ice tinkled more urgently, until Temple set the glass lightly on Bailey's outflung palm which was so hot she expected to hear it sizzle.

She sat up, took the glass—half of it gone from the sloshing it had taken to get there—and looked at the detritus that had fallen into it as Temple weaved through the bushes to get to the hayfield. She would not walk across open spaces but crept close to cover, like deer. She was on all fours now, her feet still touching the brush at field's edge; she had been able to stretch far enough to reach Bailey, but once the glass was no longer hers to bear, she had settled on her haunches, her back safely guarded by the scruffy alder growing there.

Bailey didn't bother to pick the water clean, just drank it off to satisfy Temple, who she knew would wait expectantly, crouching there, until she did so. Often as she worked she would spot Temple in the woods, watching her. The looking became automatic after a while. Had she looked for her, or looked forward to it?

She had the fish slabbed out on the counter so she could fillet it when static shot across the room. She grabbed a towel to wipe the fish glue from her hand before she picked up the unit.

"River Camp, go ahead."

"Hey," came Raina's voice as if they'd just encountered each other at the Laundromat.

"Hey, yourself."

"You up for some business?"

"No," Bailey said, and she meant it. She had cleaned her wound, swilled down an antibiotic cocktail, found her fish untouched in the boat, and now she just wanted to eat her first fresh meat in months, and get on with her life, get back to normal.

"Cash proposition, as usual," Raina said.

"Speaking of 'cash,' is his plane out again or what?"

"No, his back's out now. He ain't fit to fly and them kids is pissin' and moanin' about their stuff, which is here, by the way. Thought you could bring it up to your camp and have 'em get it from there."

Bailey sighed, shook her head. It was no use. There would be no back to normal.

"Come out, come out, wherever you are," Raina beckoned.

"Yeah, I'm here. Let me get something to eat. I'll call you before I leave."

"Big-time Roger and appreciate that. Village out."

"Camp out."

When her belly was full, she had tried to set the cabin to rights, ready her emergency pack for the flight. She went at the tasks haphazardly, picking up one thing before she finished the other. Finally she stopped, aghast at her inefficiency. She decided to boil water for a cup of tea. Perhaps a shot of caffeine would do the trick.

And then she caught a glimpse of herself in the mirror. Blood smeared on her face and neck. Hair a fright. She stripped off her clothes, leaving them in a damp pile, and warmed a big pot of water. She inspected her body as she washed, satisfied at the sight of the still lean plane of her abdomen, and the hand-sized breasts, firm and taut, a fact she was sure most women her age could not claim.

She rummaged through the dresser, scrounged up a newer pair of underwear, one that had no holes, and almost put on a bra but thought that it had been so long since she'd worn one, she'd just as soon put on a corset. Instead, she pulled on a clean silk undershirt, and finished dressing in black jeans, dark green turtleneck, and blue wool jacket. She stood in front of the small round mirror and tore at her hair, noting with horror that it fluffed out like cotton as she brushed it. She tried to smooth it down by wetting her hands and mashing them onto her hair but this succeeded only in making her look straggly.

With a hiss of disgust she turned away from the mirror. It wasn't as if the boxes would give a damn. She grabbed some meds from her kit. More antibiotics, and, what the hell, she'd donate a couple of muscle relaxers, just in case the hurt-back excuse was for real. Not that she planned to see the man. She'd give them to Raina. She washed the dishes and put them away, then found the hand radio and put in her call to the Village.

As he lay there, ears tuned for the sound of the 185 buzzing in, he suddenly got a whiff of himself. He struggled to get up, shuffled stoop-backed to the kitchen counter. He kept a bottle of aspirin there and he tipped the bottle over, skipping three, no better make it four, into his palm. He slurped them right out of his hand and gulped them down dry.

Who would have thought something as simple as undressing could hurt so much? Off went the dirty chamois shirt and T-shirt. He washed up in the bathroom sink with soap and a hand cloth, then shaved as carefully as he could. He appraised himself briefly. The chest was still strong, though the curve of his belly that began just below the pectoral muscles was more pronounced these days. The muscles in his neck corded out nicely though, and his arms were firm and well defined, the skin of the forearms darker than that of the uppers. He laid a hand on his cheek and moved it slowly down his chin and neck. It would have to do.

He returned to the kitchen, a little straighter now, where he pulled a package of caribou chops from the freezer and chucked them in the microwave to defrost. He leaned on the counter and

watched the meat go gray on the little turntable. He managed to
fry onions and potatoes in a cast iron skillet before he added the
chops, a little salt and pepper. He ate at the counter, leaning on his
elbows. The meat was good, not too strong. Sometimes the only
part of the herd that dipped close enough to the Village on the
migratory route were the stragglers, the fringes that consisted of
weaker, older animals. Their meat was rangy, tough, and often had
a strong, musky taste.

The previous winter, the herd had passed far to the north, but
this year the pickings had been good, with the bulk of the herd
passing within miles of the Village. For days there had been caribou wandering everywhere; people had had to take care on their
snow machines for fear they would plow into caribou when
rounding a bend, and a few stragglers had wandered right through
the Village, much to the delight of young would-be hunters who
harassed the animals with sling shots and BB guns. He thanked the
caribou now for his meal, a nod of the spirit so ingrained as to be
automatic, and rinsed his dishes. The iron skillet he wiped out
with a paper towel to preserve the finish that had been cultivated
carefully over the years.

Back in the windowless bedroom, he opened all the dresser
drawers and surveyed the contents. Finally, he selected a black
T-shirt and tugged it gently over his head. Absently fingering his
hair into place, he scanned the shirts hanging neatly in the closet,
all the openings to the left as he liked it. He selected maroon flannel, a newer one that wasn't as faded as the others. He looked
down at his pants. Even though the aspirin had given him some
relief, the idea of sitting and bending over made a spasm start
afresh. Besides, he thought in a sudden fit of embarrassment, did
he really think she would put herself on the line by coming up to
see him?

Back to the chair. Normally he would have had the radio on
while he went about such chores, but he'd left it off, the better to
hear the 185 when it came in.

8

At the beach, fishermen swirled in intricate knots, some working on their nets, some on their motors, others trying to re-clinch rivets that had shaken loose from the metal seams in their boats. A few of them signaled her unobtrusively by tapping a forefinger to the bills of their caps; the rest ignored her. She scanned the crowd thoroughly. His back must really be bad if he wasn't out there getting ready for tomorrow's opening. Fine. Curan was there with the boxes piled precariously on the trailer.

The boy helped her load. He'd been well taught; she hadn't even had to prompt him about how to do it. When they were done, she thanked him for his help and watched him slouch away. She was dangerously low on fuel. She dragged the hose over to the Cessna but stopped when Curan whistled for her attention, then came close so he wouldn't have to yell.

"Barge is late," he said softly. "Not much fuel left."

She was pretty sure that was the most she'd ever heard him speak. "Think there's enough for me to pinch a few gallons?"

He shrugged. "Have to check with Kash on that."

Ah, there's the pitch, she thought. A metallic taste oozed to the back of her tongue. She'd chewed her lip to the quick. Charming. She felt ridiculous just standing there. Maybe she'd catch Raina at the store. She would know what to do.

Naturally, Raina wasn't there. No choice now but to brazen it out and walk up that road. She shouldered her pack, careful to avoid the increasingly sore spot, and headed up the hill.

She'd never been to his place. Wasn't even sure how she knew it was his house. She kicked off her boots in the tiny vestibule built on to the main doorway. They called them "arctic" entries up here. Back in Maine they were simply "mudrooms." Either way, they accommodated perfectly the many changes of outer clothing and footwear dictated by living in the North.

She gripped a padded packstrap and tried to compose herself as she thumped the door twice in a businesslike manner, then swung it inward when she heard "Come on."

The interior of the house was plain, the walls simply white with a few of what she figured were his wife's handwoven rugs for adornment. The place was scrupulously clean. On the counter by the phone sat the bulk of an old wooden-boxed radio. There weren't many options for stations; mostly the one out of Fairbanks, or the gobbledygook conglomeration of a station that played everything from hard rock to Russian polkas, and every kind of talk radio in between. She noticed the microwave on the kitchen counter. Ah, the bachelor's best friend. Same here as anywhere.

He was so still in the corner chair she hadn't realized he was there until he spoke. "Sorry to drag you into this again."

She jumped, caught her breath, and felt like an idiot. "Good Lord. Thought you were part of the chair."

"Not yet," he said with a sourpuss look, and tried to get up.

"Don't bother," she said, holding a hand out to stop him. "I just need to ask about the fuel. Curan said you were low. Usual barge screwup, I take it."

He slumped back in the chair. "Yes, the usual. As for what's in the truck tank, you can try, but I don't think you'll get much but a dribble. I fueled earlier and I think I creamed it off."

"Great," she said. "I'll just take your plane."

He looked for a minute like he thought she was serious.

"I'm kidding," she said.

He smiled, relieved. She couldn't believe how pale he was. "Where's the pain?"

"Low back. Right. My father had the same thing. He handled it better, I think. Tough sonovagun."

"Any tingling or numbness in the extremities?"

"You getting into nurse mode?"

"Not willingly," she said. "Don't push it."

"There's no 'tingling or numbness in the extremities.' "

"Just a muscle spasm then, I expect. I can give you a couple of muscle relaxers. Knock back the spasm long enough for you to rest and keep it relaxed."

"*Super* nurse mode."

"Just don't say where you got them. It *is* against the law to dispense drugs without a proper license," she said.

"Yes, and we all stand on proper law out here."

"Got any ice?"

"Couple of trays."

"Plastic bags?"

"Yeah," he said suspiciously.

"I'll put some ice in a bag, wrap it in a towel, and you can put that under your back."

"Oh, God." A sigh of genuine suffering.

When she'd got the ice ready, she stood by his chair, braced a knee on its edge and slipped her hand behind his neck. She curled her fingers into the muscular warmth of it as she pulled him forward to slip the ice behind him, his face so close she could feel his breath on her neck. The cloth of her shirt tore away from the dried blood. She winced.

"Jesus, you make me feel like an invalid," he said, gasping as her chilled hands scrabbled at his clothing and reached warm flesh, hands shaking as she fumbled at the layers of shirts and pants. She felt his arm pressed to her back. It's nothing, she repeated to herself. It doesn't mean anything. She released him as gently as she could. Still, he grunted softly.

"That ice right against your skin?"

"Sure feels like it."

"Good. Is it on the pain spot?"

"I'm not telling," he said with a shaky laugh.

She couldn't look at his face. She plunged a trembling hand in her pocket and produced the pills. "Take one of these now, the other one in four hours. If they work, and you need more, call the clinic in Bethel."

His fingertips scraped lightly on her palm as he dipped out the pills. She shivered and pulled her hand away. He put the pill on his tongue and she watched it disappear into his mouth. Still she could not meet his eyes. "You want water?" He shook his head.

The phone rang and again she caught her breath, jumped. "Get that? Please?"

She found the phone on the kitchen counter and carried it slowly to her ear, paused for what seemed like an eternity as she debated how to answer. How about hello, stupid? "Hello?"

There was a definite pause of surprise at the other end before Raina said, "So, the old man sucked you in, did he?"

"Not exactly," Bailey said, relieved that it was Raina. "Curan said I had to ask him about the fuel so . . . I'm just about to leave."

"Well, that's why I'm calling. The barge just nosed into the slough. She'll be ready to unload 'bout half an hour."

"That's great news. But I don't think the 'old man' can partici-pate. I gave him some muscle relaxers. They'll help but not if he starts slinging freight off that barge." She snuck a look at him and he frowned back at her.

"Do him good to kick back a bit," Raina said.

"I'll come down and help unload," Bailey said. "Pass the time till they get the fuel off."

Another pause on Raina's end. "You don't have to do that."

"Do what?"

"Unload. We'll deal with it."

"I don't have to, or it would be better if I didn't?"

Raina cleared her throat. "Little of both, maybe."

Bailey hooked the phone over her shoulder, stared at her feet, which looked goofy all of a sudden in oversize wool socks.

"What is it?" he asked.

"Nothing. She wants to know what you want her to do."

He looked at her, his eyes narrowed slightly. "The usual, tell her. She knows the drill."

She felt rather than heard Raina's voice buzzing through the phone. Without asking her to repeat what she'd said, she put the phone back to her ear. "Yeah, Kash says you're in charge, Raina. Just like usual."

"Did you hear anything I just said?" she asked.

"Yes, I'll be down shortly."

"Okay," Raina said, the tone of her voice implying otherwise.

Bailey put the phone back on its cradle, stared again at her socks.

"Barge is coming in."

"I already got that part. What'd she say that you're not telling me?" He grimaced as he tried to shift in the chair.

Now she could not help looking at him. His eyes were black, featureless. "I don't think she 'approved' of my being here."

He watched her. "It's just business. And mercy. That's all. Right?"

"Right." She stepped back, felt her stomach re-form from where it had melted into her abdomen.

"I'd best get down there and help unload, before Raina comes up here to investigate."

"Sure," he said. "Wouldn't look good for you, hanging out with a crippled old man."

He'd said it with a twist of pique, but now that the drugs were taking effect, there wasn't much weight behind the jab.

"Soon as I get the juice I'll fuel up and skedaddle."

"Skedaddle?"

"Haven't you ever heard that before?"

"I don't know. Maybe once or twice. It doesn't seem like the kind of word you'd use."

"Guess I'm just busting out all over the place," she said.

The twice yearly arrival of the barge was a big deal in the bush. Two thirds of the Village had turned out for the show. Things that people had ordered that were too bulky or heavy to fly out had to wait for the barge, and it was the only way precious fuel could be transported; its arrival now was especially blessed since fishing season opened the next day and many a net drift would have been cut short because of lack of boat gas.

She hung back at the edge of the crowd, unnoticed, while all eyes monitored the barge captain and crew as they negotiated the balky scow close to the beach. Children weaved in and out of the crowd, shrieking with glee. From her vantage, she could see several bottles passing around. Though Ingalik was a dry village, it didn't seem to make much difference in the amount of alcohol that flowed in. The bootleggers took up where legal purchase left off, and made good money. The black market fetched upwards of sixty dollars for a bottle of cheap, Canadian-blend whiskey that would have cost fifteen in a store.

She spied Raina close to the water, but did not go to her. She had thought that there was a spark of friendship there. Nothing blood-serious, of course, but at least some kind of mutual respect. It had seemed an easy relationship, too, and that was something Bailey cherished. There were no demands going out, none coming in. Uncomplicated was the word that came to mind. But if it had been so uncomplicated, why did it bother her so much to discover otherwise?

Just as the crew was about to drop the ramp onto the sand, a float plane roared overhead, buzzing the beach. Heads ducked instinctively. The bright yellow plane did a steep banking turn over the Yukon, then came in for an across-current landing. Bailey was astonished that anyone would be so stupid, and couldn't wait to get a load of the yahoo behind the yoke. It step-taxied into the slough, just squeaking by the barge where the now motionless crew stared in disbelief at the aircraft. The pilot goosed the plane onto the sand, scattering the crowd.

The children squealed and clapped at the performance, and the tall form that unfolded itself from the cockpit smiled and took a bow on the tip of the pontoon before leaping with a flourish onto the beach. Now she recognized the man: Raina's boyfriend, Match. He lived in Shagluk, the next Village upriver, and had seen Raina on a couple of occasions after one of his visits, which left her looking like a raccoon. She had heard of his run-ins with Fish and Game on the watershed, how he blustered and swaggered and bellowed his way through most any confrontation regardless of his guilt or innocence in the matter. Most often it was not innocence he blustered to cover. He was a holy terror, near as Bailey could tell, but he seemed to revel in his despised state, or else to be completely unaware of it.

He was the kind of bush pilot for whom the saying had been coined "There are old pilots, and bold pilots, but there are no old, bold pilots." It was common knowledge on the watershed that he had smacked up two planes, accidents that had gone unreported to the FAA, and walked away from both of them. Obviously, this bold pilot had plenty of luck, and an unending supply of money. Since the previous crashes were unreported, he hadn't been able to collect insurance. Yet somehow he had been able to purchase three airplanes. He was flying a Maule now, though she couldn't figure out why. They could get in and out of spots with a third less running room than her Cessna, but they were squirrelly, nose heavy, and very tricky to fly. Come to think of it, the plane fit him to a tee.

Match spent a great deal of time and energy making himself out to be more competent than he was, the kind of person who often took credit for the accomplishments of others. He was a bullshitter, but she had to admit he was good-looking. Strong chin; full, puckish mouth; darkly rimmed hazel eyes; black hair sprawling wildly over his skull. That had to be the only reason Raina stuck with him. It couldn't be his charm, and she didn't imagine someone that crass was a good romp in the sack, either.

The crowd surged to the edge of the water as the ramp hit the sand, forming itself in two rows. Everybody jostled and nudged to be the closest to the boat. For some reason, nobody liked to be at the back so that's where Bailey stayed. Everything that could come off by dint of human strength came first: mattresses, pallets of dry goods, generators, boat motors . . . and then came the big ticket items. A new pickup truck, a couple of ATVs, pre-fab building material, insulation. The barge had to be moved in twice as the lessening load set it afloat. Finally, everything was off but the fuel. It was midnight by then, and the party atmosphere was going strong under the still-bright sun.

Unbelievably, the crew started pulling up the ramp. Bailey felt her stomach lurch. She watched as the crew made the barge fast, and offloaded themselves. She made her way to the captain who was laughing heartily amid a knot of villagers by the water. He was one of those poster-perfect alcoholic rivermen: ruddy face that had seen the worst weather had to offer, shocked-white hair escaping from a ratty old cap with ARCO stitched in yellow across the crown, and a big, meaty body that was still strong in spite of heavy abuse. He talked around an ever-present cigarette clamped wetly between his lips. Bailey had to squeeze between two older women who were vying for his attention to ask him what was going on.

"Well hell, darlin', a fella's gotta take a break sometime. Now's as good as any." He couldn't seem to say two sentences without laughing as if he'd just heard the best joke ever.

She asked him if there was any way she could tie up alongside the barge and get AV gas directly from his tanks.

"Come on, sweetheart, I been stuck on this river for three days straight. I'm taking a big break, right here, right now, right sisters?" he said, roaring at the two women who roared back at him in a higher register. "Besides, honey, my apparatus won't fit your apparatus. Know what I mean?" and he managed to wink a bleary eye at her before erupting again, only this time it trailed off in a fit of sputum-rich hacking, punctuated by his gacking a good-sized gob of it on the ground. At least he had the decency to scuff sand over it.

She tried to back out of his boozy aura, but thumped against a body before she got two steps. She turned with an apology on her lips, but stopped short of giving it to the hazel eyes that gleamed back at her.

"I don't think we've ever been introduced," he said, though he hadn't stuck out a hand. "You're the little lady bought that camp upriver, aren't you? I'm Match."

"Bailey," she said, her hands at her side.

"I get it," he said. "*Bailey*. Like Irish Cream." He laughed.

"That'd be one way to associate it," she said, unsmiling.

"What's a matter? Can't get old Cap to sell you AV gas?"

"It appears not." He was so tall and so close she had to crank her head back to look him in the face, but she wasn't about to take a step back. That would have been an admission of some kind. So she kept her head level and looked past his shoulder.

"Whyn't you stay at Raina's tonight until they get that fuel off?" He pulled a pint of something brown from his coat pocket and tipped it into his mouth. Jack Daniel's. Pretty expensive lube for out here.

"Yeah, sure." Raina's voice surprised her from behind. Now Bailey was trapped between them.

Bailey stepped aside so she could have them both in her sight. "I'll sleep in the plane."

Match looked past her to where the Cessna was tethered, then back at her. "You're small, all right, but it looks like you're going to have to get smaller to fit in that plane. It's kinda . . . loaded," he said with a wink.

She forgot she'd already had the plane loaded with the kids' gear.

"Jesus," Raina chimed in now. "Them people gonna be wettin' their britches over that stuff. Told 'em we'd be up with it hours ago."

"Kash too lazy to take care of his own business? Got to get Bailey runnin' his errands for him?"

"He's laid up or he would have," Bailey said, detecting too late the defensiveness in her voice.

"Now ain't that a shame," Match said, snapping his fingers dully. "Night's young yet. Why don't I fly it up?"

Now she and Raina stared at him while he looked back and forth from one to the other, grin as wide as his ears.

"Let's go up to my house and have a little drink or something. Wouldn't that be a good idea?" Raina pleaded.

Bailey could smell Raina's panic mounting. "Water's way low up there. I wouldn't risk it if I were you," she said.

"How'd you think you were gonna land that whale?"

"I wasn't. They would come down to my camp and get it from there."

"So Kash is givin' 'em boats now?"

"No, no, baby. Bailey lent 'em the boat when she couldn't land them at the Lodge. Kash didn't have nothin' to do with it."

Bailey could see by the set of his jaw that he had already decided to go, regardless of what either of them did. If he couldn't land at the Lodge, he'd land at her camp. She didn't think she wanted anyone messing around at her camp, particularly this prick. His intentions could be totally benign; she had no right to assume otherwise. But this was no mere assumption. The alarm bells jangling in her head were signs she knew better than to discount.

"Why are you so interested in doing anybody a one a.m. favor?"

"Why not?" he said with a shrug. "Might be fun to pop in on the tourists. Have a drink, let 'em experience a little local color."

"They're probably asleep, Match," Raina said. "Just leave this shit to Bailey. She's gotta go up there anyway."

"Yeah, Raina, but Bailey's out of gas and the customers are in a hurry," he said, looking at Bailey instead of Raina.

The unnaturally bright eyes shifted to Raina now. "Radio up there, Raina. Tell the folks I'll try to land their stuff at the Lodge. If I can't get in there, I'll go down to Bailey's camp. They can meet me there."

Ferrin appeared at his side. "What's going on, brother?"

"Ferrin. I was just going to fly some gear up to those *tourists* at the Lodge. Wanna ride?"

Ferrin smiled. "Sure."

"Too late," Bailey said, her eyes steady on Match. "He's already got a passenger. You gonna help me transfer the load or would that tire you out too much to fly?"

"No problem," he said, smiling expansively.

"I'll help, too," Raina said, glaring at Bailey.

"Suit yourself."

Bailey headed for the Cessna with Raina glued to her elbow. When they were far enough away, Raina's pinch on her arm tightened. "Are you outta your fucking mind?"

Bailey gritted her teeth and kept walking. "First of all, let go of my arm. Second, it's obvious you don't want him up there, and I don't want him up there. Third, I don't know about this guy but what I've heard and what I've just seen, and I don't mind telling you the preliminary report sucks. If your concern for the situation is of the jealous kind, forget it. If your concern is actually for my well-being, I'm surprised, but I appreciate it."

Raina grabbed Bailey's arm again and dragged her to a stop like an anchor. "If I can't talk you outta this, I'll say this and then don't say I didn't warn you. When he's drinking, he's a real bastard. He ain't there yet. But he gets there all of a sudden. Be careful."

"I'll do my best. Go radio those kids, wake their asses up and tell them to boat down to my camp, pronto. He's a lunatic in that plane and I don't want him to have any excuses to land up at the Lodge. "Stay by the radio. I'll call from camp when we're about to take off. If I don't radio you by oh-three-hundred . . ." she trailed off.

"I'll call Kash," Raina finished for her. "He'll know what to do."

"Good. Now go." She watched Raina hurry away as best she could in the deep sand, and then turned to Match, who was still where they left him, goosing Ferrin in the ribs and laughing. *"Match!"* she yelled, keeping her voice low in her chest. "Let's go!"

She could see him miming an oooooooh, knocking his knees in mock fear. Then he slapped Ferrin on the back and came on, homing in on her like the Devil himself.

She had already convinced him to go straight to her camp. Told him Raina would radio the kids and have them boat down to her place as quickly as possible. He pulled out the pint, almost empty now, and tipped his head back to get every last drop. She hadn't intended to aggravate him, but she couldn't help looking at him and shaking her head in disgust.

He glowered at her and flung the empty pint to the rear of the cabin. She tried to make herself as small as possible on her side of the cockpit, and concentrated on reducing her heart rate to a gallop.

They landed without incident. She had it all planned. Get the boxes offloaded and get him the hell out of here as quickly as possible. She was counting on the kids taking longer to get there than it would take for her and Match to unload and leave. She could just see that idiot Zach getting pissy with Match and then . . . she didn't know what. She didn't want to know what or even imagine it. To that end, she planned to be prepared. He cut the engine just before they glided to the bank.

She tied the Maule to the old cottonwood, leaned on its scabrous bole. Fatigue lurked just beneath her skin, suppressed there by adrenaline. If she could just keep him moving and get him out of here. . . . She jogged back to the plane. Match had unfolded himself from the cockpit and balanced across the pontoon wire to the passenger side.

"Whyn't you just take the door off so we can unload?"

"Why do I gotta unload these people's shit? Let *them* deal with it is what I say. Besides I gotta take a leak."

"Well, I'll unload then if you can't hold your water," she said, trying to force him to keep up with her.

"Whatever," he said, and eased himself lazily up the bank.

She did not look at him but kept every other sense tuned to his movements. She listened to him swish through the grass to the edge of the cabin, heard the soft plop of a hand on wood as he braced himself going around the corner. She wanted to follow him, make sure he didn't leave his tainted fingerprints on anything. Instead, she unhinged the passenger door so she could get the boxes out more quickly, and flung them on the grass, never mind the disorder. She had to get inside while he was still outside.

She rehung the door and climbed onto the bank. She couldn't see him anywhere in the clearing. Obviously he had stayed around back, out of her sight, probably checking out the generator for future reference. She walked to the cabin door, resisting the urge to run, and tried to breathe evenly in spite of the pulse that hammered the backs of her eyes. She slipped inside, left the door open to avoid its creaking twice. Her eyes pounded harder, adjusting to the gloom. Hurry. In the bedroom it was almost purely dark but she knew the small spaces as well as if there was light.

She bent by the mattress, slipped a hand under until wriggling fingers found their target, the 9 mm Beretta she kept there. Instinctively her finger checked the safety to make sure it was on.

Good. She ejected the butt clip, then refitted it to make sure it was set. Good. She set it on the bed, shrugged off her jacket and felt for the leather shoulder holster hanging on its nail. *He'll be wondering where you are.* She shrugged it on over the turtleneck, and cinched tight the rib band. The shoulder strap tightened and rubbed over the hook wound as she worked. *Can't think about that now.* She nosed the pistol into its sheath and grabbed her jacket from the bed.

"So, that's where you are," Match said, leaning on the doorframe with both arms. He had to bend almost in half to see into the room. *But how much of her could he see? And how had he come in without her hearing him?* She clamped her jacket to her chest, hoping it covered the straps.

"Just thought I'd grab a few things, you know, for the overnight. Ready?"

"Where are your things?" he asked, and gestured at her hands, which held only her jacket.

"I'm getting them." *Get off the defensive,* she told herself. "What I'd like to know is if you're finally ready to go?"

"I don't know." Whisper of a smile at the corners of his mouth. "Maybe I caught you here for a good reason. Like maybe the reason why you were all hot and bothered to come up here with me." *Naturally that's how he'd interpret it.*

"Are you ready?"

"I'm always ready. Ask Raina." He mounded a hand over the slight bulge of his crotch, readjusting himself for emphasis.

She imagined Broward presenting himself to Temple: *Come on, honey. Wanna play with the dolly?* his hand moving over himself. *Wanna make the dolly happy?* The leather holster creaked as she shifted her hand closer to it. As much as she detested this man, she did not want to shoot him. But if that's what it took to keep him away, she would squeeze off a round with no compunction whatsoever.

"You have Chance One to put it in reverse and back out of here."

He hesitated a remarkably long time. *Back down you idiot.* And then she heard it, a distant buzz.

Match cocked his head, then smiled. "Company," he said, and sauntered casually outside.

Bailey put on her jacket and zipped it closed over the holster. Her knees felt runny as she made her way outside into the Midnight Sun.

Whoa, Alpha thought. *That is one long, tall drink of water.* Did Bailey have a boyfriend? Here came the woman herself out of the cabin. Alpha waved like crazy but only got one raised hand in return. She turned her gaze back to the man standing on the bank, his hands tucked into the hip pockets of his jeans, one hip cocked seductively. As much as she was watching him, she realized suddenly that he was watching her pretty exclusively. Zach nosed the boat awkwardly into the bank and she had to brace herself to keep from pitching onto the floor.

"Nice landing, hon," she said over her shoulder.

She stood with the rope in one hand and tried to hold on to the bank to keep the current from sweeping them away.

"Allow me," the tall drink of water said, and took the rope from her, then one-handed her up the bank like she was a leaf.

"Thanks," she said, her face on fire. She had thought it would be only Bailey meeting them, and she wished now she had taken more pains with herself before they left the lodge. It was two in the morning for Pete's sake, but she had to shade her eyes while looking up at the fellow before her. "I'm Alpha."

"Match," he said, with a big grin and he was close enough so she could smell the booze in his reply, but he didn't seem drunk. He didn't bother introducing himself to Zach.

"Folks," Bailey said shouldering past him. "Thanks for coming down at such an ungodly hour. We figured you'd want your stuff sooner than later."

Alpha did a slow spin around. "Where's your plane?"

"Out of gas down in the Village. This . . . gentleman was kind enough to volunteer to bring your things up," Bailey said, gesturing at Match. Was that a bit of acid she detected in the comment? Maybe they'd just had a spat. God knows, *that* happened.

Bailey had already picked up a box and trundled it over to the boat, where she handed it to Zach, who was standing in the bow like an actor who'd forgot his lines. Alpha grabbed a box.

"So you're the people staying up at the Lodge? Whaddya think of our little piece of the world?"

"It's beautiful," Alpha said. "I've never been anywhere like this."

"How long you stayin'?"

"Little less than two weeks now," she said, puffing along with a heavy box.

"Not much time at all," Zach mumbled from the boat.

He wouldn't meet her eyes as she brought boxes to him. Normally she would have been beside herself to appease the dark humor, but now she didn't feel like spending any energy on it. He'd just have to suck himself out of this one.

"Well," Bailey said after the last box was in. "Mission accomplished. You guys can get back to the Lodge and get some sleep. We'll head back to the Village."

"Hang on, baby," Match said. "Aren't you going to ask these nice people in for a drink?"

"No," she said curtly. "It's two a.m., and I think these people would like to go home."

"I wouldn't mind a quick one for the road," Zach said.

Match procured a pint of Jack Daniel's from his jacket. "A little sip of this tasty brew is just what the situation calls for." He twisted off the plastic seal, uncapped the bottle and handed it to Alpha. "Here, sweetheart," he said. "We could all use a little sugar."

She didn't consciously think of doing it, she just stepped back from him. "You go ahead," and watched his face darken and whorl. So familiar.

"Let's go, Match," Bailey said.

"Hey," he said. "We're having a drink here. Relax, wouldja?"

"Let's go," she said, more quietly than before, but somehow sounding louder.

"Whaddya gonna do, spank me?" he purred.

There is definitely something going on here, Alpha thought as Match sidled up to her and slid an arm across her shoulders. "Sure you wouldn't like a little nip? It'll relax you."

And then Bailey was between them, extracting the bottle from his loose fingers and flinging it away. Alpha heard the *whoosh* of it through the air, and then a distant *plash* as it hit the water. "Alpha, get in the boat," Bailey said, her voice strained and stringy sounding.

Match snaked his arm around Bailey, looked as if he was about to waltz her before he froze, dropped his arm and backed off a pace. "That's not nice," he said so quietly Alpha had to strain to hear him.

And then Zach was beside her, pulling her arm. "Come on, Al." She wasn't sure what was going on, turned her head back to see Bailey standing tensely in front of Match who looked as if he'd been accused of something terrible.

"Bailey?" Alpha called to her.

"Go on, now," Bailey said.

Zach urged her down the bank and into the boat. "Zach, I don't think we should leave her like this."

"She can take care of herself," Zach said, slipping his way to the stern.

Alpha stood in the bow of the boat while Zach untied it and started the motor. Match stalked off to his airplane and cast it off, letting it drift into the current before he even got in and started it. The outboard roared behind her and Zach yelled, "Sit down!" She kept her eyes on Bailey whose every point was focused on Match's plane as it shot downriver, then lifted itself over the water. The last thing she saw before the first bend took them out of sight was Bailey standing on the bank, chin dropped to chest, arms folded across herself as if to ward off the Boogey Man.

9

She waited until the kids were safely away and she could no longer hear the drone of Match's airplane before she let her watery legs carry her into the cabin. She sat on the couch, mindless of the odors now. Didn't even get two deep breaths before the radio squawked at her. "Village to River Camp, do you read?"

Bailey looked at her watch. Raina was right on time. She reached for the hand unit without getting up, and pressed the mike bar.

"River Camp. Go ahead, Village."

"Request status report, over."

"Status is a Roger. I'm alone."

"You okay?"

Bailey exhaled slowly, tried to swallow down the lump in her throat.

"I say again: Are you okay?"

"Yes. I'm all right."

"I called Kash. He wants to talk to you."

"Now?"

"Yeah. He's here."

"Okay. Go ahead."

There was a long pause. She put the radio on the couch and drew herself a glass of water from the pump, drank it down in three long drafts. She set the glass on the table when she heard him, took her time getting back to the couch.

"River Camp, go ahead," she answered, the radio steadier now in her hand.

"You got a boat?"

"Roger that."

"Get in it and get down here."

"I don't think so."

"That was not a request."

She put the radio at arm's length and stared at it, made a bluff salute. *Who died and put you in charge?* but said into the mike, "I'm whipped. I'll stay here tonight."

"Negative," he said. "Too risky. You follow?"

He was worried that Match would return, maybe drunker than before, crazier. She pressed her elbow against the chubby handle of the pistol under her coat. She had to admit it was unwise to risk it coming to that.

"Affirmative. ETA two hours."

"Roger that. I'll meet you at the beach. Ingalik, out."

She'd done no more than wash down a couple of hunks of bread with cold coffee before she took off, because at that point she didn't really give a damn what she looked like. Primping was pointless anyway when you faced a two-hour ride into the wind. Her overnight pack was still in the airplane so she hadn't bothered to bring anything.

He was waiting on the beach as promised when she goosed the boat onto the sand. She stepped out of the boat and almost buckled to her knees, caught herself before she went down by bracing both hands on the boat as if she'd turned to get something. She waited a moment longer before turning again, until she was certain her legs would allow her to walk steadily toward him.

"Well," he said. "This got ten kinds of fucked up, didn't it?"

"I'm sorry . . ." but he put up his hand against her apology. He was ashen.

He turned his head slowly, a curious squint to his eyes. "I got news for you, that asshole is only temporarily defused. He's been a growing pain in my ass for months and he won't stop until . . ."

"Until what?"

"Let's put it this way: The guy's got an agenda that includes getting me *off* the agenda and ruining everything I've busted my ass over for years, my whole life. It's no ordinary pissing match. . . . Well, to him it is . . . but I know just how high the stakes are. He's got no clue about the consequences. None whatsoever."

"You're talking about the CORE, I take it."

"Yep," his lips smacked shut on the *p*. "And I'm talking about you."

"I'm okay," she said. "I took care of it."

"No, you did something incredibly stupid."

She was stunned.

"I thought you had more sense than that, getting in an airplane with that shit-for-brains, first off, and then coming up here alone, and then actually arranging to have him put on a display for those people."

Her eyes were glued to him in disbelief. She couldn't recall ever having been reprimanded in her life. Not Miss Do It All, Take Care of it All Bailey.

"You have no idea what just happened," he continued. "The success of this little venture in tourism would have proved something once and for all. And now it's all fucked up."

Because of you is how he wanted to finish that sentence. And now she found her voice, tasted the acridness of it. "Don't you *dare* reprimand me. I risked my ass to keep him away from those people. He was flying up there whether you, or I, or anyone liked it or not. If I hadn't shoved in, he would have brought Ferrin. God knows what would have happened."

"It wasn't your responsibility."

"No. It was yours. I just seem to keep getting stuck with it."

"Then don't. Don't get stuck with it."

"If I hadn't, it might have been a lot worse for you." That struck something. She saw it struggling with the anger that hadn't quite subsided. Then she realized what she'd done. Given him another big, fat sign in letters miles high. *I did it for you,* is what she'd just said, and he knew it.

"Well," he said, shaking his head until the hair curtained over his brow. "I don't know what to say."

" 'Sorry' might cut it."

He shook his head again. "Then I'm sorry." He turned that smile on her, the one she was used to, took a step toward her, then stopped, the ashenness returning to his face.

"Back still bothering you?"

"Yeah." That smile again.

"Go home," she said. "All your sheep are present and accounted for."

"What are you going to do?"

She looked at the Cessna glowing in low-angled sun. "Got everything I need right there," she said.

He frowned, looked at the plane, then back at her with an edgy awkwardness she had not thought possible of the man.

He had been thinking about what to do while he waited, and had come to a conclusion that made the most sense, yet got him somewhere he wanted to be as well. But now, when it came to presenting the idea to her, it felt like the first time he tried to kiss a girl when he was thirteen. It had turned out fine, that situation all those years ago, but only, he realized in retrospect, because of his position even then. It was a terrific aphrodisiac. Girls had never been a problem, had come willingly to him until their desires changed over time from strong, steady men like himself to the strong-minded, wildly changeable idiots that threatened the survival of the very culture—never mind his sex life. But this was about to change in both departments. He'd have to use a little finesse yet, but it was going to happen.

"Here's the plan. You've got four, maybe five hours before Captain Stumblebum comes to and offloads that fuel from the barge. You should get some sleep, and I don't think it's a good idea to stay in the plane. Not tonight." That got her. She could see the sense in it. "You can't stay at Raina's in case that asshole comes in, so you should sleep at my house. You can have my bed. I'm better off in the chair." Her eyes wandered back to the plane as if it would indicate what to do.

"Somebody's going to know about it," she said.

"Meaning?"

"Having a white girl in your house in the wee hours? Won't that look bad?"

He shrugged. "They'll have to get used to it."

"Get used to it?"

He slipped up there. "Get used to having white people around."

"Oh," she said. "Well, if you don't think it'll cause a lot of trouble . . ."

"I don't give a damn if it does."

"I do. I have to live here, too. Sort of," she said.

"Look. It's the right thing to do. People will talk no matter what. You know how that goes."

"Yeah."

He could see the fine lines around her eyes, the smoky gray circles under them. She just needed a little firmness.

"Tie off the boat and let's get some sleep," he said.

"I'll get my pack."

He watched her drag the boat onto the beach, then trudge to the Cessna where she placed a hand flat against its body while she rummaged behind her seat, then walk back to where he waited by the ATV, convincing himself all the while that the shakiness was just a reaction to the spasms in his back.

He struggled to get his leg over the saddle.

"Guess I'll have to drive," she said.

He didn't argue, just perched sideways on the tail end of the saddle.

She had driven one only once before, she told him, and that was apparent as she whiplashed him with every gear change. He couldn't help clamping an arm around her to keep himself from sliding off. He felt her stiffen at first, then relax. Her body was lithe and firm under his hand. Jesus, boy, he thought. Get a hold of yourself.

He stripped off his shirts and headed for the kitchen to get water. Since there was no door between the main room and the bedroom, he couldn't help seeing it when she took off her coat, the leather shoulder holster complete with sidearm. "What was that for?" Her head jerked up, her face looking like a caught animal, then she looked away and continued to ease the strap over her shoulder.

"Match," she said. "Good thing I had it."

He felt his fist curl and then, totally unplanned, the other hand rising to the curve of her face. "What happened?"

"Nothing happened, thanks to that," so softly he could barely hear.

She registered the heat coming off him, thumping her like a palpable fist. She stood very still, maybe shifted a hair away from him, unable to react before he'd pulled her shirt over her head.

She felt his hands gently on her, one on the near arm, one circled round behind her to cup the other elbow, shifting her gently to the edge of the bed. She sat exactly where he'd placed her, his hip so close to her face she would only have to lean a degree to reach it with her mouth.

He smoothed her hair where the wind had snarled it, then

dropped his hand to trace the swelling on her shoulder where the hook had sliced in. Clearly, he wanted to do something, but he hesitated, faced with the prospect of action. She could read it all on his face, see it in the way his tongue coated his lower lip, then disappeared behind it.

Broward had never hesitated, had moved on her before he seemed conscious of his desire. Back then, she had liked it. Thought it refreshing to know a man who knew his heart and did not hesitate. Had he hesitated in his decision to molest Temple? But when Bailey thought of how quickly he'd ingratiated himself to her, and how stupidly she'd fallen for it, she did not doubt that he hadn't faltered a moment but now doubted her ability to protect even herself.

The six years passed had done nothing to dim her sense memory, and the thin, acrid smell of him swelled in her head. Six years and she had done well by herself, blazed *keep out* signs strung on a necklace for all to heed. Why hadn't Kash? With all the factors against her—color, culture, character—why did he want her? Surely there was nothing left to take other than what was there before him.

The waxen smell of him overtook her now; a vague tremor looped languidly down her spine.

He fitted his hand to the curve of her face. "You all right?" he asked, a sickle of black hair curved over the bridge of his nose.

She nodded, spread her fingers across the pale hollow below his belly.

"You want this?" he asked.

She said "yes," her voice so coarse she hardly recognized it.

"Should we . . . do we need anything?"

She shook her head. "I can't have children."

"Wasn't worried about that."

"Oh," she said, understanding finally. "I've had all the tests. No problems." She paused. "You?"

"Same."

He had both hands on her face now, her mouth at the center of the funnel they formed, so when he kissed her it was as if he were drinking from her, drinking in long, greedy drafts. He leaned over her, drinking, his mouth as sweet as her sister's baby had been when she leaned near it before letting it go, leaned so near its mouth as to appear to kiss it but it hadn't been that. She'd just wanted to smell its sweet, unpoisoned breath and skin as an animal would its young.

He tried to lift her to him, but she'd stood of her own volition to spare his back. "Just lie down," she said. She stripped off her pants, unzipped his fly, before straddling him.

She looked at the long dusky surface of his abdomen, watched her fingers trail across it and bent again to his mouth, holding a hand across his forehead, while he moved his wetted tongue over her cheeks and down her neck, which she'd arched to him willingly. Dim light filtered around the window shade. She thought of the way his body felt under her, how his mouth tasted, how greedily he drank from her, and thought of him sucking her dry and dead until the crusted husk of her floated in the air like ash. Her hands saw him, smooth and unmarked, and saw herself as his hands moved over her.

There was a moment of pain when he moved himself into her, and then she returned to the room, to him as he was, tears of sweat dripping from the curves of his face. She gathered him into her with her legs and arms, felt and saw everything at once—a tiny piece of grit under her palm, a hair fallen from her head landing curved on his cheek. He drove into her, his spattering warmth causing her to shake. Finally, she was conscious only of contrapuntal breathing, the notes rasped and deeply drawn, before submitting to a sleep so absolute it felt like death.

And hours later on waking, she could have sworn she *had* been dead. His breath on her neck had created a damp circle of condensation that changed temperatures with the movement and cessation of air. Sweat pooled at the edges of his arm across her belly and tickled down her side. She closed her eyes. The smell of him fingered down her airway as she breathed him in, slowly, savoring every thick, sweet mote.

His free arm lay flung above his head, fingers curled loosely into the palm of his hand. One streak of hair cut diagonally across his forehead, pasted to the dampened surface. The plain, white sheet drew a stark line across the caramel skin of his groin.

She stopped breathing as the upflung arm came down across his chest and the knee of the opposite leg cocked itself up in the air, but he had not awakened. She relaxed completely now, unaware of the light sleep that overcame her.

Had she whimpered, cried out? She woke to his eyes on her. He was sitting up. The sheet tented across his knees where they splayed slightly apart, his arms draped loosely over them. He watched her without a trace of emotion, until finally she sat up, fully awake now. Fully aware.

"It's late," he said. He moved sweat-matted hair away from his face and pushed out a long, slow breath. "You all right?"

She nodded.

"Season opens today. Like to do some fishing. Ought to check those floats, too. Dinged a branch when I landed in the slough yesterday." Said it more to himself than to her, while he stretched his arms, arching his hands overhead. "Back's not too bad," he said. "Amazing."

Bailey laughed.

"What?"

"Hormones," she said.

"Hormones?"

"Medical miracles most often occur because of hormones. People with chronic illnesses suddenly go into remission when they fall in love." She could have gagged herself for letting that word float into the air. He looked at her. Did she imagine the alarm on his face? She tried to shrug it off. "It's not love, of course. Just hormones."

"Whatever it is, it works," he said.

He folded the sheet away from him and sat for a moment on the edge of the bed, scrubbing his face with his hands. She thought he would rise then, but he only propped his arms out to either side, and let his head drop forward, let it dangle from the thick stem of his spine for a moment with eyes closed. When he stood, Bailey did not look away, could not look away as her eyes scoured the contour of his back and lingered on legs that looked strong as tree boles.

There was no angularity to him compared to the men she had seen before; but power slept in the hardened protrusion of his belly, the down-slanted slope of his shoulders. He was anchored to the earth and it welcomed him. He moved before her, completely comfortable in his skin, pulling on lightweight wool pants before disappearing into the bathroom. She sat on the edge of the bed, using her ears now to watch him. She heard his water splash into the bowl, a long uninterrupted stream, and let her ears see the rough, thick-stubbed fingers holding himself. The water in the sink ran and she felt the cold brace of it roughen his cheeks and burn briefly on the shocked surfaces of his eyes.

He went to the closet, slipped a thick, flannel shirt off a hanger and swirled it on without bothering to button it. He moved toward the door as if to pass into the front room, but stopped beside her, his fingertips resting lightly on the ridge of her shoulder, his eyes on the white-knuckled snarl of her hands.

"Make yourself at home. You may want to wait until the place empties out a bit before you leave."

She concentrated on the rim of flesh that bowed over the edge of his pants, could barely stifle the urge to touch it as he spoke.

And then he was gone. No *see you later* or *gee, that was terrific. Let's do it again sometime*. It felt as if she'd done him the favors he needed doing, got the big beef, and then the old heave-ho. But what did she care if she didn't get a formal declaration of undying and undiluted adoration? They were adults. High school histrionics were unnecessary.

She dressed, stuffed the holstered Beretta in her pack, and headed down the road, praying the fuel was off so she could tank up immediately and leave.

"Hey!" she heard a woman yell.

Raina was on her porch.

"Slow down. They're not done with that fuel yet."

Bailey looked toward the beach, her face set like concrete. She felt dirty, tired.

"Come over here," Raina said irritably. "Don't make me yell."

Bailey shifted her pack to the other shoulder and headed for Raina's porch. From there, they had a clear view of the beach, and clearly Kash was there. It was crowded for that time of morning—then she remembered that the commercial fishing season had opened. The explanation would have been satisfactory but for the fact that no one was getting in their boats. They seemed to be gathered in little knots here and there, smoking, talking softly among themselves. Curan dislodged himself from the group closest to them and approached Kash, who was going over his airplane. They spoke briefly and the boy got on the four-wheeler that was parked nearby and roared off, its wide, heavily treaded tires spraying thin sheets of dirty water to either side as it went.

"Why's everybody still hanging around? Thought the season opened today."

"Christ," Raina said. "They canceled it for another day at least. Heard it on the radio this morning."

"How can they cancel it?"

"Runs are low, they can do it. And we get stopped just like everybody else. See, this is what we're fighting about. This ain't supposed to happen to us. According to yet another fine piece of legislation, we're supposed to get priority when stocks are low."

This was not an argument she wanted to get Raina rolling on. Not now. "Mind if I wait here?" Bailey asked, sitting on the steps. She didn't feel like dealing with the crowd.

"Guess not. You look like shit. What happened last night?"

If Bailey told her what a top-notch asshole her boyfriend had been, would it sound like the same old music to her? Music she didn't want to hear? Or would it be the one step too far that would give her strength to ditch him?

"Match was pretty high. The kids showed up. Situation defused."

"Whaddya mean, 'situation defused'?"

"Like I said, Match was drunk. You know better than I do what that means." She hated it when people asked her what she meant when the meaning was excruciatingly obvious.

"Did he . . ."

". . . hit anybody? No."

"That ain't what I was gonna ask."

"What then?"

"Did he . . . get slimy on you?"

Bailey rubbed the thighs of her jeans with the palms of her hands. "Slimy?"

"Don't play dumb. Did he hit on you?"

"I told you he didn't hit anybody."

"Goddammit, Bailey, did he fuck around with you?"

Bailey held her gaze. "No." And that was the truth, inasmuch as she hadn't allowed it. Was she supposed to tell Raina that he tried? But Raina obviously didn't want to know as she changed the line of questioning.

"Did he make a scene around them kids?"

"He was working up to it."

"Whaddya mean?"

There it was again.

"I mean he was working up to it."

"What stopped him?"

"Guess he thought better of it."

"Shit," Raina said. "I shouldn't have let you go up there."

"Yes, you should have."

"How's that?"

"Match, or Match and Ferrin going up there drunk was big-time trouble whether I was there or not because they're both involved with this CORE thing and they hate your brother. Would like nothing better than to shoot him down and don't mind using anybody to do it." Raina gaped at her, but Bailey didn't look away. "Now it's my turn to say 'Don't play dumb.'" Bailey had not moved from her perch on the steps, hands knifed stiffly into the pockets of her blue jacket.

She felt the ground shaking before she heard the noise, a deep, bass rumbling that seemed to come from the earth itself. Earthquake? They happened in Alaska, though infrequently. The sound grew and grew until she stood up, alarmed, and then the town bulldozer hove into view on its way down from the airstrip with Curan behind the wheel. Long, metal posts the size of telephone poles were strapped to its bucket, which was hoisted as high in the air as the mechanical arm could lift it. Raina waved both hands at her son, beaming proudly. He grinned at her but didn't take his hands from the controls to wave back.

Bailey looked toward the beach where all eyes were focused on the dozer treading down the hill past Raina's house. She could see Kash behind the crowd standing next to his airplane. It was impossible to tell whether he was looking at her, if he'd even noticed her standing there. She fought the urge to duck behind something, run out of the picture; it would have looked stupid. So she stood still, kept her eyes trained on the dozer as if it were of tremendous interest to her.

Raina's eyes shrank to slits. "Whyn't you stay at my house last night? I told Kash to bring you by."

"Jealous?" Bailey asked, trying to change the course of the conversation.

"Jealous?" Raina cackled. "Heck no."

"Glad we got that settled, then."

"It's not settled," Raina said. "You fuckin' my brother, or what?"

"What does it matter?"

"Well, I wouldn't put it past him to go and marry white just to get that land."

"I thought we were talking about fucking," Bailey said.

"Fucking doesn't get him title under white law. Marriage does."

Bailey's throat was so dry she couldn't swallow. "Your brother's a fine man," Bailey said. "But I'm sure he wouldn't go to a lot of trouble to get title to me."

"Not you he wants," Raina said. "It's the land. Bugged the Corporation to buy it before you did. It's the only parcel in our territory that ain't ours."

Bailey felt her face drain dry, turned her head so Raina wouldn't see the effect of her words. "Why are you telling me this?"

"I know, I know. I sound like a bitch, but that's not it. I didn't want to like you, but I ended up liking you anyway. You're all right. But this ain't the place for you. I can't blame you for wanting to stay here. It's beautiful country. And I can't blame you for wantin' my brother. He's a decent man. But he's my blood. So here I am caught between likin' you both, and knowing that somebody's gonna get hurt. It ain't gonna be him, and I don't want it to be you."

Bailey kept her eyes tight shut, extraneous sound suddenly magnified: men shouting and laughing down on the beach, two Canada Jays fighting over some morsel, and, finally, Raina's knuckles rapping sharply on the porch floor.

"Ya there?" she said amicably, as if they were talking about the weather.

"Long enough to say good-bye," Bailey said, and shouldered her pack before walking quickly away.

She headed down to the beach where she could see that the barge crew had finished offloading the fuel. She had come close, and the realization that she would have done it in ignorance of what was really going on terrified her. Again. She would top off

her wings, get the hell out of there, and come out guns blazing if
that sonovabitch flew low to her again.

———

Kash stared from group to group, eliciting a nod sometimes, or no
apparent response at all. He had anticipated the cancellation with
heightening dread as he checked in with Fish and Game the past
few days. The count hadn't looked good. Still didn't look good,
and they had no idea how long the opener would be postponed.
Every idle minute that ticked by was another stick of dynamite in
the can. He was beginning to feel like a one-man bomb squad. He
had hoped getting the men involved in another problem would
distract them, and checking the floats on the Cub for dings was
the perfect distraction.

The Ingalik had never been as community-oriented as some
other native cultures, primarily because they tended to be more
nomadic, traveling in small family units to follow the animals they
hunted for food throughout the long winter months. Only the
summers had brought them respite in their foraging; the summer subsistence hunt consisted of salmon almost exclusively, and
these months were spent in the Village by the river. In spite of
trouble people might have among themselves, the prospect of help-
ing someone in distress would bring the community together. At
least this had not changed, Kash thought, as the men gathered
around to help hoist the plane up on the gigantic tripod Curan
had brought down from the airstrip on the bulldozer. He was proud
of the boy. Once he'd expressed an interest in heavy equipment,
Kash had started him on anything he could get his hands on. It
was a good skill for the boy to have, a marketable one.

They managed to set up the tripod with the help of the winch
on the dozer. Metal plates two-feet square had to be placed under
the pod's feet to keep its legs from sinking under the weight of the
plane through the soft, black sand. They attached the electric
winch to the Cub's struts with a bridle, then dragged the aircraft

onto the beach until it rested underneath the tripod. A huge canvas belt cradled its belly and that was attached overhead to a gigantic block and tackle that dangled from the apex of the tripod. Kash had negotiated with the oil company on the North Slope for its purchase when they auctioned off the less than perfectly conditioned machinery they could no longer use. The oil companies, in an effort to keep up a thin veneer of political correctness, always gave first dibs on their best castoffs to the native contingent. He had outbid two other corporations for the rig and gloated in validation of the purchase every time it made itself useful.

From the corner of his eyes he caught a flash of color, Bailey's blue coat, as she headed down the beach to the Cessna. He had hoped she would find some excuse to stay another night, but something about the forward cant of her body, the way her cap was pulled low to her face, made her look as if she had something else in mind. Probably just post-first-time jitters, he thought, and tried to concentrate on the task at hand.

The pulley screeched admirably as the cable gained the full weight of the Cub. The wind caused it to swing precariously and Kash stationed a man at the tip of each pontoon to steady it. He brushed sand and dampness from the float bottoms, then let Curan do the honors of painting them with the soapy water that would enable them to detect even a tiny leak with the appearance of a telltale bubble.

"Stay to the edge of the pontoons, son. Don't get right under them," Kash warned.

On hands and knees, Curan slithered on his back, trying to paint on the slippery liquid and stay to the edges, but even the men bracing the plane at four corners couldn't keep it steady in the wind. The pulley shrieked and groaned as the plane swayed awkwardly in its cradle. Curan was having a hard time getting the soap on, crimping this way and that, lithe as an eel, to do as Kash had warned.

Bailey was already filling the second wing.

"Okay, son. Let's try another trick. Come on up now."

"Just a sec," Curan said breathlessly. "I think I got her now."

The cable groaned. "Come on up now," Kash said more urgently then shouted at the men, "Hold it still!" More men gathered around the swaying aircraft to help steady it. "Curan, out, now!" And his command seemed punctuated by a snap and whistle as the cable gave way and hissed through the pulley. Kash reacted to the sound instinctively, lunging at the nearest piece of Curan he could grab, sat down hard as he drove backward with a hunk of the boy's jacket in his hand, ended up with the boy's head in his lap as the edge of the pontoon knifed into the boy's right shin, felt him go rigid with amazement, then terror. He heard the men around them yelling as he placed a hand across the boy's forehead, *Hang on, son,* remembering the cool weight of Bailey's hand across his own forehead just hours ago.

Bailey.

He tried to get up, goaded into action by the screams vibrating into his groin but the boy's hands clenched his legs like vise grips. Ferrin had cranked up the dozer. What the hell?

"No!" he yelled. "Bailey!" gesturing frantically toward the Cessna "Over here. Rock it up on the other pontoon!"

Ferrin sprang down from the machine and grabbed a couple of milling bodies as he ran to the door of the plane and braced his shoulder against it.

"Like this!" he yelled, and the others followed the example, shoulder to shoulder along the body of the plane. "Okay, go!" A collective groan went up from the line of heaving bodies.

Kash watched the edge of the sand where the boy's leg disappeared, but couldn't detect any movement. "More!" he bellowed. Again, the unearthly groan as bodies rebelled at the tremendous strain, and now a gap appeared between metal and sand.

With his arms under the boy's shoulders he pulled back as gently as he could, the boy's scream so piercing he thought his eardrums would burst. But he was free. "We got him!"

He heard the plane *ooooffff* back to earth. A circle formed around them, a murmuring chorus of unintelligible sound.

"Curan?" he looked earnestly into his face, his hand cupping the damp cheek. "It's going to be all right, son. It's going to be okay." Kept blathering at the boy as he eased down the right side of his body until he was by the injured leg. He snapped his knife out of its belt sheath and slit the jeans to the knee. "Don't worry, son. I'll get you a new pair," he crooned.

He folded the cloth away from the leg and almost cried out loud. *Get the boot off before the leg swells,* he thought. Gently as he could he cut the laces on the boot, struggling to keep the knife steady as the boy's leg twitched in his hands.

"Curan, I gotta get this boot off, son. It's gonna hurt like hell. You ready?" The boy whimpered, eyes closed as he repeatedly dug hands full of sand and flung them mindlessly.

But before he could start pulling he heard her *"Move Move Move!"* She hurtled through the crowd that had intensified now as word fired around the Village. Sand spattered his thighs as she slid to her knees beside him. He thought he had never seen a vision so beautiful, or so welcome.

10

Alpha woke too early to a feeling dreaded by all women, a copious warm moistness under her buttocks and between her legs. If the night had not been so fractured by their hurried trip down to Bailey's, she might have been alert to the warning signs, but she wasn't due to start for two more days and so she hadn't thought of it. The familiar pitch and roll of her stomach in the imminently premenstrual hours had been chalked up to the intensely unpleasant events of the night before. Or day before. Since it never got dark, she had a hard time believing there was a nighttime anymore. Darkness had been erased from life, and relentless light would forever goad her body into constant activity.

As it seemed to be goading Zach now. She could hear him rattling around out in the main room of the Lodge. She clutched the sleeping bag around her bare chest and bunny-hopped to the bathroom. She grabbed the washcloth that had dried stiffly to its hook and turned on the faucet. Nothing. She turned the other faucet. Not even a drip. Now she'd have to get Zach involved and the prospect mortified her. What would she say? *Honey, I'm bleeding out in here. Could you get me some water?* She wrinkled her lips in distaste. Still she had no choice but to enlist him.

She called his name, hesitantly at first, then more insistently when he didn't answer the first two times. She finally got him to come to the bathroom door, but warned him not to come in under any circumstances.

"There's no water," she said miserably.

"That's because I haven't started the generator," he said.

She paused, waiting for him to take the obvious action. But he said nothing.

"Could you start it, please? I need to wash up."

"Al, we're in the bush. You don't need to shower every day and make your hair all perfect."

"It's not about that," she said. "I really need to clean up, okay?" hoping against her newfound assessment of him that he would get her drift.

"Come on, babe. Just throw on some fresh clothes so we can get going. It's late as hell already and money's flying out the window while we dawdle around here."

"Zach," she said, her voice tight, the one she sometimes had to use on her students, "this is not an optional beauty thing, okay? I need water, and I need it now. Please start the generator."

She could picture the insouciant shrug, hear the voice in his head, *gotta defer to these women*. She heard him clomp away, heard the door slam shut, and then she had only to wait in front of her own wretched image for the water.

Five minutes. Ten minutes. Suddenly a sharp hiss and spit until water came steadily from the tap. She turned on the shower to let it warm up while she washed her hands and brushed her teeth. A little heartened now at the prospect of at least getting her body clean, she stepped into the tiny, metal shower stall and bolted backward when the freezing water hit the crown of her head. Now what?

"Zach?" she raised her quivering voice as she turned off the faucets. "Zach!" her voice sounding like a howling animal. No responding clomp, clomp of boots across the floor. "Goddammit, Zach!" she shrieked, and then felt truly wretched for having spoken the ultimate forbidden word on top of everything else. Quickly she crossed herself, snatched up the stiff little washcloth and soaked it in cold tap water. She cleaned herself as best she could.

She wrapped a woefully inadequate towel around her and stepped out of the bathroom. Now, here came Zach, *whomp, clomp, clomp* and she leaped back in the bathroom and slammed the door.

He tapped lightly on the door. "You got water now?"

"Yes, thank you so much, but there's no hot water."

"Jesus," he sighed. "I'll check the propane heater. Can I come in?"

"No!"

"The unit's under the sink in there, hon. I gotta come in."

Alpha bit her nail.

"All right, but wait a minute." She rolled up the bag as tightly as she could, snatching futilely at the towel that popped off her at every move. When she'd gathered up everything and got the towel somewhat around her, she opened the door and slipped out.

"Oooohhhh," Zach said, delighted at the partially naked view he was getting, and tried to grab her ass as he gripped her in a clumsy hug, the bulky sleeping bag between them.

She couldn't even protest. Just stood there. He let go and stepped back.

"Boy, you're in a mood," he said.

"No, it's just . . . I'm just . . ." Finally she blurted it out, to hell with propriety, "I'm bleeding all over the place, the sleeping bag's ruined. I just need to wash up. Is that so much to ask?" Her chin squirmed uncontrollably.

"Oh, okay. Don't worry, hon. I'll get that heater lit and it won't take a minute to warm up. It's one of those quick recovery dealies," he said, backing into the bathroom as if he was afraid to turn his back to her.

"That's all I ask," she said, sniffling.

"Just lie down a minute, hon, or something, and I'll get this ready."

"Okay." But why oh why did it have to come to this? Why couldn't she simply ask it of him without being pushed to tears before he would comply? She leaned morosely against the wall, still clutching the soiled sleeping bag, and hung her head.

When he'd got the thing lit, he'd left her with a quick pat on the cheek.

She spent the next hour trying to clean herself and the sleeping bag in the shower but the stall was too confined to make any headway with the bulky bag. Now she had a huge sopping wet mess to contend with. She got herself dressed and started to drag the slopping thing outside. Zach was on the porch, his daypack and gun leaning against the railing.

"You ready?"

She let the wet blob slop to the porch floor, spread her arms wide and looked at him in disbelief.

"Al, I don't think you understand the urgency of the situation here. We are losing time and money every second. Forget the sleeping bag and let's go." And there was something in his voice that told her he already knew that she wouldn't just "forget the sleeping bag" and leave. He was banking on it, in fact, because he wanted to get out there without the encumbrance of hers truly, the nagging little woman who couldn't help but bleed and get in the way. A coolness settled over her, and she said in her calmest voice, "Run along, then."

And shameless as all hell he'd practically danced a jig, didn't even make the tiniest show of protest before he'd pecked her on utterly slack lips, told her he'd come back in a few hours to get her, and trotted off into the brush like a big, happy dog.

She'd stood rigidly until she could no longer hear him crashing through the brush before she'd slumped onto a bench someone had thoughtfully provided. Such a small comfort. She closed her eyes and let her head drop forward into her hands, thinking she would just cry and get it over with, but she was so drained now she couldn't bring herself to it. She curled onto her side on the not-so-comfortable bench, and slept.

But the mosquitoes wouldn't let her lie. How long had she been out? She checked the position of the sun but realized that was useless since she hadn't checked it before she went to sleep. She went inside, put on her headnet and a long-sleeved shirt, and set to finishing her cleanup chores, which included dragging the offending bedding down to the river, where she swirled and scrubbed until it was vaguely clean. She mashed the water out of it on the porch with her bare feet, and hung the thing over the railing to dry.

She had known on waking what she would do after that. She could either sit here and wait in vain for him to come back, or she could do something positive that would enable her to take action on her own. Learn something. Learn something new every day. That had been her motto since she was a child. It distracted her from the shallow anger in which she normally waded. She would take Bailey up on her offer to call if necessary. Then she wouldn't have to wait around for Zach to come get her.

She flagged a little as she thought of what doing this would entail. She'd have to start the boat, and then navigate down the river. She'd only had the brief lesson when Bailey tried to teach Zach how to run the boat. But she'd watched the channel carefully on each successive trip down and back, and she thought that wouldn't be such a problem . . . if she could just start the motor. She'd have to radio Bailey and let her know she was coming, just in case.

She turned the radio on as she had been instructed, checked to make sure she was on the right frequency and talked through the mike, forgetting at first to depress the lever.

"Hello, Bailey?" she'd said, face reddening with embarrassment that she didn't know the lingo.

"Bailey, it's Alpha up at the Lodge. Are you there?" She waited long minutes for a response and got none. Well, she could be out-

side or any number of things. Don't be such a wimp. Just do it. She scribbled a quick note to Zach and left it stuck to the door.

She sat in the boat and stared at the motor, fingering the choke button, testing the pull of the cord tentatively. Now she stood as she had been taught, hip cocked at right angles to the unit, and went through the steps. She could hardly move the pull cord. Try again. She got it out a little ways. Progress. On her fifth try the cord suddenly unwound easily and the motor growled a little. She was delighted. She rested a minute, then tried again. Success! She was elated.

She kneeled on the bench seat with the tiller in hand and shifted the gear lever to the forward, giving it a little gas as she did. The boat moved off slowly, then yanked sideways as it hit the end of the rope she'd forgotten to untie. She almost fell out, and sat there with her heart pounding madly feeling like a complete moron. If Bailey had seen that? She didn't want to think about it.

She got the motor started again, then untied the boat. Now the current grabbed the bow and she gave it more gas, shooting into the main channel like a cowboy. She slowed down as much as she dared, still going faster than the current so she'd have some control. Bailey had taught them that.

She smiled. The weather was perfect, if a little windy. The air smelled wonderful, felt good on her face. She kneeled again on the seat, the better to see the water ahead of her, and navigated her way slowly down the river, one bend, two bends. She counted that way because that was how she'd memorized the route. Ten bends would get her there. By bend five she felt pretty confident. There wasn't that much to it. Zach had made it all out to be so complicated and difficult. Like she couldn't possibly master this for lack of intelligence. They wanted to keep it all a secret, so women would feel like they couldn't do anything without them. Hah!

As she rounded bend six, she froze at the sight before her. A giant cow moose stood belly deep in water, almost in the middle of the channel, as if she was going to cross the river. Her spindly-legged calf stood in the shallow water off the gravel bar. The great ears flapped loosely as the cow shook her head. The calf blatted at its mother, who had now sighted Alpha in the boat. Growing up in Maine with a father and brother who hunted, she knew that if they felt threatened, cow moose with their young were not the amiable creatures people liked to think they were.

Alpha didn't know if she should turn around or try to slip past it, but even then she had drawn too close to turn. She eased the tiller over, thinking about Bailey's warning that you shouldn't get too close to the outside of a bend for fear the current would pin you to the bank and swamp the boat, which it appeared she was about to do. She pulled the tiller back to her but the boat was going so slow it didn't respond. The current had control of her. More gas. Her nervous hand throttled up and she yanked the tiller toward her.

Now she was on a direct course for the moose. She pulled the tiller again, succeeding in changing her course only a fraction, enough to glide her practically under the moose's massively bulbous snout. She held herself as still as possible, hoping it would think of her as a big log floating by. No threat whatsoever. Pardon me. She was so close she could count the times it blinked, see clearly the corners of its eyes oozing liquid down its face, the nostrils and most of the snout itself, which were covered with bugs. The moose snorted as Alpha was directly abreast of it, engulfing her in a cloud of the insects and splattering her shirtfront with a generous mist of moose mucus.

And then she was past it, grimy but safe. Once sure she was on the right course again, she turned back to see the creature staring at her still, the loopy calf, too. She thought for a second of telling her father about it, but the desire lasted only a second. He would not believe her, mostly likely, or deride her for having been so stupid as to get close to it. No matter. She would tell Bailey about it.

She wouldn't make fun of her, and would probably have a good story to tell in return.

Anticipating that, she was disheartened to see the stretch of bank in front of the cabin deserted. But she wasn't about to have come this far without at least stopping. Maybe if she waited awhile, Bailey would return. She had smeared up a couple of peanut butter and jelly sandwiches for her lunch, and she could eat those while she waited.

After an hour of nothing but engine noise, the silence was painful. On the bank, the grass was ankle high and shockingly green. It seemed to have appeared overnight. She threw her pack down and sat beside it in the grass. The weather was exceptional. Clear, cool and bright. Just the way she liked it. So bright, in fact, she had to keep her shades on to avoid being blinded by the surface glare from the river.

When she saw them, she thought at first they were shadows cast on the river bottom until the red filtered in and she realized all those shadows were fish. Her mouth fell open. She had never actually seen a live fish in the water. And so many of them all at once. They moved up a few feet at a time, then hung in the current before moving again, all of them moving and stopping at different intervals, but seeming to move in a group. The irregular mottling of colors on their bodies was bizarre, like something out of one of the comic books her kids were always sneaking into school in their lunch sacks. But she couldn't get over the mass of them. She tried to count them but found it too confusing as they moved and drifted from side to side in the current.

How long had she been sitting there? She began to wonder if perhaps Bailey had parked the plane somewhere else. Maybe she was here but sleeping inside or something. Alpha thought she should check before giving up her day-out-with-the-girls idea.

Maybe she would just look out back though surely the sound of the boat approaching would have brought her around had she

been there. Alpha wandered slowly around back, calling out periodically. She peered at the ridge, trying to look into the dark
fringe of spruce and larch that protected its base, but could not see
in amongst the boles. From here, she could see the trash pit.
Shredded cardboard and broken glass was strewn all around it as if
Bailey had just thrown the garbage in the direction of the pit
without caring whether or not it got in.

She returned to the cabin, knocked lightly on the door, then
opened it enough to stick her head inside. *"Hello?"* she thrust her
voice into the cool interior, unwilling to step in. *"Bailey?"*

She was struck by the lifeless quality of the air. She looked
around. Everything appeared orderly in the kitchen area: dishes
washed and spread on a towel, two chairs tucked neatly up to the
small round table. She checked the dishes on the towel to see if
there was any moisture on them, but they were dry as was the
towel beneath them.

On the wall next to the sink the glare of a tiny mirror caught
her eye; a raggedy cloth hung below it on a nail. She fingered it to
check for dampness and caught sight of herself in the oval surface.
The face there surprised her. Her skin was dark. Hair she had always thought of as dirty blond seemed to glow brightly around
her face, which receded darkly from it. The more she looked at
her hair, the less she could see of her face until it disappeared altogether in darkness. The effect was eerie and she shivered before
turning away to continue her search.

She wandered into the tiny bedroom. A single-size mattress lay
atop three rough-cut slabs of wood. The homemade slats were
supported by tree stumps that had been carefully cut and peeled
for the purpose. On top of the mattress a down-filled sleeping bag
had been zipped and smoothed free of rumples, with a pillow
propped up behind it. Another stump sat close by the head of the
bed as a nightstand. A drooling mess of a candle that had been
jammed into a wine bottle looked as if it had been used for this
purpose for years. Any glass still visible under the hardened run-

nels of wax had blackened; little clots of wax surrounded its base
on the stump. There was a flashlight and a book on the table, and
Alpha could not resist picking it up to see what it was. There was
no window in this room, and she had to step aside and cant the
book toward the doorway to catch some light.

Just outside, a susurrus of wings followed by a piercing screech.
The book slipped from her startled hands and fell on its opened
pages. One of them had creased over and she tried to smooth it
out. That's what she got for snooping, she thought, because at this
point that's exactly what she was doing. She was ashamed of herself and smacked the book shut before she replaced it on the
stump. Was it to the left of where she'd found it? She reached out
one finger to nudge it over a little.

Back out in the main part of the cabin, she was about to give
up and leave when she saw the pile of clothes on the floor. She
picked up the shirt and that was when she saw the blood. She
gasped, dropped the shirt on the floor and backed away. Something *had* happened. She knew it. Did Bailey have a terrible accident with the chainsaw? Had she then flown herself to the Village,
arm bloodied in some kind of makeshift bandage? If she'd gotten
down there then she was safe. But what if she hadn't made it?
What if she'd fainted from loss of blood, crashed the plane between here and there? That would make Alpha the only one to
know about it and her only chance of rescue.

*Twelve is the band they use to talk to each other. There's a radio in
Kash's store that Raina uses . . .*

She rifled the shelves built along one wall and found nothing
like the radio set at the Lodge amid jars of old screws and nails,
bits of electrical wire, duct tape, pads of paper, repair manuals, and
some tools. Then she spied something on the wooden box by the
couch. It didn't look anything like the Lodge radio. It was small,
like the walkie-talkie sets her kids played with at school. When she
picked it up there was a lever on the side, and some buttons on the
front. She clicked the lever bar, but nothing happened. "Well,

duh," she said out loud in exasperation. There was a cord attached to it, but there wasn't any power. There had to be a generator somewhere. She had watched Bailey closely when they started the generator at the Lodge. Bailey had grumbled that she didn't know how to start a diesel but *learn something new,* she'd said, and simply read the instructions.

Alpha could read instructions. *Come on, learn something new,* she told herself, and stepped outside.

———

"Hello? Is anybody there? Hello? Over. This is Alpha calling for Raina in Ingalik Village. Does anybody read me? Over."

Alpha set the radio down as if it might explode, then stepped away from it. She had tried three times to rouse someone with no success. It was only one o'clock. Maybe Raina went home for lunch or something. She'd try again later. It was a good thing she'd relented to anger and left Zach a note. Not that he would be back before she was.

She decided to make a fire, take the chill off the place. She could darn sure do that without directions. She had gotten used to the resinous hiss of the spruce that they burned here. She liked the smell of the smoke better than the hardwood they burned at home; it had a clarified tang to it that smelled good even afterward when it was gathered in the threads of her clothing and the mat of her hair.

Nothing to do but wait. Alpha sighed and sat at the end of the couch closest to the radio. Her nose crinkled at the smell that rose around her. Did Bailey have a dog? Surely they would have seen it at some point. Her parents' couch had smelled to high heaven for years until her father's old hunting dog had died. Then they'd gotten a new couch. It was one of the few new things her father had ever allowed her mother to buy.

11

Kash stood on the abandoned beach, staring blindly at the spit of land across the slough where moose liked to browse. Sun spewed gold-speckled light at his back, casting his silhouette long across the sand and onto the water. The shadowed apex of the tripod connected perfectly with the shadow of his hand. The impression looked like a pictograph in which the three bolts of life shot forth from the shaman's fingertips.

Bailey had proved herself admirably. Of course she had medical training, but somehow "nurse" just didn't include doing what she'd done for Curan. She had talked him so smoothly through the whole thing in spite of the boy's hysteria.

And Raina. He'd expected a wailing mess but she had remained fairly calm, listening to Bailey's monologue as she talked her way through the procedure. The boy probably had an unstable fracture of the lower leg. She would traction it into position to help ease the pain, then splint it so they could fly him to the hospital in Bethel. She had instructed Kash to remove the backseat from the Cessna so they could lie Curan down in it. The boy had begun to calm down listening to her steady voice. By the time Kash had the plane set up, she had the boy ready to go and somebody had brought down an old door to carry him on. Kash assumed he'd be the one to go with them, but Raina had stopped him. She was his mother. He needed her. And she'd climbed into the plane and sat on the floor beside him, gathering the kid's shaking hands into hers.

Kash was still waiting on the beach when Bailey returned two hours later. The boy would be fine. It was a bad fracture as she'd suspected, but they didn't foresee any complications. He would have to stay there overnight and Raina remained with him. Raina had told her to clean up at her house, which she planned to do, and she had left him with that businesslike report stinging in the air around him.

He knew it wasn't just the fatigue in her dark-rimmed eyes that had made her so curt with him. He'd had plenty of time to think about it. He'd acted like an oaf that morning. Or at least he'd acted as he was accustomed to doing. He'd neglected to factor in the culture gap, the age gap—hell, he hadn't really thought of anything but feeling better and getting to work. In his world, that was the way it went. You had your "time" and then you went to work. And when there was "time" again, you did it. He would have to explain this to her. *Wanted* very much to explain it, because he wasn't about to fuck this up now. The possibility of an alliance between them was too close.

He walked up the road to Raina's house, his boots sucking mud at every step. He relished the pull of it, liked to feel his quads flexing against it. Errant, high-pitched squeals floated on dreamy air around his head; the children never seemed to stop in the summer. Nobody did. It reminded him of the James Fenimore Cooper novels he read in the American Literature class he'd had to take in college. The action took place without any sense of time cast over what used to be a vast prairie. The professor of the class had been uncomfortable teaching to him. Perhaps he'd expected an open insurrection of some kind. Kash had attended the lectures, written the papers, and said nothing. What was there to say that would make a penny's worth of difference? He had held his counsel and saved his rhetoric for a time when it could matter.

He clomped up the steps to Raina's door and thumped his

knuckles gently on the wood frame. Maybe she was still in the shower and wouldn't hear him. He rubbed the flats of his hands on his pants; he was sweaty and filthy, black sand still clotted on his knees. His hair straggled down over his forehead and he was about to smooth it back when the door drafted inward.

———

Bailey posted herself at the picture window in Raina's living room, absently toweling her hair. She watched Kash staring across the slough, thought that he didn't look like much if she just squinted her eyes and saw him there, dirty and rumpled; didn't look capable of cruel intentions. But there was something about the stillness of him that hypnotized her until she actually was squinting, the act of it tiring her retinas to the point where the surrounding tableau burned away, leaving the image purified of the world around it.

She had watched him turn and walk slowly toward her, invisible to him behind the glare of glass, mesmerized yet by the stillness of him even though his body was in motion. Fingers teething through the snarl of wet hair that had left darkening stains on her shoulders ceased their activity; probably she stopped breathing as he got close enough to decide whether or not he would stop, though he had come on so purposefully it never looked to her as if he had decided at all. Her breath had stayed trapped in her until the soft thud of his hand on wood released it, allowing her to respond to the knock.

The door swung in to her, wafting her shampooed smell away and bringing with it something so rare to her, so pungent, it coated the membranes in her nose and would not be breathed away. She stepped back into what she hoped was shadow, damned if she'd let him see how his scent made her skin ripple and hive. He propped one arm on the doorframe and smiled. In the tiny wrinkles at the corners of his eyes she saw something she had not noticed before. It was as if he had not stopped looking out at whatever he had seen from the beach.

"We finished checking those pontoons. Watertight. Not even a dimple."

"How nice."

"You know I'm kind of old," rueful smile, "and I'm not used to . . . haven't done anything like this in a long time." He indicated the space between them with a flick of his hand. "I was probably a little . . . clumsy this morning. I hope it didn't seem as if I didn't appreciate . . ." He hesitated. "I hope it wasn't too 'unromantic' of me." He dropped his voice and leaned closer. "I would really like to make it up to you. I'm one old dog that can learn new tricks with a little guidance." Sheepish smile.

She looked at him, astonished that he could go about the greasy enterprise of sucking up to her with not even a hint of discomfort. But what was she thinking? Of course he wouldn't experience a moment's moral dismay. He was a predator, and nothing stood to lessen that ancient urge in a man. But she didn't plan to get flattened by it. Not again. Not ever.

"Hey," she said softly, gathering his eyes back to hers from where they'd wandered uncomfortably away, because she wanted to make certain he was looking her square on. "Spare me the old-dog bullshit. In fact, spare me all of it." She closed the door against him and turned away, her face crackling hot, and finished combing out the mess of her wet hair before braiding it so tightly it felt as if she were smiling. She stuffed her gear into her pack and swung it on, careful to ease it over the sore shoulder, and stepped onto the porch.

He stood on the bottom step, his back to the door. She moved past him, careful not to let one molecule touch him as she went.

"Hey," he said. "Where are you going?" She kept walking. "What about your boat?"

"Shove it up your ass," she said over her shoulder. "There's plenty of room."

"What the hell's that for?"

She would have liked to turn on him and unload the stick of dynamite that sizzled in her throat, but it was pointless. Instead she moved on, savoring the sweet, forward momentum she had gained.

Alpha stretched out on the couch, hoping to shut up the fearful noise in her head. She had sat up straight for the longest time; if Bailey returned, she had not wanted to be caught in her personal quarters, much less sprawled on her couch. Now she thought it wouldn't hurt to just lie there a little while, see if she could doze off for a few minutes. She shimmied uncomfortably on the stiff, smelly cushions for a while before deciding it was the little bit of light shafting through the small windows that was bugging her. She rolled onto her side, away from the light, and tried breathing deeply.

She ricocheted between being angry at Zach, frightened at being alone, worried about Bailey, then outraged that she'd been put in this position in the first place. How could Zach just up and leave her without any visible signs of remorse? She had tried to justify his behavior by rationalizing that he had their best interests at heart, that he had become so obsessed about getting the gold because ultimately his eyes were on their future. But there was something in the way he had been so quick to abandon her yesterday, and again this morning, that alarmed her. It was as if she had tried to step out of a place he expected her to stay in. Trouble was, she had counted on him expecting otherwise.

That freakin' Zach's a lunatic. She had discounted her father's opinion of Zach because she was sure it was based in his distrust of anyone who was different, anyone who could possibly want Alpha to be *with* him, not beneath him. The thought crossed her mind for the hundredth time in the last couple of hours that her father's assessment of Zach was pure mirror recognition. Takes one to know one, isn't that what the kids used to say in school when taunted? If she shoved that thought away, then whatever horrible thing had become of Bailey popped up to take its place. She didn't know which was worse.

Her body grew more rigid by the second. Sleep was out of the question. She wandered around the cabin in search of something to occupy her mind. If she was home, she could have listened to the radio, or watched the tiny black and white TV she kept under her bed for just such occasions. She could walk in the woods, woods that weren't full of bears, mosquitoes, vast untracked acres that would swallow her whole if a bear didn't get her first.

She could practice splitting wood, but if she hurt herself, who knew when anyone might show up? The sting of those thoughts again. She checked the woodstove. It could use some stoking, which task took her all of ten minutes. She wandered into Bailey's room where she remembered the book beside the bed. Maybe it was a good one, something that would engross her. Maybe it was a romance; a tiny giggle bubbled from her lips. Good Lord, what a hoot that would be.

She snatched the book from the table as if it might be booby-trapped and turned back to the main room where what little light you could find in the cabin gave up all its glorious wattage. In turning, her foot caught something at the edge of the bed which cartwheeled into the middle of the room, spilling its contents. She clamped a hand across her mouth and froze, her shoulders hunched to her ears as if somebody might step from the shadows and scold her. She dropped her hand. *Tighten up.*

She scraped up the little bits of paper that had fallen out of the box. No, not paper, she saw, but photographs. She scrunched them together and put them back in the box. But how had they been placed in it to begin with? She couldn't possibly know, but if she didn't put them back the way they were. . .

A young girl frowned daringly out at her, dressed up in a little cowboy outfit, hat cinched firmly over dirty brown hair, and a pair of six-shooters strapped onto her child's hips. Her figure took up the entire frame as she stood spread-legged and square to the camera. Her hands clutched the pistol grips like she was ready to draw, but the expression on her face was what really caught Alpha's eye. The child should have been imitating the look of tough, cowboy endurance, but this kid didn't look to be faking it. The downward curl of the corners of her mouth and the deep furrows on her brow looked natural. Alpha thought that if the guns had been real, the child would have plugged whoever took the picture. That was one unhappy little girl. She sighed a maternal sort of noise and before she knew it she had piled the photos willy-nilly in the box and carried it into the light. At the little round table, she sat and picked through the images.

Two girls sat double bareback on a horse. Alpha was pretty sure the one up front was the same as the kid with the pistols; she sat rigidly aboard, holding the reins in tight fists, presenting only a stony profile. The second rider was bigger, probably a little older, and sat half-cocked to the side as if she was about to get off. One arm encircled the kid in front, while the other reached for the picture taker. A look of pure delight animated the face surrounded by a halo of bright hair.

She squared that one up with the cowgirl. The look on the cowgirl's face unsettled her, but the other picture drew her in. She looked at it closely. There was something about the other child. That bright hair, the smile. She smiled back at the tiny face. It was irresistible.

As she looked through more photographs, she sorted them into piles. Little kids, bigger kids, teenagers, family shots. She had figured out pretty quickly that Bailey was the cowgirl. Fit her to a tee.

She picked up a picture of two young women, one of whom was Bailey. The other was the grown-up version of the delightful child Alpha kept smiling at. She must be Bailey's sister. Alpha turned it over. Nothing written on the back, not even a date. All of them were blank. But when she remembered, it was as if invisible ink came clear on the white surface before her. That name, town of Medford. She had read all about it in the newspaper, what, six years ago? Seven, maybe? She was in high school then, had had a report due on local government. Sifting through the newspaper for results of the town council meeting, she had been distracted by the cover story in the local section. It was the farm fire in Medford. Somebody had been caught in the burning building and died. Obviously not Bailey, but who was the other person? There was an investigation to rule out foul play. Was it Bailey they suspected? Alpha gnawed absently at a fingernail as she stared at the blank surface.

She picked up another picture and looked hard at Bailey in it. In all the snaps she appeared as stony as Alpha had seen her in real life. Maybe once or twice the picture taker had cajoled her into something resembling a smile that was about as inviting as a guillotine.

Yes, she remembered the whispered consultations the next morning in study hall. The article had mentioned that the sister was retarded. They had painted the most gruesome portrait of Bailey as the murderer of her retarded sister. The girls panto-mimed a poor, drooling, mess of a human chained to a bedpost as the evil sister poured gasoline in a ring around her, then struck a match. The reporter had noted that Bailey had been the sister's guardian for years since their parents were both dead. Guardian. As in angel, Alpha thought, and shivered. *She just couldn't take it any-more*, the girls had said as they conjured the secret story. *A young woman in the prime of her life, tethered to a future with this pitiful retard, no men willing to come her way. She cashed in the only way she knew how. Violently. Crime of passion.* They had fallen silent on that note, looked slowly, searchingly at each other, their fable already be-come truth in their constricted minds.

While now she recalled the fallout, she couldn't remember the follow-up, the conclusion to the investigation. Surely if she had been found guilty she wouldn't be here now, Alpha thought. She must have been cleared and come here to get as far from her grief as possible. Isn't that what people usually did? Tried to outrun the things that hurt them? Hadn't Alpha done the very same thing by moving to Massachusetts?

Now it was clear why Bailey had been so cagey about where she was from. She must have thought Alpha knew. The image of her white face coming out of the dark of the kitchen that day drifted into Alpha's thoughts and she couldn't help wondering what it masked, or what grim scenes were branded on those eyes, just beyond the reach of her own. Goosebumps erupted on her arms. What if she had done it? People got away with stuff like that all the time. Alpha had been about to spend the day with this woman. Alone. The whole thing really gave her the willies.

She folded her hands together on the table. The crystal face of her watch caught the light from the small window and cast a darting patch of brightness on the dark logs. It startled her. The time, she thought. Holy mackerel it was five o'clock. She needed to radio the Village again. She tried to pile the pictures carefully into the box, but the dog-eared corners of them kept snagging. Finally she got them all in, mashed the cover down and tucked the box under the sleeping platform. She stepped back from the bed and took a look to see if she had pushed it under far enough, a useless exercise since she hadn't seen it there in the first place.

The beach was deserted and Match's boat was nowhere in sight. Good. Much as she hated the inevitability of talking to Raina, Bailey figured she'd better call the hospital in Bethel to see how the boy was doing. She'd stop at the store to make the call and grab something to eat.

A cliff swallow swooped past her head, leaving the whoosh of its passage to echo in her ear. She hugged the side of the road so her boots didn't get so heavy with mud. She rolled her head, tried to stretch her neck as she passed tiny houses, the Corporation offices, and more tiny houses in-between without raising so much as a whine from the chained gargoyles.

A small knot of children was still gathered outside the Store by the time she arrived. One or two glanced at her surreptitiously but their faces remained impassive as they scattered.

Lenora Richardson sat at Raina's big desk.

"Hello, Lenora," she said.

When Lenora scanned her up and down over the tops of her bifocals Bailey felt as if she'd been stripped.

"Hello," Lenora said.

Bailey put down her pack.

"Mind if I use the phone?"

Lenora shrugged. "Fine with me. I don't guess Kash would mind."

Bailey moved to the desk. "Would you get me that phone book in Raina's desk drawer? I want to call and see how Curan's doing."

Lenora dutifully pulled out the stapled sheets that contained the entire populace of the Yukon watershed. It could hardly be considered a phone book, but that's what everyone called it. Bailey thumbed the pages. "You still baking those wonderful sweet twists?" she asked, not looking up.

"Oh my, yes," Lenora said, and Bailey could hear the grin in her words. "Had a coupla batches out this morning until all this crazy mess happened and Kash called me to mind the store. I brought some down with me for just in case."

Bailey wished she would stop saying Kash's name. "I don't suppose you'd let me buy a couple?"

"You can *have* as many as you want. I wouldn't take money for them. Not after what you did for the boy."

"Well, that was my business, or used to be. I didn't do much but make him more comfortable for the ride. The doctors will fix him up right. But those sweet twists, they're your business. And I'd be happy to pay for them." Lenora frowned at her. Bailey had as much as insulted her, and she was quick to backpedal. "Never mind. Just let me put one in my mouth right now so I can think straight."

Lenora smiled again, and pulled a large paper bag from under the desk. When she opened it the smell of the freshly baked bread wafted into Bailey's face; she closed her eyes, the better to savor the smell. When she opened her eyes, Lenora had one of the delicious twists shoved practically under her nose. Bailey received it with both hands and took a bite. "They're better than I remember."

Lenora blushed proudly and slid the phone across the desk. "Now you can think straight enough to dial the phone."

Bailey smudged her finger down the page and found the hospital number again.

"Here," Lenora said, taking the pages from her. "I'll dial it."

She handed the receiver to Bailey as her pudgy finger found the numbers.

She finally got through to the ward room where they'd put the boy, and got Raina on the phone.

"Just called to check on Curan," Bailey said. "What's the prognosis?"

"Whatever the hell that means," Raina said. "Anyways, the doc says the X ray showed it was a hell of a break, my words, not his. If we hadn't seen to it so fast, there could have been some serious damage." She paused. "He said you did a great job."

"How long in the cast?"

Raina rattled off what she knew. Said the boy was resting fine, eating ice cream like there was no tomorrow and having a great time. "Listen, there's something I wanted to say before you flew back to the Village."

"Save it, Raina. You said what you felt and you meant what you said. That's all there is to it." Bailey plunked the receiver back in its cradle.

She was dimly aware of the radio crackling with a static-laden transmission. Lenora fiddled with the squelch. The radio spat in earnest as Lenora swore softly and turned the dials this way and that.

"Aw heck," she said. "I don't know how to work this darned thing." She put her hands on her hips and stared at it.

Automatically Bailey leaned over the desk and adjusted the set, and was halfway across the store when she heard it. "*. . . anyone in Ingalik Village. This is Bailey's camp.*" She was hardly conscious of having moved back across the room. She loomed over the desk.

Lenora held the mike out to Bailey.

"Go ahead, Camp," she said.

There was no answer.

Bailey pinched the lever in so hard she thought the handset would shatter in her hand. "Village to River Camp, we are responding to your hail. Do you read? Over." She released the lever, letting it spring away with a satisfying *thwack*. She waited for what seemed like an eternity, was about to hail again when she heard what she dreaded, Alpha's voice, barely audible but clear, repeating her previous message.

"Alpha, this is Bailey. What's wrong?"

"You're there?" the girl said.

"Yes, I'm here. What the hell are you doing there?"

"I came down to visit. I waited for you. Thought you were hurt."

"I'm fine. Where's Zach?"

"Upriver." There was a long pause.

"Alpha, you're alone?" Bailey asked.

"Yes."

She saw Lenora shaking her head, whispering *"Oh Jesus."*

"Just sit tight. I'll be there in twenty minutes. Village out."

She couldn't believe that twerp left her alone again. She spun the mike across the desk. Lenora stared at her.

"You want me to tell Kash anything?" she asked.

Bailey tried to will some life back to skin she knew had gone colorless and cold. *Tell him to fuck himself* is what she wanted to say, but didn't see any good in rubbing Lenora the wrong way, so said aloud instead, "I already told him all he needs to know."

She kept her eyes on the Cessna as she walked to the beach, thinking only of flying now, of going home. She unlocked the door and flung her pack behind the seat before doing a careful external preflight check, something she had been unable to do in the rush to get Curan to Bethel.

"How's our little white savior this evening?"

Her hands froze in the guts of the engine. She didn't know who she would have dreaded seeing more than Kash until just now. And where the hell had he come from, anyway? She hadn't seen his boat on the beach.

"The whole watershed's just buzzing over your deed of the day. The way people are carrying on, I should ask for your autograph."

Bailey closed up the engine and stepped down to get a handful of sand with which to cut the grease on her hands. Match dodged back.

She laughed. "If I was going to get into it with you, buddy, a little handful of sand would not be my first choice." She rinsed the gluey grit in the water and turned back to the plane.

"So I hear you're fuckin' the chief."

A dangerous buzz in her head now. She stood on the pontoon, fingers curled into the handle pocket. Faintly, a voice in her head, *Hold tight. Squeeze with all your might.* Knuckles ground hard to metal, she tried to make herself open the door and get in, but the fuse had spluttered to its end. She exploded off the pontoon and was at him in one thrusting leap, hurling herself into his chest so hard his back met sand with a muted *whumpf.*

"I am none of your business. Sell booze to whoever you please and go on with your pathetic excuse for a life, but leave me alone. Why can't you do that?"

Match lay calmly where he'd fallen, staring at the sky. "I can't leave you alone," he said. "You're part of it whether you wanna be or not. Everywhere you go, you're part of it. If you didn't want that, you shouldn't a parked your white ass in our country. If you want to stay alive, you gotta take what's coming, no matter what. But if you really want to be left alone, the thing to ask for is death."

Tears stung her face like alcohol on raw flesh. She stumbled backward as he stood and gently brushed the sand from his pants, his arms swinging in impossibly slow arcs. Where was the predictable, leering humor, the rippling, boozy curve of the Match she knew?

He walked away from her, his back so straight, he appeared to tower over the landscape, obscuring with his shadow a judgment she now realized was completely wrong. He was worse than the Devil. He had read her like a genius of souls.

12

Kash watched her walk down to the Store, watched until the door closed behind her, thinking her reaction was way out of proportion to his crime. In fact, whatever he'd done or not done that morning was far from crime status; he couldn't imagine what could have happened to freeze her to the level of rigidity he had encountered just now. Probably, he should go after her and push a confrontation, but in this state, it was bound to be messy and he just didn't have the will for it at the moment. He shook his head, figured it was best to leave it be for now until something came clear.

He turned and walked the short distance up the hill to the Corporation offices to find out if there was any word from Fish and Game about opening the season tomorrow. Several fishermen were gathered there already, waiting for news, arms clamped across chests in bitter resignation. He gripped the receiver so tightly his hand began to cramp as he finished dialing the hotline number. He listened to the recording and hung up, composing himself while he rubbed the twisting ache from his fingers, then put on a pot of coffee and called the men inside where their anger had less room to swell.

Forty-five minutes later he had them damped to a smolder and muttering amongst themselves as they filed out. There was still a chance the season would open in the morning, he told them, and he'd be there at 7:00 A.M. to get the first word. They were appeased for the next twelve hours, anyway.

Halfway through the meeting he'd heard the Cessna roar out to the Yukon for take-off. Sounded like she was pushing it. Not like her. He locked up and went down to the store. Lenora might have some information. The woman had her ways.

"Hey," he said. "What's going on."

"Whew!" she said, exhaling loudly through the flared portals of her nose.

"What?"

"You missed the knock-down-drag-out of the century, mister."

"Christ, what now?"

"Well, Bailey was here talking to Raina at the hospital. Conversation was kinda tense if you ask me. When she hung up the radio started spittin' and that girl calls from Bailey's camp. . ."

"You mean the Lodge?"

"No. I mean the camp. Said she came down there for something and was waiting for Bailey to get back. So Bailey tells the girl to sit tight and she'll be there in a few."

"What about the knockdown?"

"I'm gettin' to that, Kash," she said.

"Sorry," he said, trying to swallow his impatience.

"Bailey goes out to her plane, and I'm watching all this because you know how I love to watch them things take off on the water."

"Yes. Go on."

"So she's checking her plane when guess who shows up."

"Just tell me."

"Match," she said, a little disappointed that he wouldn't play.

"Terrific," he said, not sure he wanted to hear what was next given the mood she was in and the already thorny disposition between them.

"It looks like he's talkin' to her and she's ignoring him until all of a sudden she comes off that airplane and tackles the guy. No kiddin'. Tackles him like she's a football player, and down he goes flat on his ass in the sand."

"Christ," he groaned.

"And here I gotta give him some credit because he doesn't come back at her. It just looks like they exchange words and then he gets up and walks away. When he passed here I seen his face pretty clear and I can tell you it was some weird lookin'."

"Weird looking?"

"Like . . . I don't know what's the word for it, but it looked like he had an idea, a real serious idea."

Kash couldn't picture it, but he knew it wasn't good.

"But here's the bad part," she continued. Could it get worse? "He goes on up to Ferrin's, then comes back down to the beach, hops in Ferrin's boat and heads upriver."

"Good," Kash says. "Maybe he'll go home and stay there a while." ·

"No, honey. He went up the *Ingalik*. Not the Yukon."

"You sure?" Lenora looked at him like she'd been slapped.

"Okay, Okay," he said. "I'd better get up there. Lock up for me, would you?"

"No problem."

He jumped on the ATV and ground hard up the hill to Ferrin's. His dog team put up a tremendous roar as he cut the motor and leaped up the steps, banging the pulpy edge of his fist against the peeled-paint surface of the door until it swung inward and there was nothing left for his fist to connect to. Ferrin shifted deftly back for a man his size when he saw Kash there with his fist raised, and when he dropped his face from Kash's stare and turned side-ways, Kash knew he was as guilty of whatever trouble Match was up to as Match himself.

"What's the plan?" Kash asked.

Ferrin stared at him, wolfish wariness turning his eyes to slits. Were it not for the children crouched in front of the television in full sight of them, Kash would have pumped him one right then, felt his fist balled and angry at his side. Vida came out of the kitchen, her eyes questioning, frightened.

"Vida." Kash said her name by way of greeting.

"Kash," she said, smiling hesitantly. "Everything all right?"

"No. But Ferrin was just about to help me make it all right, weren't you?" he said to Ferrin.

Ferrin shifted uneasily from foot to foot. "Sure," he said, finally, looking fleetingly over his shoulder at Vida before closing the door.

In the yard Kash said, "I've been fighting for you. Everything in me has prayed that you wouldn't fall to this shit." Ferrin grunted, braced his hands on his hips. "For starters, opening those boxes was a federal offense. Now you've let that idiot go up to her camp to do God knows what. Set us back a hundred years."

"Look. You want us to do it your way, but your way don't do shit," Ferrin said, voice low, quivering. "They're lookin' for gold up there, and they'll use the magnificent, twentieth-century contract you insisted would make a difference to wipe their asses. When did a fuckin' contract ever mean dick in all of our history? It still don't."

"There's no gold up there for them to get in the first place, and in the second place how are you so sure that's what they're after?"

Ferrin started to reply but abruptly clapped his lips shut. He'd been about to fall into Kash's trap, would have admitted to opening the boxes and seeing the gear. "This is not worth going to jail over. It is not worth risking everything we've fought for."

"Nobody's going to jail for anything because nobody knows anything."

"I know it."

Ferrin's face burned. "Yeah, right. Go ahead and narc on your own kind while you're fluffing that white bitch. Some leader you are."

It was all Kash needed. Ferrin hit the ground sitting. Kash saw the countermove on his face before the man's body could respond.

"Don't," Kash growled, his spread-wide hand inches from Ferrin's eyes. "You're a shame, damn you. You've shamed us all."

He drove the four-wheeler as hard as he could down the soupy road, cursed and bullied it, using all the force of his will to make it go on. He left it where he skidded to a stop and pocketed the keys. He skipped the external preflight check, then perused the dash gauges so cursorily he could not have said seconds later what they read, knew only what years of practice told him were green lights and let it go at that.

The engine chuffed as always, then choked and fell silent. He reprimed and tried again. Nothing but a gutsy wheeze this time. Again. Nothing at all. He'd had the thought before he was conscious of thinking it: somebody had tampered with the engine. He was lucky it had quit so soon. Otherwise, it might have taken just enough time for him to taxi out and take off before killing the engine, and possibly himself.

The realization boiled to a level of rage that he did not think himself capable of; he could not think through the chaos it wrought on his brain. He fought for control. He needed to get upriver fast and the only other recourse was by boat. His boat was useless on a river the size of the Ingalik. The propeller on his motor needed deep water, like the Yukon. He would have to borrow a jonboat with a jet unit.

And there it sat, not thirty yards away, water lapping lazily at the stern. She would need the boat up there anyway. She would have to fly him back down. Somewhere in there, he was bound to find out what the hell was going on.

He spun out of the slough full-tilt and headed up the Ingalik, his rage bled out and nothing in his focus now but the stretch of river before him. He monitored every wind-driven wrinkle from which he wove a telltale composite of wind and current and motion. All he could do now was read the water right, move on, and hope.

———

Kash had spent his fourteenth summer alone on the upper reaches of the Ingalik River. He already knew the lower river well after hunting and fishing it with his father. He wanted to know what was up there. A few staples—sugar, tea, flour, ammo, a rifle and a shotgun—were all he'd brought. Later, when he'd read all the books and tracts that trumpeted the bounty of nature he'd been perplexed. What nature had those writers lived in? Where was the bounty after centuries of starvation? Where was it still? Nature wasn't too forthcoming in the boreal north. It was a fact those writers had failed to grasp.

He'd survived at first on rodents, moss, lichens, and pan bread, which he'd learned to make on the trail with his father. He'd been able to shoot a few birds when they came, and hares. The spring migration of caribou had passed nowhere near him as far as he could tell, though he scouted many miles for sign of them. By midsummer, a few salmon reached the upper watershed, and he'd netted and dried as many as he could get. He was hungry all the time. At one point he'd gone for three days without food. He huddled in the little shelter he'd built by weaving willow for a frame and lashing a tarp over it. He'd been asleep for most of a day, waking every now and then to thoughts of his father, home, and the rich, bubbling caribou stew that his mother made.

He could not say later whether he was awake or dreaming, but he'd recalled vividly a time with his father—Kash but a boy—in late winter. They had snowshoed upriver a few days before to stake out a beaver drainage that his father knew the moose favored as a crossing when it was frozen hard. The family's meat supply was low because his father had shared their game all winter with an elderly couple whose children had gone, and who now had no means to get their own grub. Though the meat would be tough

this late in the season, one good-size bull would feed them all until the salmon came.

Kash relished the opportunity to go alone with his father to
hunt. He seemed to know everything from curve of land to sky.
They were on the return trip, swinging along single-file in the
hypnotic stride of the snowshoe, the old man moving tireless, efficient, in spite of the nearly two hundred pounds of meat humped
under tarp on the sled he dragged behind him. Leaning heavily
into the pulling collar as he did, he looked small and gnarled from
behind where Kash occasionally looked up to mark his presence—
the boy liked to stop and regard the scalloped trail their snowshoes
made in sharp-grained snow, sunken edges bluish in the low winter sun. The trail was beautiful, a temporary mark, the way his
father taught Kash to be in the bush.

They were within ten miles of the Village, almost well into the
braided channels when they came to Rigel's trapping cabin. Two
men stood in roiled snow in front of the cabin, hair lank and
pasted to the dampness of their skin here and there. The slim-
tined caribou racks on their heads were shaggy with loose velvet,
bare in some spots from repeated impact as they sparred. Kash
stared, astonished, to watch the fight. The half-men battled on,
unaware of their audience.

It was not the fact of their nakedness that amazed Kash (consid-
ering the ambient temperature that day hovered near zero), but
the whole of the apparition that caused him to gape until the cold
ache in his teeth reminded him to close his mouth. The men's
hides were unearthly tapestries of white and red, mottled in inde-
cision of whether to react to the exterior cold or the heat within.
Steam rose about them, sometimes shrouding their heads so
thickly the high-curling racks could scarcely be seen.

He could not tell how long he watched before the men ceased
their fighting at some undetectable signal. Neither seemed victori-
ous, nor to have lost. They stood in their shrouds of steam, heads
hung so low the tips of the antlers skived into the snow. He'd

turned to his father in amazement to ask if he knew the men, but his father was far down the trail, still pulling steadily. That's when he knew what he'd seen was unseeable.

Kash hurried to catch up. The images played so vividly in his thoughts he hardly felt the remaining ten miles pass. They had hung the butchered quarters of meat in the shed behind the house, stowed their sleds upright against a tree, facing them east to invite another day. He had stomped wordlessly into the warm house after his father where a blood-broth stew *gumped* unctuously on the woodstove.

His mother sat working a caribou hide to the pliant consistency that would allow her to sew it into moccasins and mitts. She didn't need to ask if their hunt had been successful. She could smell the blood and the heavy sourness of the animal's fat on their clothes when they came in.

He had been relieved to see Raina already curled in sleep on the bunk they shared at night, relieved because she always chattered madly when they came in, asking questions and giving details of her time when none were asked for until her father told her to be silent. She would cry bitterly in the corner of the room until she was done, then go about whatever chores she had to do in stony silence. He had felt sorry for her, knowing he would be unable to tell her about his vision.

That summer, he hadn't spent much time on the river itself because he'd brought very little fuel. Could not afford more, anyway. So he had grown to know well the land that bounded the river. Had scouted the tributaries and eskers and found the gold that no one suspected existed there. The small creeks were full of it. But only in their upper reaches, places that were impossible to access by boat, could only be reached by exhaustive hikes with very little gear.

When he'd come back in September, he'd told his father what

he'd found, knew before his father said it to him that he would tell no one else. It was not for the taking. It was the tribe's future. When the parcel of land that had become the Lodge was purchased by the doctors' group from Anchorage, he was beside himself. His father was gone by then, and already people looked to Kash for answers. He had fought the purchase, but the land claims had not been settled, and there was nothing he could do. He needn't have worried. The land mass itself was not indicative of the kind of structure and makeup that produced gold, and the terrain was too forbidding for anyone to make the effort when there was no good reason.

So he'd had no good reason to fear Zach and Alpha's perambulations up there. They didn't strike him as being ambitious enough, or knowledgeable enough to find anything. The day he'd left Bailey's camp and flown over he'd seen them back in the bush behind the Lodge. Still, he hadn't worried. They wouldn't find much if they did get to the stream. It was just too tricky. If he chose to make a stink about it, the situation might demand the information be shared and he was unwilling to do this. It was his ace in the hole, his secret. His and the land's.

All his life he had continued to explore the river and the land around it. He knew every gravel bar, every bend and land contour that caused each quirk in the river's hydrology. No one knew this river or this country as he did.

As he raced upriver now, he knew that disciplinary action would be in order. A dirty fight might be fun, he thought. He wouldn't mind flexing those muscles a little more. Whatever it took to keep the community together, keep it strong and alive, was reason enough to employ any strategy necessary as long as it did not smirch their future.

Expecting the confrontation at the Lodge, he was surprised on rounding a bend to see Match sitting desultorily in the boat, which was anchored in a shallow run, its motor tilted out of the water. He had obviously run aground and sucked gravel into the impeller, successfully choking the motor. Kash notched his outboard up to shallow drive and let the motor and current ferry him closer.

"Nice day for a ride," Kash said, noticing the red, runneling mess on Match's upper lip. He must have taken a dive into the console when the boat shrugged to a stop. "Need some help?"

"Fuck you."

"I'd say you're the one who's fucked, my friend. I'm just trying to help."

"Fuck your help." A gobbet of crimson mucus arched into the water between them.

"Where you going?" Kash asked.

Face gone foxy, Match smiled at Kash, dark-stained teeth making him look even more treacherous. "Nowhere at the moment," he said.

Kash pulled up his hip boots without bothering to buckle them to his belt before he chucked out the anchor and slithered into the knee-deep water. The current surprised him, even in this shoal water. He steadied himself against the gunwale, let his legs recognize what they were up against, before picking his way carefully to the stern of Match's boat.

"Hand me a screwdriver."

Match looked down at Kash. "Well look at you, just dishing out orders like your tit's not in a wringer. You're just dying to know if I messed with your little white girlfriend, or your little white customers. Treat them like royalty but you got no respect whatsoever for your own people, your own kind."

"With shit like you in our gene pool, it's a miracle we're still a race. But I'll tell you what. If you continue to fuck with me or anyone, I will lay you out for the sorry, bootlegging killer you are. You will be banished from the community."

Match's face contorted. "Bootlegger?" He laughed so hard he choked on the back-slag of phlegm in his throat. "Banish me?

Stupid old man," he gasped. "Who the hell do you think you are?"

"I'm a man who's given a life to this community. You've given what little you have to killing it. You think you've got everyone hoodwinked with your bullshit CORE talk while you're out here ripping them off. All you've managed to do is divide and discredit us, but once everyone knows where your politics really lie, you'll be lucky to get away with your hide."

"I guess all your college education failed to clue you in to the fact we're in a different century. People don't get banished anymore. You are not the law around here."

"That's right. The law is still in Juneau. And D.C. If you make it off the Yukon alive, they'll be waiting for you, more eager than I am to break your balls, and I'll be happy to see it. My kind? You're not my kind. You're worse than white."

He watched helplessly as Match's body arced from the boat, the shadow of him blocking the light steadily until the weight knocked Kash off his feet. Forty-five-degree water sucked the air from his lungs. His eyes bulged at the mess of swirling cloth before him, saw the anchor line sliding by and his hand curling around the furred rope as if it were detached. When his grip yanked them to a stop, the weight of Match clinging to him and the drag of the water in his boots nearly ripped his arm off. He squeezed his eyes shut against the cold as it froze the oxygen in his blood, his heart clenched in agony. He felt Match's grip slide from his waist to his hips, the circle of them tightening around his knees, sliding down his legs and taking Kash's hip boots with him as they slid off altogether. He got hold of the rope with both hands and dragged himself into the air, then pogoed off the bottom and slithered over the gunwale, lying aflop the cold metal like a fish in reverse gasping for life.

Kash heaved himself onto the bench seat, water creaming off him into the boat. He spotted Match floating down on his back, spitting and hissing like an outraged wolverine. Something about the image alarmed him, made him pay attention. *Like a wolverine.* They were the indisputable kings of hostility in the animal world, tenacious as hell, and capable of inflicting tremendous physical damage though they were no bigger than a medium size dog. A formidable combination of abilities right there, but they were also intelligent which made them, finally, downright dangerous. Even the big browns and grizzlies didn't compare to the wolverine in these regards. Had anyone asked which he'd rather face, he would choose the bear because they, at least, might back down.

Match had floated into shallow water, gained his legs and begun to slog to shore. Kash thought of pulling the anchor on the other boat so it would float down to him, but didn't. Instead he searched the dry well in Bailey's boat, hoping to find some dry clothes. Nothing. He swore at the thought of the careful stash of dry clothing in his own boat, and tried to wring out his sodden shirts. Hell of it was those hip boots Match had so kindly taken with him had been practically new.

Kash hauled anchor and continued upriver.

⌐────────

On rounding the final bend below her camp, he ducked reflexively from the figure poised on the bank in classic rifleman's posture. He throttled down completely, his head still low. The wake caught up to the boat and slopped over the transom. That would be the perfect ending to the day. Show up to save the distressed damsels looking like a drowned rat and get his ass shot. He shut down the motor and shouted to identify himself. When he peeked up, he could see she'd lowered the rifle, had it resting on one hip like a gunslinger in a Western.

He cranked the motor and eased upriver, hung the boat in the current opposite the cabin. She kept her eyes on him but had not raised the rifle again.

"Thanks for the boat. Been raining downriver?" she called to him.

"Took a little swim with one of the locals a ways back. Little chilly yet." Tried his best to jolly up in spite of his foul mood.

"S'pose I'll have to fly you back now?"

"Or later," he said.

"Now," she said, and started toward the cabin.

"What about the girl? She alright?"

"I made sure she got back to the Lodge safely. That seems to be my job around here anyway. Take care of the customers, bang the chief's drum every now and then . . ." She stood at the door, the rifle held like a slash across her chest.

Try again. "A hot cup of coffee would sure take the chill off these bones."

"There's a fine establishment about sixty miles thataway," she said, pointing downriver. "If you'll tie my boat off, I'll take you down."

Her eyes strayed over him a moment longer before she disappeared into the cabin leaving only the blank windows in reply.

13

As he'd hiked back to the Lodge the day before, Zach had made a plan. He would make a spike camp up at the stream to save them the time of having to hike back and forth. Now all he'd have to do was convince Alpha. By the time he'd reached the Lodge, he was exhausted and prepared for a major rasher of shit because he hadn't come back at lunch as promised, plus he was going to have to take that rasher of shit and convince her to go along with his plan.

But he was not prepared for what he'd found instead of his angry girlfriend. When he saw what was left of the sleeping bag, not to mention the friendly piles of crap left as calling cards, he'd figured it out pretty quickly. He'd actually laughed at the shit piles, which were flecked with bits of white fluff and the red remnants of sleeping bag. Those guys must be big-time hungry, he'd thought.

And then the territorial rage had kicked in; he had felt it flush up his spine and practically stand his scalp away from his skull. His shelter could have been destroyed, his food supply jeopardized. He realized later with a shudder that he had been so focused on his material goods, he hadn't even considered Alpha. Of course he'd found her note on the door and everything was all right. She hadn't even been there. That's what got him thinking. If she knew a bear was running around, there was no way in hell she'd go for his plan. He'd thrown his pack on the porch and proceeded to clean everything up as best he could. This was not something she needed to know about. The bear was probably way the hell and gone to Anchorage by now anyway. He didn't know what he'd tell her about the sleeping bag. He'd figure out something.

Since she'd got back from Bailey's the night before, they'd fought and slept and screwed and he still hadn't got around to telling her the plan, in spite of the fact that he'd devised a great story to explain the destruction of the sleeping bag when she'd told him she'd left it to dry on the porch. That wasn't very smart, he told her sternly. The wind had blown it into the trees and bushes until there was nothing left but tatters. Two hundred fifty smackers down the tube.

Painted in morning light, Alpha crouched now by the wood-stove, humming a little now and then, looking perfectly contented. There was something changed in her that he couldn't quite put his finger on. Though she had been perfectly cheery with him this morning, there was a distance that he could not step into. He circled it warily, testing it here and there, finding at each point that he could not cross it. Probably it was just fatigue and anxiety. All they needed to do was get on with the business at hand, to achieve their goal, and then things would be different. That thought settled across his shoulders like a favorite old shirt, which only reminded him that he felt ridiculous standing there stark naked. He'd almost cupped a hand over his genitals in a fit of modesty but consciously resisted doing it for fear of looking prissy.

He scurried back to her and kneeled on the couch cushions he had placed in front of the stove so they could lie together in some modicum of comfort and warmth. The curve of her waist flaring to buttocks was so beautiful his hands moved of their own accord to mold themselves there; he felt himself getting hard again. He lowered his mouth to her shoulder, brushing his lips smoothly along the crest to the nape of her neck; her skin ruffled under his hands and she shivered just perceptibly before settling back on the cushions with her legs tucked under her. He turned himself to face her profile, moved his eyes like fingers down the slope of her breasts to the apex of her thighs, flushed pink from the heat of the stove.

Alpha looked at him, drifted two fingers across his cheek, then stood abruptly.

"We'd better get going," she said in the tone he recognized as business. He sighed in dour acceptance of the dull ache he would have to endure in his groin for the next hour. She was right, of course, and that soured him even more.

Alpha asked him to turn on the generator so she could shower. She spoke to him now in a high-pitched, cajoling voice and he knew she was trying to brush past his sullenness, but he couldn't help holding on to it for a while longer. He grunted at her in answer and shoved his legs into his jeans. Once he'd finished dressing, he made himself a sandwich for breakfast; anything but do immediately what she'd asked him to do.

After eating, his sulk subsided and he went outside to start the generator, then carried in a few armloads of wood. By the time he was done, Alpha was dressed, had brushed her hair and swept it up, emphasizing her bright, doll's face which she turned on him with her I'm-ready-for-anything smile that made him weak. He bent to kiss her, cradling her head gently as if her hair might break at the least pressure. She had gone limp the first time he'd tried that move. He'd balked at trying it because it seemed like a cheesy movie gesture, but mere moments afterward she had capitulated to some irksome thing that bristled between them, so he'd filed the move for future use.

"Ready?" she asked.

"There's still some stuff I have to get together."

"I've got our lunch ready, and some water."

Zach hesitated.

"Listen, hon. I've got an idea that'll make our time more profitable. Let's sit on the porch."

"Okay," she said. He tried to gauge her tone of voice. With

women, some *okays* were not really *okays*. "I'll get my pack and meet you out there."

Zach sat on the porch fingering what was left of a Forget-me-not that had been crushed on the bottom of his boot, his skin purpling from the blood of the flower.

"Hope that's not for me," Alpha said, pointing at the tiny bruised bloom in his hand. "It looks pretty sad."

"No way," he said. "Nothing but perfection for my gal." He got up and cantered down the bank, returning quickly with a fresh bunch of flowers. "They don't come any fresher than that," he said, bowing as he stretched out his hand, remembering just then that she hated having wildflowers picked. Had always said if they were grown cheek by jowl to be cut, it wasn't so bad, but she preferred to see wildflowers where they were supposed to be. He flushed with irritation and prepared to just have out with it before she even had a chance to look upset, but she had taken them, blushing as cutely as ever he'd seen a girl do, and tucked the tiny bouquet into the sweep of her hair.

"*Now* I'm ready," she said.

In spite of everything—lack of sleep, hard work, few amenities, bugs—she stood there looking at him, hair wisping charmingly at her temples, making him stiffen in his pants and feel like complete shit. He snatched at his hair, and cocked a hip sideways.

"Okay, this is what I'm thinking. We brought a tent, right? It takes me a half hour to hike up there, and that's if I'm really moving out. It'll take the two of us at least an hour to make the trip, one-way. Then there's the trip back at the end of the day when we're whipped. That'll take longer. I'm thinking we should take the tent and sleeping bags . . ."

"Sleeping *bag*," she corrected.

"Whatever. One's big enough for both of us. Anyways, we'll take our gear and camp out up there. We'll bring enough food for two or three days and come back here when we really need to. It'll save us boocoo time, maybe make up for all we've lost already." He watched her face closely, the way that half smile had not changed one iota while he spoke. It was that frozen-in-disbelief smile, the one that preceded a woman saying, *I don't think so, buster,* keeping the smile on so it wouldn't look like she was being bitchy.

"Shit," he hissed, angry adrenaline flooding his system. "Look at this friggin' situation," he said. "We are running out of time faster than you can say 'gold,' and we haven't found a goddamn thing. I mean I'm on the spot here. The stuff is definitely there, but I can't get at it for walking and walking and worrying about you and all this other freakin' crap." He had both hands in his hair now rubbing hard down the back of his neck.

"I know, Zach. But let's think this through."

"I've already thought it through is my point, Al. Done all that so you wouldn't have to deal with it. The logistics are the same one way or another. Time is wasting and it's still wasting."

"I'm worried about the bears. Bailey said there were a couple at her camp We're not that far away."

"Sure. Now everything this wacko woman says is the law. Al-pha, do you hear yourself? You sound like a parrot."

"She's not wacko, Zach. She lives here. She knows what's going on."

"But she doesn't know what we're trying to do here. Nobody does but you and me. All our money's at stake. How are we gonna buy a house and get married and do all that shit when we're in debt for what we spent to get here?" It was a dirty card to play but he had to do it. He knew what she expected to get out of this, and he wasn't above using it to get his way, especially since it was the right way.

"I understand that," she said. "I'm not saying we shouldn't do it, I'm just saying that there are things we have to take into consideration. We have to be careful. Take some precautions."

"You're absolutely right," he said. Telling a woman she was right was another effective move he had filed away.

"How are we going to get our stuff up there? We may need to make a couple of trips."

He knew she was trying to be helpful; there was nothing smug or derisive in her suggestion, but he couldn't help snapping. "No shit, Sherlock, which is why I suggest we cut all this arguing and get on with it."

Alpha said nothing, just looked at him, questioningly at first, then her face changed as if a windshield wiper had cleared something away, taking with it the soft girlishness he had seen glowing there so brightly not long before; knowing he was responsible for that made him madder still.

"Fuck." Sometimes it was the only word he could say that was even vaguely satisfying, and he said it again, harder, "Fuck!" Alpha flinched. "It's not like I'm leaving you in the bushes somewhere with no food or shelter. Now you can help us or hurt us with the attitude. Your choice." She shrank away from him and he could have kicked himself for going off like that. He was just making it worse.

"Look, Al. Don't worry. We'll stay close together so you won't ever be alone. I'll take care of any cranky bears that even think about taking a bite of my sweetheart." There. That was pretty diplomatic.

"It doesn't seem as if I have a choice," she said. "I mean, if it's the right thing to do, then that's what we have to do. So, okay. We'll try it," and put on that half smile again, the one that said okay was not exactly okay. But at least she had agreed and they could get started now.

"Okay," Zach said. "That's my girl." He patted her shoulder awkwardly and went about gathering together the things they would need to camp out.

There was another thing he hadn't told her about that still bothered him. As he'd explored the stream yesterday for the site that Arnie had described to him, he'd stumbled onto a sort of clearing in the brush by the stream. He didn't remember Arnie mentioning any clearing. It was obviously the place in the stream he had described though, because the low ridge had intersected it there, and the little pool below a riffle was exactly as he'd imagined it would be.

The clearing was definitely man-made, which was what bothered him. There were grayed stumps of alder all over the place, obviously chainsaw cuts, and two weathered looking rocker boxes. He had never used a rocker box himself, but he had read about them in the mining magazines, seen plenty of pictures. He had wanted to bring one for his operation, but they were too bulky in cost and size. Arnie had said he could do the job with a camp shovel and the gold pans, and indeed there was a broken-handled shovel at the edge of the brush, as if it had been flung there and forgotten. Most disturbing had been the piles of slag all over the place. He'd known what those were, too—gravel that had been washed through the rocker box and left on the ground after the gold was extracted.

Arnie hadn't told him he'd done such a thorough job of checking the place out, though it didn't surprise Zach that he hadn't. The little weasel had to have taken some gold out to know it was there. But that reasoning didn't quite satisfy Zach. Wouldn't Arnie have used the clearing as a landmark instead of all the other geographical bullshit he'd told him instead? Well fuck it, is what he'd finally decided. The guy was half out of his mind on pain pills and booze most of the time anyway.

It could all end up being for nothing if he couldn't find the stuff. He had to keep reminding himself that a good showing of glitter on the surface didn't necessarily mean there was a mother lode, or even a beer bottle's worth of gold, but he couldn't give up now. He would run himself and Alpha to tatters before he'd come out empty-handed. So he hefted a load of gear onto his back and struck off, centuries worth of cocksure thrumming his white heartstrings.

Kash had never in his life felt foolish until he'd raced upriver once again to save the woman from the menace of the century and been held at gunpoint by the woman herself. She hadn't held the gun on him exactly, but he sensed something chambered and ready behind her eyes that would have killed him as surely as a projectile from the rifled barrel.

She hadn't let him come in for coffee and effectively stone-walled him right to the moment the pontoons touched sand in the Village. Wouldn't take her earphones off or let the engine idle low so he could talk. Even his top-of-the-lung shouting departed as air. He'd climbed down out of the plane with a plainly spoken *fuck it* and ridden the ATV like a wet, barefoot, bat-out-of-hell to his house where, surprise, surprise, there was one piece of good news. The fishing season would open the following day, and the atmosphere was not quite so taut as a result. The prospect of action was always good for the soul. Raina had called to say she and Curan were flying back that evening, so he'd picked them up when they came in and he'd been so happy to see the boy he laughed out loud. He didn't blame himself for what happened. But he was responsible for the boy in all ways, good or bad. If the boy suffered, it was his vicarious burden to suffer also.

Curan was eager to show off his designer cast, couldn't tell Kash fast enough how they did it and how they had all these colors to choose from now, even camo, and he'd pointed proudly at the sure-enough camo-colored cast that sheathed his leg to midthigh.

Kash had scooped him from his seat in the plane, the boy's lanky teenaged skeleton sprawling over him like a vine had grown there. Kash thought he'd never felt anything as energizing as the boy's living self gathered to him. "Good to see you, son," he'd whispered, and felt an arm tighten around his neck in response. He'd nested him in the trailer which he'd stacked with pillows and blankets—much to the boy's dismay: *Geez, Pops, I'll look like a woos*—and with Raina hugging him from behind he'd driven back down the hill feeling graced as the wealthiest of men.

It hadn't taken long to fix the plane, which he'd tested with a couple of touch-and-go's. Right as rain. With that done, he'd been able to settle himself in bed, exhausted enough to sleep without thinking of her.

But he'd spent much of the day now fighting to keep her image at bay. Much as he'd hashed over the events of the past couple of days, there was still nothing to merit the bone-chattering chill she exuded. He had considered interrogating Raina—she was a woman, after all—but he couldn't go over with her the most salient features of the problem. That was out of the question for now.

Besides, there was something in his gut that told him her feelings had not shifted as far off course as she wanted him to believe, that the look on her face as she watched him dress the other morning more accurately echoed what was under her skin. His own skin prickled to remember it as he had a hundred times already. He sniffed her desire as surely as a bear did a meal, and he could not help thinking about having her. The worst thing was, the thing that had made him feel foolish, was that he still wanted her. It made him uneasy, made him feel as if he couldn't just let it lie until the time was right to take care of it. Had made him feel as if, instead of loading his nets that morning for the beginning of a process ingrained as breathing, he should have been piling into the plane to fly upriver and make everything right.

His unease was mitigated somewhat by the events of the day. At least Match hadn't had the total lack of good sense to show up and fish with them as he'd boasted of doing for weeks. He'd sworn that first day's catch to Raina, something that Kash usually did. It had rankled him like hell, but he'd swallowed it, figuring the man was so inept and unreliable that Kash would end up doing it anyway.

On opening day, most of the fishermen gathered at a spot on the Yukon for the afternoon meal to discuss the health of the salmon run and to give thanks for their bounty, regardless of how bountiful it was. Just about everyone had showed up, even Ferrin. They motored downriver to a high bluff exposed to wind that would keep the mosquitoes at bay. From this vantage, he could see for hundreds of miles: the Kuskokwim Mountains loomed behind him, the stony, horizontal spine oblique to his own, snowcaps looking like clouds in the haze of distance; across the river, westward, the horizon was bounded by the Nulato Hills, golden flanks gently ridged and gullied, protecting the Ingalik from the Bering Sea weather that lay beyond them; southward, the Yukon made its way through the land to where it jigged west to the sea, and at that juncture rose the top end of the Kilbuck Mountains, also still snowcapped; northward, the land undulated and drove on to where he fancied he could see the end of the trees, and beyond that, the Brooks Range sending its cold, imperious spires skyward where they touched heaven and gathered power for the earth on which he sat, his spine straight as a lightning rod to receive it.

That day on the river had been more like the old days when his father was still alive. He had felt the old man's presence strongly as they sat on the high bluff taking the meal, talking, smoking. He had felt at moments the eerie sensation of the shade of the man slipping in and out of his own living self and honored the perception with wonder and attention.

They had told stories with their usual candor, about women they'd fucked, or women they would like to fuck; he had tensed at first over the stories, then relaxed when he determined that there was no subtle point to it. He kept his face closed to the questions he knew wanted to surface, refused to give the matter power by giving it voice, and felt sure he had conveyed an air of easy authority. After the meal, it was customary to sit quietly for a while and give up your ghosts to the air, your thanks to the spirits, and your malevolence to the Bushman.

They were well into the sitting when the noise cut into his meditation. There was so much boat traffic on the river this time of year he was annoyed that he'd noticed it. Though it was a hundred yards distant, he recognized the figure immediately. He was not in the big fishing boat, but in his shallow-water jonboat, which meant that Kash had been right and it was a good thing he'd fished well today. He watched Match go on by, not even noticing them on the bluff, and continue toward the Village. No doubt he wanted to sweet-talk Raina before Kash got back. He'd ascertain first how much syrup he'd need to add, because he wouldn't know whether Kash had told her about the day before. Ferrin had caught his eye, shrugged as if to say, *I got no idea what he's up to.*

Then Bailey had cast herself onto the map of his thoughts, finally obliterating the possibility of regaining his trance. He concluded the ceremony with a thanks mumbled in Athabascan, then rose to make his way back down to the river. He stood for a moment at bluff's edge to drink the land. The heat would come soon. He could smell it.

The boat was logy as hell with its load of salmon, so he'd had to take it slow on the way back to the Village. He was as happy as he'd been in years. He was convinced he could make it right with Bailey. She had been overwhelmed, frightened by all the craziness with Match. Because of the way she handled herself, it was easy to forget that she was vulnerable. Patience was what he needed in this situation. Play it right and you will pass GO and collect your due. He smiled at the memory of the ridiculous game fellow students had tried to introduce to him in college. Monopoly. It didn't get any whiter than that. He smiled into the warm wind, smiled and stretched expansively and held the boat on course with a knee wedged under the wheel.

He turned into the slough and ground his boat hard onto the beach, an uncustomary act of assertion. Most everybody else was there, and he had automatically taken note of the fact that his boat had the better catch by far. Match's boat was nowhere to be seen. The little prick had bolted to avoid seeing him. Good. He didn't think he could stomach the man just then. He'd had a bellyful of bullshit.

The prospect of physical work heartened him, and he rose to begin the task. He would deal with the rest of it later. And here came Curan racing down the beach on the four-wheeler, camosheathed leg stuck out before him, trailer jouncing crazily behind. He had not been given permission to ride yet, not to mention he'd been told a hundred times to take more care with the trailer, but just now, the excitement and vigor on his face made Kash smile, and he called out to the boy in Athabascan a greeting his father had made to him when he came home from a successful hunt.

───

When Bailey returned to her camp after the fight with Match, she had thought her anger would be boundless, consuming, make her unable to deal with the girl in a civilized manner. But once she'd got inside her cabin and seen that everything was in order, and Alpha was all right, she had felt the venom leach from her blood, leaving her pliant, exhausted. There was still the startling resemblance between the girl and Temple that unsettled her. When the girl had started talking to her, she had braced herself for a sickening surge that did not come. During the flight up, she had catalogued a hundred ways the girl could get hurt, had thought if something happened to her because Bailey had not been there, she could not bear it.

And why? She had already convinced herself that it was impossible, that Alpha could not be the grown face she'd scented twenty-two years ago. It was too coincidental even for coincidence. Even so, there she'd stood talking at Bailey with the resemblance that wouldn't let her leave it alone.

She'd done what she could to make her comfortable, taken her fishing and fed her, and she'd seemed to buck up. She thought the girl was strong enough then to take the possibility of it. And she needed to say it, because maybe saying it would spring the frightening forms from the blackened shadows of her imagination and into light. But she'd sent the girl upriver instead, telling herself: *It's not what you think. It's what you want.*

She'd let her go, but not before promising to come check on her. Bailey watched her maneuver the boat awkwardly into the current, a curiously buoyant sadness pressing her sternum.

When she woke the next morning, the memory of what Raina had told her fouled her thoughts. She stewed over how Kash had played her. She had known all of her life what it was to want things in a rapacious way, but this kind of desire was unfamiliar. It had a neediness in it, a helplessness that was horrible. She tried to relegate it to a darkened apse, but found that the darkness there was not as complete as it had been once. Dim forms crouched in the gloom, and when she tried to dress, her hands trembled at the task. Her carefully constructed haven had been violated by the wraiths of her past, and she'd been made a fool of, all in a few days' time.

Normally, being alone was a balm. People couldn't understand what you'd do out here to keep the boredom at bay. But there was always too much to do, it seemed to her. Just the endless array of chores one had to perform to keep oneself alive was staggering. The body had to be fed and sheltered. The sheer amount of organization it took to make sure that she had what she needed in operating order to survive was boggling. For two years, that and the occasional social moments in the Village and with Kash had sufficed aplenty. Now, it was not enough.

She needed to work, to push her body so hard there was only the physical sensation of tendon against bone, her body against gravity, until nothing remained to feed spectral thought.

There was the chainsaw to retrieve and dry out. And the root cellar she'd been digging off and on needed to be finished this summer. She hoped to have vegetables to store one day, and a pressure tank so she could use an electric pump on the well head, have running water. She eyed the trapdoor in the floor that led to the four-by-four-foot hole she'd got dug so far and thought that would be the perfect place for her today. She would close the trapdoor over her head and relax in the gravelike must and damp. The prospect perked her up to the point her appetite returned and she made a big breakfast to fuel herself for the day. She thought about how much Alpha had enjoyed the fish. Perhaps she'd invite her down for a meal. She could even bring the lout if she wanted. The prospect of gunning his ass around a little cheered her immensely.

But first, the chainsaw. She grabbed her jacket off the peg by the door on her way out. She could smell the pitch rising in the spruce, fresh grass exploding from still cool earth, the river and its bright, ozonated aroma. There was something familiar in the air that she hadn't smelled the day before. She cast her face from side to side like a dog trying the wind. The heavy, sweet smell was everywhere. And then she remembered the wild roses; they would riot the riverbanks for miles. Maybe she'd pick a few for the dinner table. That was how she'd intended life to be: nothing more than the decision to do something and then doing it. She followed the scent, keeping her face uptilted, as if the smell of life could flush the long-dirty corners of her heart.

14

Alpha was more relaxed about being alone. When Zach decided to work farther up the stream, she had set herself the task of tidying the camp. Zach had stopped only long enough to pitch the tent, leaving her to deal with the niceties of making a fire pit, and unrolling the sleeping bag and pads. The clearing was big enough to accommodate a comfortable setup, and she was grateful to Arnie for having done it. She was surprised at how little things regenerated in this country. Fifteen years was a long time for nothing to have grown back, not even the groundcover.

She was relieved of the horrible suppositions about Bailey that had clouded her thoughts. She hadn't wanted them to be true because she had actually liked the woman, in spite of her prickly exterior. She was strong, independent, capable and that was something Alpha admired and aspired to, though she knew she'd never achieve Bailey's level of tenacity. Bailey had a tempered steel core that Alpha did not. Alpha knew she could be strong, but she'd never be tough. Not like that.

So she had been flattered that Bailey had spent time with her the evening before, taken her out to the river and showed her how to fish, then made her dinner. Alpha had been a little nervous at first after being alone so long with her memory and imagination. After all, Bailey was a woman about whom stories had been conjured. Terrible stories. Surely she could not be the creature of the imagined scenarios played out by her and her girlfriends those years ago in high school. But as the revue of the last couple of days played helplessly to her, she watched her beliefs shift and crumble. Zach, Bailey, this place, even her sense of herself . . . All of her perceptions were skewed.

But she intended to sort it all out, starting that morning. She had balked at Zach's "plan" initially. If she cleared the fear away, she knew he was right. They were running out of time and all their money was at stake. All the things that she wanted depended on their success here. So she'd flung herself into the move, packed as much gear on her back as she could manage and carried more in her hands. The hike had just about done her in, but she'd made it without stopping. When Zach had decided to move upstream and work down, suggested she work the stream next to camp in case he disturbed something that washed down, she'd had to bite back the response that leaped there to make itself heard, had supplanted that with a simple *Okeydokey* and a smile.

Banishing fear wasn't as easy as simply making up your mind, however. She had gone about her chores, aware that her senses were hypervigilant to noises and smells around her. Finally, she forced herself to grab one of the plastic green gold pans and walk downstream a ways. She had made as much noise as she could before edging through the brush to the water's edge, then slipped gratefully into the water, felt it cooling her even through the thick rubber hipboots. Now she worked upstream slowly, panning as she went.

As she bent to the water, the sound of it mesmerized her. Carefully she scooped matter downstream of any rocks as Zach instructed. When nuggets were washed free over thousands of years, they would tumble downstream with the water, but being heavier than mere rock, would lodge themselves in the eddies of larger obstructions. It all made complete sense to her. She loved the dance that accompanied the swishing of sand and gravel and water in the pan. She had thought the people in the videos that Zach made her watch looked ridiculous, like they were dancing with an invisible hula hoop. She tried to use only her arms to swirl the plate, but soon gave in to her body that wanted to swirl with it, found that it actually made the panning easier.

Zach would be more bearable now that he was on his mission. But when he was there, it seemed that a part of her whirled away and turned to watch. She wanted to close those eyes but the detached part would not allow it. That part saw him in three dimensions where before she had only seen him in two, like the cutout cardboard figures that she had the children make in class.

Hours later, she straightened up and braced her hands on the backs of her hips. She didn't think her body could take much more right now. She was sunburned and mosquito-bitten to a fare-thee-well and she decided to bathe herself in the tiny pool by the campsite. She shucked off her clothes, and only paused slightly when the water level reached the tops of her legs before she submerged herself.

The cold was painful. Her eyes ached against closed lids, but she forced herself to stand and dip several times before she gathered her things and ran back to the tent, flinging water from her body like a dog. She lay on top of the sleeping bag and let the dry heat evaporate what wetness remained. Her hands smoothed down goose bumps, surprised to feel how firm she had become.

She remembered her bleeding and sat up, trying to think where her toiletries were, was so intent on digging through her duffel that it took her a while to register the unusual sound. She froze, her hands still deep in the canvas bag, listening, trying to register what it all meant. The tightening of her muscles had caused blood to trickle from her, but she did not move to fix it.

"*Relax, you idiot. It's probably Zach.*" She called his name but there was no response.

Minutes passed and she had not heard the sound again. She chastised herself for being so paranoid, and was about to get her clothing and get dressed when she heard the sound of metal clanging loudly in the still air. The tensed muscles in her back cramped sharply. She tried to lick her lips. Maybe it was Bailey coming to visit as promised, though how would she know where they'd gone? She felt the cramped muscle in her back slacken a little.

"Bailey?" she said softly. She bit her lip hard, thought: *that was stupid.*

Her nakedness became suddenly paramount. Every rustle of the sleeping bag was like fireworks as she slipped on a flannel shirt then lay back slowly so that she could pull on her jeans. She no longer had any thought for her bleeding. A sharp snort. It sounded like the warning blow of a deer in the woods back home. Were there deer in Alaska? She couldn't believe she didn't know. There was another loud snort, closer, and a large, indistinct outline cast itself against the tent like the shadow puppets she used to make on her bedroom wall at night.

The first growl was soft, almost a purr followed by slurping noises. The rank, greasy odor was strong now, and she knew without doubt what was outside.

The snorting intensified as the bear snuffled around the edge of the tent, her every sense tuned to its movements. Surely it knew she was there and was sounding her out. She tried to take stock of the food and where it was. There was nothing that resembled food in the tent, not even toothpaste; they had known better than to distribute invitations. Most of the food was in the cooler outside; she knew a bear's sense of smell was remarkable and its eyes were bad. This, she thought, was her only hope.

After it had made its way around the tent, she heard it lumber away, breathing in loud, humanlike sighs. When she heard the unmistakable sounds of the bear trying to beat its way into the cooler, she moved slowly, on all fours, toward the flap. The zipper was excruciatingly loud, and her progress was slow. She had just got it all the way down when she heard the bear's frustrated cry and a booming *thwump.*

The cooler hurtled through the tent flap and would have hit

her full on had the cloth not altered its course slightly. Instead, it clipped her as it passed and rolled to a stop at the back of the tent with its top flopped open, bits of food strewn in its path. Alpha had fallen to the side and lay still, unable to figure out what had happened, then felt as if her blood froze entirely when she heard the bear give voice and realized it was there at the tent and then had no time to think when it catapulted itself through the flap in pursuit of the cooler.

The ridgepole snapped, causing the tent to conflate and drape itself across the bear's forequarters. Alpha rolled to the side, clawing desperately at the nylon in an attempt to make a hole so she could roll out but instead was stretched slinglike, and yanked around as the bear groped and swiped at the cooler. She could see nothing from her swaddling. Instinct caused her to wrap her head in her arms and lie as still as possible lest her movement draw attention.

The bear began to buck through the tent, successfully getting its head and shoulders out, while the rest of its body was caped in the nylon. Then she was being dragged, *bumpety-bump*, across the ground, as the bear tried to outrun the apparatus that had attached itself to its body. Alpha kept her arms wrapped around her head.

The dragging stopped as suddenly as it had begun. The cloth tightened and loosened around her, the bear's outraged voice was so close she thought her eardrums would shatter. She could hear cloth ripping as the bear tried to shred its cumbersome burden, yard by yard.

She was so intent on imagining what was happening that she had no sense of danger for herself, and so the contact of claw to skin came without pain, but with otherwise incredibly heightened sensation. She felt she could sense exactly how deep the claws had sunk in her flesh; fancied, from some greatly removed and carefully ordered place, that she could hear her skin tear, feel bits of thread embedded into tissue and most of all, felt distinctly that the bear was not trying to hurt her. She just happened to be in the way. She meant it no harm, was completely unafraid, numb, wrapped in her cocoon when she heard the shot crack out, heard the air *whoof* out of the bear's mouth from the bullet's impact. The following seconds of silence and stillness were horrible; without noise and movement she had nothing to go on.

There was another shot, louder now in the stillness, and her ears rang so hard she felt more than heard the huge, ursine body hit the ground, then heard, as if from a great distance, groaning of such agony that she felt compelled to give solace. It thrashed for long moments, tightening the sling around her. A tremendous ripping sound and then all was still.

The sound of her name filtered into her addled mind. Adrenaline surged anew, and she began to struggle in her cocoon. Something pulled at the tent around her, rolling her this way and that as it tried to find an opening. She was aware of a light stinging sensation across her back that increased when her weight was forced onto it. When the light shafted into her wide-open eyes she did not even blink. Once sure she was free, she rose to her hands and knees and scuttled along the open ground until Zach caught her and tackled her down. She stopped fighting and sat still on the dry, sunbaked earth, her legs jutting out before her, and focused her eyes on her lap, afraid to look any farther for fear the creeping hope that she had had a nightmare would be shattered.

<hr />

Zach scooped and hooped till his ass ached, certain with each dip that when the plate washed out, there would be the nuggets, and found nothing but more pea gravel and sand than he'd ever seen in one place. The scene had lived so precisely in his imagination, he didn't know what to do with the possibility that it might die there, was so shaken he couldn't even get mad about it. He would cover the ledge and the pool below it with a fine-tooth comb before he would stop. The stuff was here and he would stay till he starved to get it. But just now, he had to quit, get back to camp and rest awhile. Then he'd start fresh.

The prolonged rush of excitement leaching to disappointment began to weigh on him as he stumbled over grassy hummocks of frost-heaved earth. He wanted to look around at the landscape as it seemed the only thing that could mitigate the grittiness of his mood. Now, with the sun piercing the evening air, the tundra was serenely beautiful. But every time he looked up he lost his footing, and the pause to recover his balance brought down hordes of mosquitoes on his unprotected skin. In his hurry to start panning, he'd forgotten to put bug dope in his pack.

He had bought what seemed at the time to be ridiculous amounts of the stuff but now he worried that he might run out if the clouds around him were any indication. He remembered that little smart-ass Winston back home at the feed store who gave him enough shit about it to fill a dumptruck. *Christ,* he'd said. *Don't sound like much fun to go nowheres you gotta use that much bug dope.* And hadn't he cackled, the little raisin-faced fucker. He had had it in for Zach from the day he bought the shop and moved there. Couldn't get enough of calling him an outsider when he'd grown up not fifty miles from there. But it was fifty miles closer to Boston, the big city, and that was enough for folks in those parts to suspect you of having an extra head growing between your shoulder blades.

But he wouldn't have to worry about that for long, he reminded himself. When he flashed the nuggets under Winston's nose, he'd be ready to kiss Zach's ass dipped in Tabasco. He could buy Winston's store right out from under him and stand there laughing while the little bastard shriveled on up and evaporated. Zach let out a whoop at the idea and picked up the pace.

He was still caught up in the image of Winston's pathetically in-blown face when he heard the ruckus.

He stopped, listened intently, heard nothing for a long pause, and was about to go on when another sound made the hair on his arms prickle through the butter of sweat congealed there. He started to run, his daypack banging away at his rump. As he ran, he unslung the rifle from his back and carried it with both hands in front of him, the way he had seen guys carry it in army flicks.

When he crested the little rise behind their camp, he stopped, gaping, gasping. Had this been another place, a circus ring perhaps, he would have laughed out loud. It would have been hilarious, really, to see the bear wearing their tent like an unwanted robe, bucking along in an effort to rid itself of the cumbersome garment.

He cocked one leg forward, leaned his weight into it, and raised the thirty-thirty. With the crosshairs he followed the humping figure until it stopped and turned on its train in an effort to shred it away. He had almost taken one shot, a lung hit, then reconsidered and gone for the heart. Figured at this range the high grain bullets would easily penetrate bone, and then he would go for the throat if the bear insisted on living. He waited until it paused a moment in its flailing, then he'd squeezed off, letting his shoulder stoutly absorb the recoil.

He watched its body curve around the point of impact, and the head come around in amazement, ears pricked in his direction. Not twenty yards separated them so he heard clearly the air *whoof* from it after the hit. He waited for it to go down and when it did not, he got the long throat in his sights and fired again. Then it did go down, hard on its side. *Mosquito bite, my ass,* he thought, Bailey's words ringing hollow in his memory. He lowered the rifle, confident that that was the end of it, wasn't even looking when the bear struggled to its feet. It was the nylon tearing that got his attention again, and he stared in amazement as the bear ripped the tent away from its body with one slash of a huge paw and ran into the brush, its hind end corkscrewing wildly like a rodeo bull. He was so surprised, he hadn't even raised the gun. But he was sure the bear was a goner. There was no way it could be otherwise, not with two good hits.

He almost raised the gun again when the tent began to move and wriggle. He was reminded absurdly of the chrysalis his fifth grade teacher had made the class watch when it was about to open and release the adult butterfly. He couldn't believe it didn't hit him until then, *Alpha,* and ran toward the squirming mess of nylon, calling her name.

He had a hell of a time untangling her, and when she did pop out she ran from him like a lunatic until he tackled her. She had seemed to come around as he spoke to her in rapid, senseless syllables, and then she had turned to the fringe of brush behind her and puked.

The injury had gone unnoticed until she turned. Zach had no idea whether to deal with the blood or the puking and fluttered around her, touching first her back then scrabbling for her hand to hold. Finally, he was able to calm her until she stood, quivering and wild-eyed.

"Sweetheart, I just want to have a look at your back." He talked to her slowly, clearly. She nodded, then closed her eyes as he unsheathed his knife and slit the shirt up the back, trying not to move it away from the wound too quickly. The claws must have just grazed her, he figured. The edges were ragged and welted, but they were not mortal wounds, at least not now. Infection would be the thing to worry about; he should flush the wound with clean water, he knew that much, but then they'd have to get some antibiotics, and he gritted his teeth as he thought of who he'd have to turn to for that.

He looked around, bewildered. The camp was a disaster and the mosquitoes were maddening. Alpha seemed not to notice as she stood there, her skin bristled with the gray-black bodies. Zach rubbed his hands over her face and neck, succeeding in smearing more blood over her.

"I'll rig up some shelter, get you out of these bugs," he told her. "The cuts aren't too bad, but if these mosquitoes keep at you, you might bleed to death anyway." He wanted her to laugh at his stu-

pid jokes like she always did, but she only nodded, panting and
hiccuping alternately.

"Where is it?"

"Where's what?"

"The bear. Where is it?"

"Well he ran off in the brush that way," he said, pointing.

"He's still alive?"

"Oh no, hon. He's a goner for sure. I plugged him twice."

"Then how could he run away?"

"Oh hell, they do that sometimes. It's just a nervous system reaction. They'll run a ways and drop."

She stood on the far side of the clearing, facing the direction in
which the bear had run, while he looked at what was left of the
tent. The body was a total loss, and he balled it up and winged it
into the brush. The rain fly was shredded in places, but he thought
if he could get it stretched and draped just right, it would make a
passable shelter. Remarkably, the sleeping bag was unscathed. Well,
thank God for this littlest of favors, Zach thought. He cobbled
some of the tent poles into a cross-hatched hump over which he
draped the rain fly, then he spread the sleeping bag on the ground
under the wilted dome. It would have to do for now.

He moved about as quickly as possible to keep the bugs off, split
up some kindling, and got a fire going. He rummaged through his
daypack and found a few crumbly aspirin in a baggie he'd kept in
there for the hangovers he inevitably had during hunting season.

He got on his hands and knees and passed the white-creased
plastic to her. "I'll be back in a minute with clean water for those.
We'll wash you up a little, okay?"

While waiting for the water to boil he worked frantically at
straightening up the camp. He didn't know what to do about the
gigantic carcass he was certain lay in the brush a few yards out.
When he had gotten their fishing licenses and a copy of all the
regulations in Anchorage, the rangers had made sure to impress on

him the penalties for taking game out of season. One old prospec-tor at the Mining and Marine store had told him you'd get less hassle for killing a human than for shooting a bear out of season.

But how the holy hell was he going to get rid of this carcass? He could argue that it was self-defense, but he remembered saying that to the prospector, who replied, *Hell, son, that's what everybody says.* Should he skin it out and butcher it? What to do with the meat? It's not like he had access to a freezer or anything. Thinking about the fresh meat reminded him of how hungry he was.

He got the pot of water off the fire, just warm enough to do the job, and crawled under the dome with it. She was still sitting up, and had managed to let go of the gun long enough to get her shirt off. He was appalled to feel himself stirring at the sight of her naked from the waist up. She tapped the contents of the baggie into her mouth and dipped her face right into the pot to drink.

"We'll have to hide the body," she said.

"I was just thinking about that," he said. "I don't know how I'll hide it. Don't even know where the freakin' thing is."

"You said it didn't run far."

"Yeah, but it could have run in circles or anything. You never know."

"When we find it, we could bury it."

"Ground's too frozen. I don't have time for that."

He squashed a few mosquitoes against the nylon, leaving little trails of blood here and there. The question arose that had tickled darkly at him. What would happen now? Would Alpha want to leave?

"Cut some brush and cover it. Nobody will know. We'll be staying at the Lodge now anyway." She'd said it matter-of-factly, so he knew there was no point in arguing, but he brightened consid-erably. It didn't sound like she would insist on leaving.

"I'll get rid of the bear, Al. But first I'm taking you down to the Lodge. We'll radio Bailey and get some antibiotics for just-in-case. For now, we'll wash the cuts and see how it is."

Zach was glad he hadn't eaten; plucking the bits of thread from the gouges made him gag. Alpha was silent during the cleaning, but he could see her hands like whitened strips on the gun.

"There," he said, letting out a deep breath. "Did you take those pills?" She nodded, sniffling a little. He stroked the back of his hand across her cheek. "You're one brave little sweetheart. I gotta hand it to you." He tried to pull her toward him, but she hissed between clamped teeth which ended in a hiccuped sob.

"We gotta get you out of here," he said.

"We'll radio Bailey," Alpha said. "She'll know what to do."

Zach frowned and rubbed his face. "All right, but let me do the talking."

She had only closed her eyes in response.

He had loaded himself up with so much stuff, he felt like an Okie without the beat-up truck. He had called to her when he was ready, and she'd wormed out on her side, the gun held across her. He couldn't help but laugh. "Geez, hon, relax. That bear's dead as a doornail."

She hadn't even looked at him as she tottered to her feet. "If it'll make you feel better, you can carry it," he said. "Just be careful how you hold it when you're behind me so I don't get one up the butt." She hadn't even cracked a smile.

There were three more bullets in the magazine. He scanned her grayed face, thought he'd better give a little more instruction or else he might end up getting his ass shot. He'd showed her the safety, stressed the "on" position in particular, told her how many bullets there were left and how to bolt a round into the chamber so the gun would fire.

"You got all that?"

She nodded.

He struck off first, her following close behind him. It was going to be a long-ass hike and he'd only managed to wolf down one peanut butter and jelly sandwich. He'd tried to get Alpha to eat but she'd grimaced and turned away from the proffered tidbit. At least he'd remembered to get out the bug dope which he'd greased on so thick he was burning up within minutes.

When he turned to check on her she had lagged far behind. He waited until she caught up and started out again. Twice more he stopped to wait for her and then forgot about it altogether.

He could see over the tops of the brush to the Nulato Hills where they ranged the horizon in the distance. The air smelled bright and tangy and it could have been a lot hotter. He didn't think that anything could possibly change the tableau in which he felt frozen as the hero who had saved his girlfriend from a savage grizzly bear, and who was this close to finding gold in the wilds of Alaska. He clucked his tongue lightly in amazement, and felt like he had really accomplished something, was still clucking when he heard the brush snapping twenty yards in front of him.

All he could think of was that the gunshots must have alerted somebody. He stopped dead in his tracks, figured he'd best get his story together.

Yes sir, good evening sir, my girlfriend and I are just out for a hike. She fell through the brush by the creek bank and scraped herself up some, but she'll be fine. We're just heading back to the Lodge now. Oh, all this stuff? We were going to camp out but the little woman got nervous after she fell so I decided against it. Nice day for a hike though, eh? Gunshots? Oh heck, I was just popping off for fun. You know. Guy stuff.

He was ready to sing like a canary to whoever it was thrashing inexorably closer, didn't even put down the things he held in his hands.

15

Kash unloaded his catch at the processing plant in good time, then rode up to the burial ground on the hill. He made his way amongst the too many graves to John Knik, earth looking a bit grayer now even in two days. He carried with him a plastic garbage bag out of which he emptied the largest chum salmon he'd culled from his catch. He kneeled and clawed away hardened chunks of dirt, made enough room for the body of the fish, which smelled of Yukon silt yet, and placed it in the shallow bed. He slashed its spine and gills and waited while the dark blood oozed into the dirt before carefully covering it.

He sat with his legs folded under him, rocking slightly with his heartbeat as he stared away to the north. Clouds scudded across the land, green turned black in their shadows. Though he could discern no detail at that distance, he sensed the life there: a fox skipping down the sandy ledge below Dead Man's Curve, scavenging fish; might be a wolf denned in that gravel blow out on Porcupine Hill; a moose would graze quietly today in that big open marsh behind the ceremony bluff, her calf cached secretively in the edge brush, while a pike lazed in the warm shallows of the lake, looking to the casual eye like a log fallen there. Through it all, thousands of silver-mottled bodies surged up the creamy silted waters of the big river, survival predicated on their purposeful, inexorable wills.

He nodded. All as it should be.

On his way down, he decided to check in with Raina at the store, let her know that he'd brought her plenty of fish to put away, as usual, and drive home the fact that, as usual, the Dick with Ears had failed to make good on his boast.

When he pulled up to the store, the door was closed and locked. He picked out the key from the heavy bunch he kept clipped to a belt loop, and let himself in. He didn't bother flicking on the lights; the dimness was a relief after spending all day in the sun. He felt the top of the radio at Raina's desk. Cold. She'd been gone a while. Prickle of annoyance bristled his forearms. She was supposed to stay open until after the bulk of the fishermen returned. The annoyance strengthened when he pictured the inevitable: Match had coerced her away, probably more to piss Kash off than because he wanted her company.

The ATV slopped heavily in the mud as he paused in front of Raina's house. He knew instinctively that she wasn't there. He tried the Community Center. Curan was there with Stan's boys, watching basketball on the big screen TV, all three wearing the Bulls caps he had brought them last year. He had told Curan he was off-limits to any machinery except something he could watch. The casted leg was propped up on a chair, though the camo had been virtually obliterated by magazine cutouts of animals that the boys had glued to it. He dropped his hand on Curan's shoulder.

"How's it going, boys?"

Group chorus of "good" in response, not even a turn of heads. He leaned close to Curan so as not to disturb the others, "Where's your mother?" The thin shoulders rucked up under his hands. "That idiot been around?" Again, the shoulders arched into his palms.

An ineffable unease settled over him though he could not distinguish the elements that caused it. Signs as subtle as a slight shift of light had shivered the flesh of those long before him. He was conditioned by generations of life in extremis to assemble signs and react. But this was no weather-generated alert.

"Go to Lenora's house for supper after the game. Have one of the boys drive you. I'll tell her you're coming, so don't forget."

"Okay, Pops." A warm, smooth hand covered one of his briefly before sliding back to his lap.

He yanked the handlebars this way and that to steer out of the road slop, shifting his weight fully to one side or the other. When he gained solid ground, he twisted the throttle as far as it would go and clamped himself to the leaping machine. He gunned the bike straight across the yard to his porch steps flinging a leg over the saddle before it had stopped rolling. The darkened interior caused his eyes to ache and water. He closed them and let memory guide him to the kitchen. His hand found the light switch over the kitchen stove; again, his eyes adjusted painfully.

Even through the squint he caught the gleam from the corner of the room, then the vague outline of her there in his father's chair. He forced his eyes wide, hoping that what he had seen so vaguely was a trick of the mind. But she was there still, slumped in the chair like a sulking child, head lolling sideways, the bright bubble of liquid forming on her lips as she breathed, glinting again in the light.

He kneeled, turned her face to him. A rope of pink phlegm drooped lazily from her mouth to her chest where a dark stain had begun to form like a bib on her shirtfront. Her eyes gleamed at him from their frames of purpled flesh. He pressed the fingertips of his free hand to the side of her face, the pressure just barely dimpling the swelling skin. Raina tried to smile. The bubble popped wetly, splattering moisture across his cheeks. He dragged his bandana across her chin, swiping away in its folds the saliva that drooped there.

"I know," she said through thickened lips. "I knew it before he started in."

"Where is he?" Kash asked, gentle hands belying the chill hardness in his belly.

"It's too late," she said.

"Not too late to pay for this."

"You were right. It's going too far. I tried to stop him."

"From what?" Kash felt the chill in his belly invade the muscles of his legs and arms.

"From going up there."

He had to close his eyes before he could ask "The Lodge?"

"Yes," she said, and sounded almost irritated though he knew she could not be that. Not now.

"Add a little murder to his mayhem, do you think?" Kash asked her, trying to connect his gaze to what was still visible of his sister's eyes in their contracting rings of flesh.

"No . . . Christ let go," she whined, tried to pull her hand out of his grip that had tightened uncontrollably. He stood.

"What, then?"

"He figures they won't be there. Thinks they're back in the bush looking for gold. He's going to burn it while they're gone. Scare 'em outta here."

"Jesus." He covered his face with his hands, scrunched them tightly as if to obliterate the sights cast there by his imagination.

"I tried to stop him. I took him up to the house, tried to get him drunk, stall him off," she groaned as tears welled over the lipped swelling and trickled into the cuts on her face. "I begged him not to go up there, and that's when he started on me. Christ, Kash, you know I got no chance against him like that."

He was moving through the kitchen then, throwing food into a paper bag.

"Where's Curan? I came here so he wouldn't see me."

"Down at the Center. I told him to go to Lenora's for supper."

Kash chucked the paper bag by the door, then stood over Raina, hesitated seconds before lifting her from the chair. He couldn't believe how easy it was, how thin she'd become.

"Don't take me out there," she pleaded.

"I'm taking you into my room. I'll tell Lenora to keep the boy for the night."

"Kash, he's in a way like I never seen him. Hasn't even been drinking." She clung to his neck like a child and for a moment he had the absurd urge to sit her on his knee, rock her softly and tell her it was all right, but the anger boiling just behind his skin would not let him.

"I'll take care of it."

He put her on his bed, propping two pillows behind her. He wet a towel and brought it to her, then packed another towel with ice and put it in her hand. "I'm bringing you some water. Don't drink anything else. It'll make the swelling worse." She knew what he meant.

Lenora Richardson didn't ask questions, only agreed to feed the boy and make him comfortable for the night.

"I'll be back," Kash said to Raina. He pulled their father's old .12-gauge from under the bed and laid it alongside her after racking in two shells. "It kicks like a sonovabitch, remember? Hang on tight."

She nodded. "Kash?"

He turned back to her.

"There's something else."

He looked at her, face stitched in question.

"He'll have to go by Bailey's camp. I begged him to leave her out of it."

"He ought to know better than that," he said with a pinched smile.

"He don't. He's got it in for her big time."

Kash slumped against the doorframe.

"You want me to call somebody?" she asked.

"No," he said, almost a whisper. "We need to keep this in house. I don't know if it can be done now, but I'll try."

"You try so hard. I know I . . ."

He heard the knot come up and choke her off. He moved quickly to the edge of the bed and leaned to the top of her head, pressed his lips to her hair that smelled like sun.

"I'll do better," she said, gulping. "He's out. I hope he's out all the way."

"It may come to that," he said. "For somebody, anyway."

"Don't let it be you. Don't risk yourself. Not for them kids, not for her. We need you."

"How much of a start has he got?"

"Two hours, maybe."

"By boat?"

"Said the plane drew too much attention."

"I'll take the Cub."

He ran the ATV slopping and sliding at full throttle down to the slough. The plane was fueled and ready to go. He had only to taxi out to the Yukon and point it at the sun.

Had the hole not been so dark, the work lamp would have been blinding. Every undulation of earth was etched clearly as if drawn on white paper. Bailey had closed the trap door to mute the noise of the generator that she had to use to run the light. She had tried going at it with an axe, but stones nicked the blade and ruined it. So she'd switched to using a shovel with the handle sawed short. There wasn't enough room to use anything with much of a protrusion.

With the hole the size it was now, the shovel was pretty handy. She could stab it into a section, brace against the opposite wall and kick the blade in deep, using the strength of her legs. Like that, she had been able to clear another foot-deep section of earth running the length of one wall in just a few hours.

She had not been able to stop thinking about Temple's pregnancy, the delivery in particular, because her mother had insisted that Temple have the baby at home.

Why, Momma?

Because we don't want this all over town, do we?

Do you really think people don't know?

Good chance they don't, she'd said. *Child never goes off the place.*

You've been keeping her out of sight when the propane man comes, like I told you?

She'd nodded resolutely. *But that doesn't mean nobody knows. You don't think they know something's wrong out here, you're crazy.*

I'm crippled and I'm dying, but I'm not crazy.

Her mother never had been able to take a turn of phrase for what it was. She always had to address it literally. "I just about died," you could say, or "That just kills me," and she'd come back at it like you meant it for real.

On the other hand, there was Temple. Bailey was never sure what she'd understand literally or figuratively. When the girl had started her monthly bleeding, Bailey just about had to strap her down she'd become so frightened at the sight of the redness on her pants. And every month thereafter it was the same thing. Always a surprise, always cause for hysteria. She had tried to explain to her why her belly was growing, but couldn't tell if she got it or not. She patted herself constantly, fascinated by the smooth, hard roundness of it. Stroked it and patted it until Bailey wondered if something like that would hurt the fetus, traumatize it somehow.

Surprisingly, her mother had directed her to contact a private agency about the adoption. *Just make sure it's a Catholic agency. Ten grand is nothing to sneeze at. We could use the money.* At the time, Bailey was appalled. Later, she was grateful.

The birth was a nightmare. Temple would not leave her mother's bed, and her mother could not leave. So there they'd been for eighteen hours, Temple shrieking at the pain, her mother directing, trying clumsily to hold Temple who clung to her so desperately her mother cried out in pain. Halfway through it all, Bailey couldn't tell who was yelling. Thought sometimes it might be herself, and then did join in just to relieve the pressure in her head. When the baby finally came, Temple had shrunk in horror from it when Bailey tried to give it to her to hold while she saw to the cord. She had tried to stagger out of the bed, run from the wrinkled, cheesy mess of it. Bailey had had to knock her back on the bed so she wouldn't drag the baby away by the cord. Had yelled at her mother *"Hold her. Can't you just do that?"* knowing that her mother hadn't the strength or the muscle control to hold a pencil anymore, much less a writhing human being.

After she'd cleaned up the baby, wrapped it in a clean towel, she'd hoped Temple would take to it enough at least to let it feed, but she'd run at the sight of it out to the woods or the barn and not come back for hours. Bailey had had to feed it cow's milk until she could get the adoption people out there to take it.

She kicked the shovel into a fresh patch of dirt and groaned when it resisted her with a *chink*. She pulled the shovel out and tried to introduce it a little to the side. Again, it *tink*ed against rock. Must be a big one. She could just see herself digging around and around some massive rock obstruction. This would cause the wall to be uneven and that rankled her sense of orderliness. She worked farther and farther to either side of it, finding that it was at least two feet wide. Hopefully, it was just a clot of gravel that she could chip away. She used the hand spade to clear the surface of it, see what was there. Finally she had a two-by-two-foot area of it uncovered. She ran her hand over the bumpy uneven surface, too bumpy to be a rock, but it didn't feel like gravel either. She fumbled behind her for the whisk broom to brush away the dampened earth that clung in its crevices, then adjusted the work light so that it shone directly on it.

The piece appeared to be solid, not clotted gravel, and as the bristles did their job, the rock appeared lighter and lighter until it seemed almost white except for the darkened streak that bisected it almost in half. She put the broom down, moved her eyes to within inches of the surface. She pulled the light closer, wetted her fingertips with spit to wash away some of the drying earth and thought in the moment she knew what it was, *Why me?* And in the following moment the barely audible hum of the generator ceased and the light flared and dimmed, flared and dimmed again before extinguishing completely. She was kneeling with her face so close to the rock, she could smell the ore in it.

In utter darkness she sat back on her heels, and waited for the brilliant green afterimages to fade. It could not be possible. You had to be looking for gold to find it. It was something to which you gave up your life, not something unearthed while making room for canned goods and pressure tanks. And then she couldn't help thinking that Kash knew about it. That was why he wanted this place badly enough to take her on. But how could he know? How could anyone have known?

She scooted as far from it as the space allowed, dug in her heels the better to press her back to the damp earth wall. She heard the solid thump of her heart in the silence, marveled that it did not gallop apace with her thoughts, heard the scrape and *screeeee* of the cabin door on weathered hinges but thought that was impossible until she heard steps. One, two, three slow steps taken with quiet purpose. Blood surged into her head at a deafening volume. She blinked hard, had no thought for the possibility it was not someone she wanted to see. If it had been, they would have called out.

She waited, willing her heart to slow down so she could hear better the steps moving slowly about the cabin, could only pray the intruder would not wander across the trap door where the change in pitch would reveal that there was no solid ground underneath, where a glance could discern the outline of the door. Her eyes strained wide in the darkness as if to see what was happening above.

The steps receded, moving into her bedroom. Something hit the floor and she flinched, almost sucked air but stopped herself. She tried to take stock of what she could use, her hands sifting the dirt for the shovel and spade, the whiskbroom, and throwing the last aside. Useless. She thought of the rifle hanging over the door, calculated how much time she'd have to burst from the hole, grab the gun, load, and swing.

She took three deep breaths in preparation, and stopped short,

breath held as the steps came back into the main room. She had
waited too long. They paused at the doorway to the bedroom,
then crossed to the outer door and out as she willed them to. She
let go the breath she'd been holding, panted as lightly as she could
so she could hear what was going on outside. She forced her hand
to let go of the shovel and rose to a stoop, cracked the door. Clear.
She sat and took off her boots so she could move quietly.

She opened the hatch just enough to jack herself into the open,
her head caroming left and right. Clear. She made the door in
three quick bounds and reached for the gun. Her hands encountered empty air. Her visitor had availed himself of it already. The
Beretta was still in the airplane. She could have kicked herself for
such sloppiness, thought she had nothing to defend herself with
now, then thought the hell with that, she could still think. She slid
across the wall to the window that fronted the river.

There was no airplane tied up next to hers. She could not see
over the bank to where a strange boat would most likely be tied. If
it was Alpha, she would have sung out. If it was Kash, the plane
would have been there, or at least he would have called to her. She
could think of no one else it would be other than Match. Obviously he had gone into the bedroom to look for the pistol he now
knew she kept there.

A shadow crossed the floor by the window. She scurried,
hunched low, back to the root cellar and slipped in. Heard the
door creak open as she crouched in a darkened corner, her hand
over her mouth to keep her breath from *whoosh*ing out. The boots
crossed to within inches of her. Something dropped lightly on the
floor, metallic. A softly spoken *"shit"* reached her ears, a male
voice though she couldn't make out whose for sure.

The noise took her by surprise. She scuttled to the opposite
corner thinking the floor was about to come down on her. She
stared blindly in the direction of the banging, knew before she
could give it words in her head what it was, waited in silence,

the backs of her closed eyes blenched white as she listened to each of the four nails crying into dense wood.

Then the sound of the hammer falling to the floor, hands clap-wiped against one another, and steps moving to the door and out. She waited, as still as her banging heart would allow, until she heard the outboard motor start, rev hard, and move off upriver toward the Lodge. *Alpha.*

She felt around the rim of the door for the nail ends so she could whack them with the flat of the shovel but could find none. She slumped to her knees. He'd driven them in on a hard angle, sinking them deep in the two-by-fours she'd cribbed the hole with, wanted to make damn sure she didn't get out. But she would get out, and when she did, all the blackness in hell would not save the mongrel-hearted sonovabitch.

She tried ramming the shovel against the edges of the door, hoping the blows would loosen the frame, give her an edge, but couldn't get enough of a swing going in the small space. For once, she cursed her thoroughness. She flung the shovel away, heard it thud into the loose dirt and squatted, her own sweaty fear rising around her.

Her teeth ground in the darkness, and she thought at first the crackle was her jaw protesting the abuse. She listened. Nothing for a moment and then a series of cracks, and another until it was clear to her what the snapping was. She'd lived with the sound all of her life. Feared it, respected it, fought her sister away from it, then lost her to it. She saw with searing clarity the old, checked logs, knew they would go up hot and quick. Knew that if she didn't get out now, she would lose herself to it, and that Alpha would be lost, too.

She hurled herself upward, letting the back of her shoulder take the impact. Again, she sprang, willing every fiber in her legs to project her through the planks. Her shoulder flattened on impact. She sprang at it again and again like a berserk jack-in-the-box, the fire audible to her now even above her ragged suspirations and the blunted groan that burst from her at each blow, then felt the bones misalign and a pain of such sweet agony she didn't know whether to smile or scream. She switched sides, offering the still good shoulder in place of the battered one so she could project herself upward again, fighting for the light.

Once more she'd pushed up, expecting only the ungiving wood to meet her, but found herself in cold, sopping folds of singed wool, something binding her within it and moving her. She'd given up to it, couldn't imagine what had happened until she lay supine, and the blackened cloth came away from her eyes to reveal a sky as blue as any color she could imagine, and Kash kneeling over her saying *"Jesus, Jesus, Jesus."* She thought he was singing, and it made her cry.

He had already played out the scenario in his mind: fly low to the camp, see that Bailey had the bastard pinned to a tree at gunpoint, land, march the idiot into the back of the plane, tie him up and leave. Hopefully she'd keep the rifle trained on Match and not on him. If it had only gone that far, then the aftermath was manageable, and he was able to hold the illusion until minutes before gaining sight of the place, when he'd seen the first thin wisp of gray furling lazily over the spruce tops.

He flew clear of the ridge behind her camp and leveled out for the landing. The lower courses of logs were ablaze and it was only a matter of minutes before the roof caught. The cabin was so old it would combust in a hiccup. The Cessna and boat were both tied at the bank. He scanned the clearing, looking for humans, living or dead. Saw nothing. He focused on his gauges now, throttle down, ailerons trimmed. Superheated air mixed with cool air off the river kept the plane skittish as he tried to settle it to water. He touched down unevenly on one float and fought to keep the weight up until he could get the other float on water.

He'd grabbed a blanket from his emergency supplies in the back of the plane, dredging it in the water as he crossed the wire, whipped the catch rope around the tree a couple of times and prayed it would hold before running to the cabin door. Even over the sound of the fire, he'd heard it—sounds like he didn't think a human voice could make.

He swirled the sopping blanket around him and kicked in the door. The fire hadn't breathed through to the interior yet. He leaped the margin of low flame that had licked across the doorway, and whirled around, couldn't figure out where the noise was coming from until he saw the floor boards hump up slightly after a crash. He grabbed the hammer and jammed the claw under a board, started to lever it up when they all gave way and she'd shot up, inches from his face. He grabbed her in the blanket, and half crawled to the door, only able to gain his legs when they were out. He dragged her to the far side of the clearing, thinking of the propane tank, and the cache of gas he knew she kept for emergencies, was surprised they hadn't gone already.

The face that appeared to him when he'd peeled the blanket back was so changed from the one he knew he was stunned. It was shining and clear in spite of its dirt mask, eyes rounded, huge, like a child that had just seen its first magic trick, was overjoyed at the possibility of it. He scooped his arm under her neck, whispering *"Jesus,"* like a chant, and tried to hold her to him but she'd struggled weakly away. His heart sank, thinking she was still angry but realized when he saw her face again that she was not. She'd taken his hand and guided it to her shoulder, cupped it gently over the baseball-sized knot there. And he understood then that she was hurt. How could he not have thought to check that first?

"Alpha," she said. "He's up there."

"What about this?" he asked, his hand on her shoulder.

"It'll wait," she said. "He's up there. Take my boat. Don't risk the plane."

For the first time in his life, two points of action were perfectly pitched, both of equal importance to him. She needed help, but the time it would take to see to her as he should and wanted to might be the time in which the situation upriver escalated from bad to deadly. She would understand why he heeded her demand that he leave her for now, would be waiting for him when he came back.

He curled his hand under her neck, bent close to her face. "I'll go. Be back for you as soon as I can. Okay?"

She nodded, closed her eyes. "Counting on it."

When the propane tank blew, the explosion thwacked him on the back like he'd been punched. He hunched over her, lips accidentally grazing the grit on her forehead. He felt her good arm around him, hand splayed protectively across the back of his head. She moved her mouth close to his ear. "Guess I've got my work cut out for me. Good thing I've got the rest of the summer."

"You'll have help. You know that," he said.

"Raina told me. I know what you want."

"What?"

"If I were another kind of person, I would give the land to you, but I'm not. I can't go back out there." She spread her hand across the slope of his shoulder and tightened it around the muscle, tensed and corded in the curl of her palm.

"That why you gunned me away yesterday?"

"Sorry."

"A few months ago that was true. It's not about that anymore." He strained against the emotion, the words. He knew the art of oratory. Could speak eloquently to points of history, culture, politics, anger, but he did not know how to make this kind of talk. "You understand?"

She nodded. "Hurry."

He smiled, "See you."

"Wait," she held him back. "He took my rifle. You got anything?" He shook his head. "The plane. Under my seat. Clip's full."

He rolled his head back, took in the space around him, felt the heat from the burning cabin soak almost pleasantly into the tired muscles of his back. He'd only used long guns for hunting, something he needed to do to survive, had never even used a small arm before. They were for killing people and that was not part of his plan. Everything in him was bent on survival, for all of them.

"No," he said, finally. "You might need it in case he gets past me."

He smiled, patted her awkwardly, didn't know if he should try to kiss her. He squeezed her hand. She'd be safe enough with the gun. The fire would burn itself out on the cabin, wouldn't have anything else but new grass to feed on. He fetched the gun from the Cessna, the chubby grip uncomfortable in his hand, and brought it back to her, folded her good hand around the butt.

"Be careful," she said.

"Count on it."

The last time he'd been on this section of river in a boat had been the previous summer. He'd had to bring up some things for the Lodge that were too bulky and heavy for the plane. The watercourse had great character in its upper reaches, undulating back and forth, braiding here and there around small islands formed by the river at flood stage when it was choked with breaking ice. It was beautiful to him, intimate as the curves of a woman's body.

His mouth was so dry he couldn't swallow. He didn't know how he would be able to keep this situation under wraps. If Match had gone this far with Bailey, there was no telling what he'd do besides mere arson up there. If truth was anywhere in the man's bones, he hoped it had been in what he told Raina when he said he was just going to burn the Lodge and scare them off. If he ended up getting physical with them, there wouldn't be much he could do to keep it from outside law.

He beached the boat on a gravel bar at the bend below the Lodge. With the water as low as it was, he could sneak up the shoreline, use the bank as cover. At least he would be favored by surprise.

16

Alpha had waited for what seemed like hours, quivering in the brush with the gun to her shoulder, her back throbbing more horribly each minute she sat with nothing else to do but acknowledge the pain and wonder what happened to Zach. He was out there somewhere. She couldn't see where he'd fallen through the thicket. Snot trailed from her nose, tickling the furze on her lip. She didn't try to wipe it away, was afraid if she made the tiniest noise, the bear would hear her and come back.

She was so far behind when it happened, she hadn't been able to see anything, only heard the awful voice, and a squirt of a shout from Zach before it ended abruptly. She ran in the direction of the noise, thrashing through the brush, the gun catching maddeningly in the branches. And then she'd stopped, called Zach's name in the silence, and backed into the thick brush where she crouched now, trembling so hard the leaves started to rattle.

Two young males that hang out together. They're bold in numbers. That's what Bailey had told her. Why hadn't she reminded Zach about that before they left the campsite? Maybe he would have listened to her then.

A familiar scent settled in her nose, the sour onion sweat of her father. Had he come to save her? Tears dribbled down her face. *Now what, smart-ass.* The brush, which had seemed protective before, pricked her. She tried to pull away but it snagged at her shirt and tensed the cloth across the claw marks. Her face crumpled, and she sagged on her haunches, let the gun settle slowly to her lap.

Her only hope was Bailey. Her head lolled forward as she prayed, tried to remember anything she'd memorized in Sunday school. *I believe in one God the Father Almighty, maker of heaven and earth, and of all things visible and invisible. And in one Lord, Jesus Christ, the only begotten Son of God . . . Light of Light . . . the Lord and giver of Life . . . I look for the resurrection of the dead, and the Life of the world to come . . . Please make Bailey come today. Amen.*

She tried to calculate how close she was to the Lodge. If Bailey came in the boat, called out for them, would Alpha be able to hear her? She could no longer escape what she had to do. If she didn't try to get to the Lodge, get help, Zach would die. She eased the compass from her back pocket. When she flipped it open, she couldn't help catching herself in the mirror, saw there the face of a frightened child. A frightened child was not going to get her or Zach out of this. *Buck up. You're in charge. You have the gun.*

She rose as quietly as she could, holding the gun before her. Once she'd got clear of the brush, she could see around her, walk faster. About three hundred yards distant was the grove of spruce behind the Lodge. She kept her eyes on the dark green line of it.

By the time she'd got into the grove of trees she was exhausted, nauseated. She leaned heavily against the bole of an old spruce, big enough to be the parent tree of this whole grove. She had been raised on the terminology of the forest by her father, the ultimate paper company drone who drove a skidder forever, and then got "promoted" to the pulp mill. Funny she should think of him now as she leaned against the cool bark, sweat beading from every square inch of her as she fought to keep from vomiting.

She held her breath. Thought at first it was the drone of the mosquitoes getting thicker, but it had grown louder and more mechanical by the second. Never in her life had she believed that prayer went anywhere but into your own heart, making you stronger for whatever the outcome was to what you were worried about. But today her prayers had been answered. She drew herself heavily upright and began to trot as fast as she could through the grove toward her salvation.

The trees began to thin and she could see the Lodge but couldn't hear the motor anymore. She started yelling Bailey's name, thick grass tangling in her bootlaces as she tried to run. She was almost there, trying not to cry she was so relieved, when she'd fallen flat. She scrambled to her feet, riffling the grass for the gun she'd flung aside.

"Lose something?"

She straightened, her eyes searching for the source of those words, found it leaning against the building as if nothing in the world was wrong.

"Zach's hurt. He needs help."

"Whyn't you come on into the Lodge and rest a minute. Calm down so I can get your story straight."

"But we have to hurry. Zach's hurt and we need to call on the radio."

"Come in or go, suit yourself," he said, and disappeared around the corner.

She couldn't believe it. She took a step forward, felt something hard under her foot. The gun. Should she carry it in with her? She'd been around enough drunk men in her life to know you didn't do anything to set them off if you could help it. She propped it carefully against the wall and hurried after him.

She swung around the corner, saw gas cans scattered on the lawn out front and wondered what they were there for, then leaped onto the porch and went inside. Match sat on the couch in the main room, long legs crossed as casually as if he were at a cocktail party. Alpha tried to catch her breath as she turned on the radio. Nothing. She cursed. The generator must have run out of fuel.

"Would you please start the generator, at least? I can radio for help."

"Sit down," he said, pointing at the chair across from him. "We need to talk."

"Zach might be bleeding to death out there. I've got to get help."

"I'd say you're in more trouble than he is if you don't—sit—down."

"Why are you doing this?" her voice had risen to a shrill pitch. "Why won't you help me?"

"Today, *you* help *me*," he said. "That's how it's going to go now. Sit down. I'll tell you all about it."

She looked at the radio like it was a drink of water in a desert, then did as she was told.

"Very good. Maybe you white bitches can be trained after all."

"Look, mister, there's a life at stake."

"You got that exactly right. Your lives for ours. What do you say?"

"I don't know what you're talking about."

"Let me explain. You and your boyfriend come out here on the pretext of camping out. That's what you tell our world-class leader, anyway, right? You sign a legal document to the effect that there are certain things you will *not* do, and like all your fucking kind before, you do them anyway. Am I making sense so far?"

Sweat trickled into the cuts on her back but she didn't move. Zach had said nobody would find out. *We'll be out in the middle of freaking nowhere. Who the heck's going to know?* And how did Match know, anyway?

"How do you know that?" she asked.

"Because I know that spot. Did your boyfriend tell you he made that clearing or something?"

"No. He . . . he . . ." She didn't know if she should bring up Arnie's name or not. Was what he'd done illegal, too? "He didn't say. I didn't ask."

"That's what I like to see. A woman who knows her place. I bet he liked it, too. Bet that's why he brought you along."

Alpha squinted at him, then turned to the window and kept her eyes on the river. If she could get to the boat, she could get to Bailey's. But Match had to come by Bailey on the way up here. If she'd been there alone . . .

"Bailey's coming up today," she said, testing him.

"She sends her condolences." He looked blackly around the room, then back at her. "It's time to get down to business." He rose from the couch, stretched like a cat without taking his eyes off his prey. "I thought we'd have a little barbecue, just you and me. Then we'll take a trip. How about that?"

"I'm not going anywhere with you," she said.

"Careful. I'm not in the best of moods today."

If she could just make it out the door, she could get the gun. She didn't know if she could shoot it, but he didn't know that. She stood abruptly and ran for the door, the chair rattling to the floor behind her. But he was on her before she could get it open, pinning her flat to its rough, splintered surface, his belt buckle grinding into the cuts on her back. She cried out.

"Ah, that's what I like to hear." He stood away from her. "Sit down. And pardon me if I don't pick up your chair."

He rummaged in a kit bag she hadn't noticed before, pulled out a roll of duct tape and proceeded to strap her to the chair, her arms twisted behind it. He made it tight, cutting into her belly and chest, grinding the wounds into the chair back. She winced but did not cry out.

"What do you want with me?" she asked.

"First of all, I don't want to fuck you. I hope you don't mind. Warriors don't fuck the day of battle. Bad vibes."

"Lucky me," she said.

"You don't know what you're missing," he smiled and winked at her. "But I'm gonna explain something to you because you're ignorant. Ignorant and guilty all at once." He kneeled next to the chair, braced his elbow on her thigh and leaned into his hand.

"You people have this ridiculous idea of Indians sitting around

smoking the peace pipe, communing with nature, you know, being *spiritual*. When you get a look at what life's really like around
here, then you know the truth. The truth is that justice for the Indian has never been anything but a joke. We have been trampled,
and bled and beat to hell and back by *you*." He pinched her cheek
hard between his thumb and forefinger. "You have stolen everything from us, mostly material shit which really ain't what we're
about. But the thing you've stolen from us that we cannot live
without is our core."

"What does that stand for?" she whispered.

"It don't stand for anything," he said. "It is what it is. Our
CORE. You people use all them buzzwords, sovereignty, subsistence rights, blah blah blah. But all that is what makes up our
CORE. That's the truth we're fighting for, at least some us are
fighting, the warriors left in us. The rest of 'em have gone soft.
Like our fearless leader, Kash. Thinks if he deals with white people like a white person, we'll get what we need. 'Violence gets us
nowhere. Patience and truth must be our guides.' Truth, hell.
Truth is we're the poorest of the poor, shit on, ripped off, disre-
spected, and powerless from Day One you people landed here till
Day Now. The longer we talk about truth, the farther we get from
it. Well I'm not walkin' anymore. I'm ridin', and you're comin'
with me."

"With you? Where?"

"Anchorage. We're going to go to Anchorage to play a little
poker. And you, green eyes, are the kitty," he said, dimpling his
forefinger into her cheek.

"We didn't take any gold," she stammered. "There wasn't anything up there."

"I know that," he said. "I've already worked that stream. It's
dead now."

"I thought we're the ones who ripped you off?"

"Difference is that gold is mine. I can't rip myself off, can I?"

He rose to his feet, towering over her. "Well, you're a little less ignorant but still guilty as hell. How do you feel?"

"Helpless," she said, staring straight ahead.

He bent close to her face. "Now you know just a tiny speck of what it's been like for us for centuries." He backed away, eyes slitted, then seemed to wash himself of the emotion. "You wait here while I get everything ready to go. If that ain't chivalry, I don't know what is."

She strained at her bonds, couldn't believe that a bunch of tape could keep her from escape, from getting help for Zach. She hated this helplessness. Hated it with the force of a lifetime of helplessness behind it. "Goddammit," she moaned and didn't care if it was wrong to say. What difference did it make, anyway? She was only saying it to herself.

She hung her head. She wished she were somewhere else, but couldn't imagine where that would be. Someplace safe, warm, where she knew what was what. But that place didn't exist anymore because she didn't exist anymore. She moaned again, wordlessly.

She felt something tickling her fingertips, then her wrists, and flung up her head in fright. Something was crawling on her. She caught her breath when she heard the *"Shhhhhhhh,"* behind her, and did her best to obey as her heart jackhammered her ribs. She felt the left side loosen, and the right. *"Shhhhhhhhh,"* came the sound again, and the tape ripped quickly from her arms, which smarted like crazy. Then he appeared, squatting in her peripheral vision.

Kash, thank God, she mouthed the words, her eyes blinking slowly as if bliss had descended on her. He worked at the tape on her legs as she continued to pull the stuff from her chest and belly.

He squatted in front of her now, his hands on her knees. "You okay?"

She never knew a man's voice could be so soft and clear at the same time. She nodded.

"But Zach," she said. "He's hurt."

"Where?"

"About thirty minutes northwest, toward the stream." She was so hoarse it was hard to whisper.

Kash scrubbed his chin, his eyes darting toward the windows. "Can you drive a boat?"

She nodded.

"Bailey's boat's downriver, just below the bend."

"Is she okay?"

"She's alive. Hurt. I want you to sneak out the back and follow the bank down to the boat. Get to Bailey's. I'll find Zach. Meet you there. Got it?"

"Okay," she said, brushing her hands over her face.

He squeezed her leg to get her attention. "Don't stop no matter what. Just keep going."

His hands were pulling her up, pointing her at the back door. As she turned she saw daylight in the front door, and then he shoved her so hard away she was running just to keep from falling and his voice loud as all hell now, *"Go!"* and she did, knowing she would not run away.

—————

They circled each other, hackles raised, hands curled like claws, except for Match's one hand, which held the rifle at his hip, pointing straight at Kash.

"You won't stop me," Match said.

"I may not be able to stop the movement, but I'll sure as hell stop you."

"Goddamn, old man, you are one ballsy fella. Standin' there telling me what's going to happen when I got the gun."

"I'm not afraid of you and I'm not afraid of you with it."

"You ought to be. Because like I told that silly white girl, I'm not in the best of moods today."

"What were you planning to do with her?"

"We were gonna take a little ride into Anchorage and play some poker with the big dogs."

"Meaning?"

"She's the ante in return for some fucking progress on our situation."

"In spite of everything that leans to the contrary, you just can't be that stupid."

"Guess you don't know everything."

"You will be caught and jailed or gunned down like a dog. Either way, we don't get shit but more misery because of what you do."

"Somebody's gotta try. Somebody's gotta do something."

"And you're taking her to do it?"

"Soon as I knock your ass out of the picture. She won't get far."

"But first, you gotta 'knock my ass out,' right?"

"That would be the idea."

"Then come on. Do it."

"I don't need to 'do it,'" he said. "This here'll do it." He squeezed off and the bullet pocked into the wall behind Kash. "You gonna sit down and play nice or what?"

Kash had moved closer by millimeters as they circled and now he was close enough to lunge forward and flip aside the barrel, hurling himself at Match's legs as he went. They went down, the rifle skittering aside. Match had his hands behind him, trying to squirm away, but Kash wasn't going to let him go. Not yet. He was up on his feet again, following him.

"This is your chance, warrior boy. Like the old days. Like when warriors were men."

Match bared his teeth and pushed up at Kash, locking his arms around his neck, the pose almost brotherly. With foreheads together they scrambled, Kash locking his arms around Match's body to lift him and throw him down.

"Come on you little bastard," he gasped, but he hadn't seen Match make the move, hadn't thought of the big fish net hung on the wall behind him until it was too late and the net swooped over him, air swishing through its mesh as it engulfed his head and upper body. He flailed helplessly as Match yanked him off his knees and he went down heavily without his arms to break the fall. He couldn't breathe, struggled feebly at the restraint and then Match stood over him, the rifle jammed into Kash's chest.

He wheezed as his lungs suddenly reinflated. "Heart shot," he said, fluid crackling like wax paper in his throat. "That's the one to take."

Match's eyes glittered vacuously at him from an impossible height.

"Get up, Kash." He heard the words but Match's mouth hadn't moved. Thought maybe he'd been deprived of a little too much oxygen lately, but there it was again, a woman's voice. Had Bailey got up here somehow? He clawed the net over his head and stood, swaying. And she was there, all right, not Bailey but the girl. He gaped at her, then at Match, his perception taxed to the limit.

"Come by me," she said to Kash, the thirty-thirty trained steady on Match, who stood now, arms limp at his side, the rifle barrel nosed to the floor.

Kash did as he was told.

"Put the rifle down, and sit," she said to Match.

Match edged himself onto the chair.

"Good boy," she said. "I like it when a man knows his place. Kash, tie him up."

"Can do," he said, casting about for some rope.

"Behind you," she said. "Use the duct tape. Use a lot of it. I want it to hurt when they peel it off."

Kash just shook his head and got the tape. Match would not meet his eyes as he bound him to the chair. Much as Kash wanted to castigate him, he didn't have the stomach for it now. Didn't have the time. He worked silently, quickly. There were other things to take care of yet.

When he finished, he almost stumbled over the net as he turned away. Smiled. Couldn't resist the final gesture and capped him with it. "Keep the mosquitoes off, anyway," he said to Match.

Alpha leaned on the doorjamb, her face pale but hard set. She handed him the rifle. "What about Zach?"

"We got two boats out there," he said. "I'll go after Zach, you get down to Bailey's."

She nodded, her eyes transfixed on him. He'd never seen eyes that green before. They were kind of pretty, he thought. Unusual. "Go," he pushed her gently out the door. "I'll take care of Zach."

She turned to him, gripping his arm. "He didn't think it would hurt anything. He was going to buy us a house, so we could get married. He did it for me. But we didn't take anything. Didn't find anything to take. Match said he'd already got it all."

"Match? Got what?"

"Gold," she said.

He should have known that's what all this was about. He couldn't figure how Match had found it. Couldn't believe he'd had the gumption to look.

"I'll take care of it," he said, and waited on the bank till she'd got the motor started, cast her off, and watched her follow the channel down, wake furling off to the sides until it lapped onto dry gravel.

The epiphany was so strong his hair crackled. All these years, all these years since that day on the trail with his father, he'd had the vision in his heart, those two men steaming in their warriors' trances, fighting color to color. Knew it was a vision but never once knew what it meant until today. No one would win, and all would be lost as long as they fought each other.

~~~~~

She rose in the Phoenix through wet, suffocating clouds of pain. The vibration, the reassuring thrum of the engine, centered her, made her feel as if she were in control. The names of things, details, seemed to slip past her in the mist and she could not grasp them, could only seem to keep the gyro level and continue to hurtle through the clouds. Pictures slowly filled themselves in, and there was Temple beside her in the cockpit. *Take care of your sister. Be gentle with your sister. You know she hasn't got everything God gave you.* They were wrong. She had something that Bailey had not. That's why everybody loved Temple, and Temple loved everybody, even Bailey. Now here was the burden again, when she thought she had taken care of it all. Here she was right next to her.

It's all right, she said, trying to edge her voice with efficient authority. *I'll get us out of this.* And she had done her utmost to keep true to that promise. Had kept her from drowning in the river when she'd walked into the cool, inviting water with not the slightest notion of how to stay on top of it. Had fought off the bullies, then the boys who threatened to take advantage of her when she got older. She was so beautiful, so sweet, it could hardly be helped. And Bailey was always there, had always to be watchful. *Take care of your sister. She doesn't have everything God gave you.*

Their mother was right, but Bailey had nothing God gave Temple. Neither of them could make right in the world. They were two useless halves of gunk, flying around in the clouds.

When her eyes strained open she thought she saw the bright hair emerging from the darkness. She tried to grasp the apparition next to her, touch the bright halo, but her hand would not obey. Her body was failing her; she was failing again.

—————

She relaxed her neck, rolled her head back, and let the sun beat on her face as she fanned the branches madly first over Bailey, then around herself to keep the mosquitoes off. She heard sniffling. Bailey was awake, staring at Alpha, tears washing dirt in dark, watery tracks down her neck.

"Didn't think you had it in you," she whispered.

Alpha tried to smile.

"Thought you'd be like your mother."

Terrific, Alpha thought. She's delirious. Alpha could understand that. She felt a little delirious herself. "It's okay," she said. "Where are you hurt?"

"Pictures. Just like her," Bailey said with a dreamy sigh.

"Bailey, it's me, Alpha. We're at the camp."

She seemed to focus on her more clearly. "What happened?"

"Those two bears you told me about. One got me in the tent . . ."

"Let me see." Alpha turned her back to Bailey and hiked up her shirt.

"Zach washed it out for me. He said I should take antibiotics."

"We'll get you something. What else?"

"Zach . . ." she dangled on his name, swallowed hard. "He's still out there," she continued, tears trembling in her eyes. "I walked back to the Lodge, to radio for help and he was there."

"Kash? Is Kash all right?"

"Match. He was going to kidnap me or something. There was gas everywhere. And then Kash came. I got away. They were fighting. I got Zach's gun, and made them stop."

"Kash?"

"He's okay, I think. We tied up Match, and then Kash told me to come here with you. He went after Zach."

Bailey dropped a hand heavily on Alpha's leg. "Kash'll get him out."

Implicit words hanging in the air. *Dead or alive.* Alpha started to tremble again.

"Hell of a mess," Bailey said, trying to pat her leg, but the jarring motion caused her to shrink back, close her eyes.

Alpha had forgotten Bailey was hurt. "Is there something I can do to help?"

"Dislocated my shoulder."

"What can I do?" Alpha asked. "There must be something we can do."

"Shelter," Bailey said.

Alpha looked around. There wasn't anything she could see that she could make a shelter out of.

"Emergency stash," Bailey said.

"The Backup Plan," Alpha said.

"Rule Number One. You got it."

"Where?"

"Behind the fire pit, tree with a ladder against it, there's a cache. Tent in red bag. Food and meds in the plastic cooler. Duct taped. You can throw it down. Don't throw the tent. Might puncture."

Alpha frowned.

"No bears," Bailey said as if she had read Alpha's mind. "Smoke runs 'em off."

Her hands shook. She couldn't help it.

"Believe me," Bailey said. "No bears for miles."

Alpha looked at her.

"You can do it. Pain meds, antibiotics in the cooler. Then Easy Street."

"Right," Alpha said. "Bonbons and tea."

Bailey's laugh trembled. "Bourbon for me."

The wind gusted suddenly from downriver, draping heavy, sweet-scented motes across her face. She huffed a deep breath, exhaled loudly. "Wow," she said.

"Wild roses," Bailey said. "My favorite."

<hr />

Alpha set up the tent as near to Bailey as the heat from the cabin would allow.

"Let's get this over with," Bailey said. Her skin whitened as she struggled to her knees and crawled into the tent.

"Is this something we'll need?" Alpha asked, handing the Beretta in to her.

"Leave it out there. Damned dangerous." She levered herself into a sitting position. Her eyelids fluttered woozily.

"You all right?"

Bailey's mouth widened a millimeter. "I'm here."

Alpha opened the cooler and tipped it over. "Okay, what do we need?"

"Med kit."

She found the red nylon pouch with a white cross on it. "Bingo." She gripped it with her knees and buzzed the zipper back, then dumped the contents on the floor, but didn't even need to wait for her to I.D. what she needed because the baggie with the small bottle in it was clearly marked PAIN in bold Magic Marker. "You drink this stuff or what?"

"Inject," Bailey said.

"Inject? As in needle? I don't know anything about that."

"Simple," Bailey said. "In the muscle. No veins."

"Just a muscle, she says. Simple, she says."

"It *is* simple," Bailey said. "Pay attention. Little blue case. Get the smallest syringe."

"Got it."

"Take up two cc's. Marks on the syringe."

Alpha held the small bottle between her knees, and pushed the needle in, following Bailey's directions. When she'd squirted a little of the liquid out, she turned to her. "Okay. Now what?"

Bailey instructed her how to hold the syringe, how to poke it like she was throwing a dart into the muscle of her upper arm, then inject the drug slowly. "Won't pass out. Just loose."

Alpha cocked her wrist back and forth several times before she got the nerve to press the needle to her skin. Bailey winced.

"Punch it."

Alpha repositioned her hand, took aim and let it fly. She closed her eyes as she pushed the plunger in slowly, listening to Bailey, "Good. Now pull it out straight." She opened one eye, certain she would see blood spurting everywhere, but only a tiny bead of red appeared at the puncture site. Bailey continued, "Break the needle off in the case. Close it tight and put it back in the cooler. Ten minutes. Then we'll go on."

"Go on?"

"Shoulder. We can fix it." Bailey coughed, more a slow, hard exhalation. "I'll take my shirt off, get into position."

Alpha turned discreetly aside. Outside, a gut-wrenching sound. Metal screeching as it twisted and fell into the coals. She shuddered and couldn't help thinking of Zach out there alone, hurt, at the mercy of the bugs and possibly a wounded bear. What goes around comes around. Match was right. They were as bad as anyone who had come before them, had thought of nothing but themselves, as if their actions had no consequences whatsoever. She could argue that Zach had talked her into it, bullied her into complicity, but that was wrong. For all her anger against the "place" her father had assumed she should occupy, she had let herself stay there.

"Ready."

She turned and saw the hard knot on the front of Bailey's shoulder, flesh swelling around it. "I'm here," she said, feeling more calm than she had in, what, days? Weeks?

"Move my arm like I'm going to throw a ball, till the back of my hand is on the ground beside my head. Go very slowly. It'll take about twenty minutes. Hold on at the elbow and pull a little. Traction. It'll hurt like hell. Don't mind what I say."

She started out too fast and Bailey hissed, arched back her head. Alpha let go of her arm.

"This isn't going to work."

"Yes. Go slow. Talk to me."

"I'm sorry about your sister," Alpha blurted out.

Bailey was silent but for heavy, splintered breaths.

"I remember from the papers." She tried to concentrate on a steady motion.

"What is it you remember?"

"That there was a farm burned in Medford. One person didn't make it out. Your sister, I guess. You were her guardian since your parents were both gone. That's pretty much it."

"How old are you?" Bailey asked.

"Twenty-two."

———

Bailey nodded. She had been eighteen when her mother finally died from complications of multiple sclerosis. The fact that she'd been left legal guardian to her sister was nothing to her. She'd been her guardian for as long as she could remember, anyway. Her mother's death had been a relief. Then she was free to get her nursing credits, something she was never allowed to do before, since her mother would not let her put Temple in day care or have a baby-sitter, or sell off any of the farm so she could afford it.

She had put the "land for sale" ad in the paper the same day she handed in her mother's obituary. She didn't really have to run the ad. The farmers in the area had been itching for a piece of that land ever since her father had run off ten years before. Had fully expected it to come their way once there was no man around to take care of the place. But her mother had resources no one knew about, and she had Bailey.

She'd wanted to go to nursing school since she'd had to start caring for her mother. She had learned a lot about the body on her own and from books and doctors. Then had to learn much more when Temple got pregnant. She was a beautiful young woman, Bailey knew, but only realized the consequences of that when the farmer's son down the road went to such tremendous lengths to get at her. Bailey was only seventeen then, but already her responsibilities were so great, her mother's Catholic insistence that Temple go through with the pregnancy was only one more burden. At least she hadn't made them keep the baby.

Temple was almost always cheerful, sweet, loving, if you could call it love. This had been good for her mother. Temple ate with her, bathed when she bathed, slept in the bed with her until she died and would not sleep anywhere else afterward. Toward the end of her mother's life, when the spasms were near constant, Temple's body next to her seemed to ease their violence somewhat. The difficulty was in saving her from consequences that most children learn by age five. Don't touch that, it's hot. Don't go outside without a coat when it's freezing, you'll get cold. Don't play with sharp things, they'll cut you. There was no discernment or discrimination in her. Everybody was nice. Everybody was loved. Even the farmer's son. Even Bailey.

Later, after her mother died and she was able to hire a baby-sitter for Temple so she could work at the hospital, she'd started to meet people. Had met a particularly congenial, understanding fellow who was a medic for the local ambulance service. Broward took her out to dinner, movies, and paid for the baby-sitters. He had done all this in spite of the fact that the baby-sitters were there for a grown woman. Didn't seem to mind at all. He had bought Temple a puppy, a mongrel collie-retriever cross. Temple went nowhere without it or it her. It slept in her bed where she cradled and soothed it as if it were a baby. And Bailey wondered sometimes if the dim memory of what happened lurked somewhere in her head, or if it were just her natural predisposition to love.

Sometimes, Bailey had to change shifts, or work doubles. One time, she'd been unable to get a sitter and Broward had volunteered to watch Temple. When a major schism at the hospital caused a lot of job vacancies and she'd had to work doubles to keep her job, he had volunteered cheerfully whenever there was a lack of sitters.

She had finally understood his unstinting generosity when she'd come home early one night and found him enjoying the new game he'd taught Temple, the "dolly" still upright between his legs. Bailey could fathom it coming from horny, teenaged sons of farmers, but she could not fathom it from a grown man, one who had professed to love Bailey and had taken her body freely in the name of it. She could not get over feeling as if she should have known it, should have known that, young, old, educated, or illiterate, they were all stupid in that one way. Every cussed last one of them.

Temple was entranced by fire. Matches, candles, cigarette lighters had to be kept in locked drawers. The house was heated by a woodstove around which a cage had been built to keep Temple away from it after the first time she opened the door and pulled embered logs onto the floor so she could watch them glow. She'd burned her hands horribly, but hours later had no memory of why her hands hurt.

Bailey had to work another double shift one night. A local girl on whom she depended for Temple's care had said she could be there. Trouble was, the girl had acquired a boyfriend unbeknownst to Bailey, one who smoked. The sitters knew about Temple's attraction to fire and weren't allowed to smoke in the house. But hormones overwhelmed the girl's better judgment. Bailey knew all about that. The boyfriend had come to the house with her, left a cigarette not quite stubbed out in the sink with his lighter beside it, and taken the baby-sitter for a stroll in the woods.

Smoke curling lazily from the sink would have been unbearably attractive to Temple. She had taken the cigarette and the lighter upstairs to her mother's room. The bed had caught up first. The forensics people had been able to fill in the rest of the story. The couple hadn't even noticed anything was wrong, so engrossed were they in their woodsy haunt, until it was too late. They had run down the road to the next farm and called the fire department.

But Bailey had got there first. Disoriented by the smoke, she'd followed the sound of the dog barking, barking, barking. When she found it with her hands, she felt its face, the direction in which it was pointed; that's how she knew Temple was under the bed. She'd grabbed the first thing she'd been able to get hold of, she hadn't known whether it was an arm or a leg, and dragged her out, again following the dog's voice, which had seemed to lead her to the stairs.

Temple allowed herself to be dragged at first. It had been so easy, Bailey thought she was unconscious. But once she'd started down the stairs, Temple fought her, struggling back to her mother's room. When the beam came down and broke her grip, the hallway erupted into a vortex of flame that bellied out to the stairwell. Bailey had already fallen, already knew it was useless to go back up, useless to go back there. She had never heard Temple cry out, or scream. The only thing she remembered hearing was fire coming at her like hell in the dark.

<hr>

Bailey coughed, a gacking sound in her throat and swore words that Alpha wasn't sure existed.

Alpha kept her eyes on the pale curve of Bailey's face, her hands gone numb.

"Don't quit on me now," Bailey hissed.

"I'm sorry," she stammered, trying to regain the traction.

"No," Bailey said. "I'm the one who should apologize. I've never told anyone and I should have kept it that way."

"Please don't say that," Alpha said. "I was just . . . I'm just . . ."

"It's all right," Bailey said. "Talk to me."

"I'm sorry about that baby, your sister's baby. I had all kinds of ideas about you when I read that article. We all did. But after what you told me, I know that was wrong. You've had a hard time. A lot harder than me. I know how you got to be so tough. I wish I was tough. I mean I thought this trip to Alaska would show everybody I'm more than what they think. Maybe they were right."

"If I had a kid, I'd be happy it was you."

"Not if you knew what we did," Alpha said. "When Kash gets here, he'll probably turn me in."

Bailey's eyes opened to slits, focused on Alpha's face questioningly.

"Zach and I signed a contract that all we were doing was camping. But we came here because Zach's friend used to work on that oil pipe thing. He was a geologist or something. He scouted places for the company, found gold in some of the streams on this river. The one behind the Lodge. He didn't report it because he planned to come back for it himself, but he got hurt working on the pipe. Lost a leg. We were after the gold. We lied to Kash about it."

Bailey was silent but for hissing breaths.

"Guess you'll think twice about me now," Alpha said.

"We'll work it out," Bailey whispered.

"Your hand's in position," Alpha said.

"I didn't feel it pop in. That knot in my shoulder gone?"

"No."

"One more step."

"Will it hurt?"

"Like ninety-nine daggers. But the payoff is immediate."

"What do I do?"

"Traction," Bailey said. "Get a good grip on my elbow with one hand. Brace the other flat against my ribs, just by the armpit. Don't pull the elbow. Just hold it steady while you push against the ribs.

Alpha didn't want to hurt her. She grasped the elbow, pushed tentatively against the heaving wall of ribs.

"You're gonna have to do better than that."

"I don't want to hurt you."

"Do it."

"Shouldn't we wait?"

"Do it!"

Alpha shoveled into her ribs then, and felt the thing go back in, a distant thud that registered against her hand, and Bailey made a sound like a bird trilling in long, stuttering syllables.

He'd had to slow to a crawl, could hardly keep his eyes open for the smoke that had drifted upriver from the cabin. He'd shielded stinging eyes with his forearm. When he came out of the haze and saw what used to be the camp, he had to squeeze his eyes open and shut several times before he was certain there was a tent set up on the bank.

He scrambled up the bank to the tent. Through the mesh he could make out the two women lying there. He unzipped the portal and crawled in halfway, put a shaking hand on Bailey's leg. "Hey," he said gently, trying still to squeeze the sting from his eyes. "You all right?"

He thought of all the things he had willingly killed, how he always touched them to know for sure they were dead, how it only ever took one brief contact to know that a body was without life. He had learned the Latin name for it in prep school. Anima. Life force. Soul. When he'd touched Bailey that first time in his house, he'd done it to convince himself she had a soul, because until then he hadn't been so sure. It had been there, all right—a tangible aureole of warmth encircling his hand as it did now. He crawled in farther to reach her head, curving two thick fingers around the arc of her neck to reach the carotid pulse. Life thrummed against his fingertips.

He jostled the girl's body, trying to remember her name but could not. And then she'd come to, pushing herself up on one arm, grinding the heel of her free hand into her eyes.

"Wow," she said. "Bailey gave me some pain stuff. Knocked me on my rump."

"Apparently."

And then she'd come to herself fully, sat up straight. She clutched his arm, the question on her face so clear she did not need to speak it. She'd squeezed his arm so hard *Tell me* he thought it would snap.

But how could he tell her that he'd smelled the blood before he found the body? That he'd known without getting too close that the extent of the mangling precluded any possibility of life? That he'd hightailed it out of there, his heart in overdrive, because the last mistake you'd ever make was to mess with a bear's kill?

"Your friend didn't make it. They'll send a chopper for the body," was all he managed to say.

He braced himself for her response, tensed his arm against the vise grip she had on him. But she'd surprised him, dropped her hands in silence, her features softening into the seamless, rounded contours of a child's face. He'd forgotten how young she was.

"Can you make it to the airplane?" he asked her. "I've got to help your friend here. Looks like she passed out." He moved backward to clear the portal and she followed him, scooting on her butt until she got in the open.

She straightened her clothes and smoothed her hair idly, face creased into serious lines. "Yes, I can."

He grabbed the heels of Bailey's boots and slid her gently over the nylon until he had her on the scorched dry grass. From there, he picked her up in his arms, the muscles in his lower back writhing in rebellion. He would sure as hell call the clinic in Bethel for a stash of those muscle relaxers. He eased down the bank onto the pontoon, directing Alpha how to take off the door and unclip the seat to stow in the rear of the plane. He had her spread his emergency sleeping bag over the floor before he laid Bailey on it. Alpha sat on the floor behind him. She leaned against his seat, clutching Bailey's hand to her chest like a rag doll, face eerily blank and dry. But as he went through his preflight check, he could feel her body vibrating his spine right through the seatback.

Kash taxied upriver, giving himself plenty of room for takeoff. Smoke hung in a lazy layer a few feet off the water, the Cub cleaving it perfectly once he arrowed down under full power, and then seeming to float on it as they rose. He tilted his face to the sky, blinking rapidly over the burnt coals of his eyes. So many questions, but none of them had to be answered now. There would be a great reckoning that he would have to direct. But for the clarity of his destination, the task would have seemed overwhelming.

He scanned the land below, caught the outline of the plane cast there by the sun, and watched his shadow self slip smoothly over country he knew blind.